McPHEE

A FAIR EXCHANGE

Gillian Bouras was born in Melbourne in 1945. She worked as a teacher in Australia before moving to Greece with her husband and children in 1980. Her first book about this experience was *A Foreign Wife*, published in 1986. Gillian still lives in Greece, and is a regular contributor to various newspapers, magazines and journals, both in Australia and overseas.

By the same author

A Foreign Wife

A FAIR EXCHANGE

Gillian Bouras

McPHEE GRIBBLE

McPhee Gribble
Penguin Books Australia Ltd
487 Maroondah Highway, P.O. Box 257
Ringwood, Victoria 3134, Australia
Penguin Books Ltd
Harmondsworth, Middlesex, England
Viking Penguin, A Division of Penguin Books USA Inc.
357 Hudson Street, New York, New York 10014, USA
Penguin Books Canada Ltd
10 Alcorn Avenue, Toronto, Ontario, Canada M4Y 1E4
Penguin Books (N.Z.) Ltd
182–190 Wairau Road, Auckland 10, New Zealand

First published by Penguin Books Australia Ltd 1991

1 3 5 7 9 10 8 6 4 2

Produced by McPhee Gribble
56 Claremont Street, South Yarra, Victoria 3141, Australia
A division of Penguin Books Australia Ltd

Designed by Meredith Parslow
Typeset in Bembo by Bookset, Melbourne
Printed in Australia by The Book Printer, Maryborough

National Library of Australia
Cataloguing-in-Publication data:
Bouras, Gillian, 1945– .
A fair exchange.
ISBN 0 86914 210 0.
1. Bouras, Gillian, 1945 – . Australians – Greece –
Biography. 3. Women immigrants – Greece – Biography. 4.
Immigrants – Greece – Biography. 5. Greece – Social life
and customs – 20th century. I. Title.
305.8240495092

McPhee Gribble's creative writing programme is assisted by the
Australia Council.

For my parents, brother and sister, who gave me the
memories.
For Katie and Ismini, who helped shape them.
For my sons.
And, once again, for George.

Acknowledgements

The author wishes to thank the Felix Meyer Scholarship Selection Committee of the University of Melbourne. Without the scholarship award for 1988, substantial parts of this book could not have been written.

'It is the image in the mind
that links us to our lost treasures;
but it is the loss that shapes the image,
gathers the flowers,
weaves the garland.'

Colette

The Faces
and Places

Chapter 1

WHEN they talk of lame Spiro, my elder sons use many words, some printable, some not. They also often have words *with* him, for Spiro is a crusty character. 'Like the bread he sells,' I suggest, brightly. But Dimitrios moves from simile to metaphor.

'He's a tough egg,' says my seventeen-year-old, rue-fully. 'A real twenty-minute job, Spiro is.'

'Moody, temperamental, changeable, volatile,' adds Niko, practising his English vocabulary. Another thought occurs to him: 'Spiro's like the little girl with the curl.' And indeed Spiro is, but he dotes on Alexander, whom he has watched grow from babyhood. Between them, there are few words, for words do not seem necessary.

I thought I knew Spiro well. I knew his story, knew all about his daily routine, knew his wife, thought there was little left to know or learn. Crippled in a boyhood accident, he keeps a shop where he sells cigarettes, maga-zines and newspapers, paper tissues and serviettes, a few lines of confectionery, and bread. Every day he makes four slow, wearisome journeys back and forth to the shop, helping his artificial leg along with a walking-stick. One thing I can only guess at: pain.

Even occasional pain produces irascibility, irritability and sheer bad temper in all but the most patient sufferer.

I imagine that Spiro is never without pain, but that some days are worse than others. On bad days he mutters, mumbles, swears and shouts. On good days he is benign, even merry.

'A great many good mornings to you,' he beams, then, 'and may you be sound and in good health from the tips of your toe-nails to the crown of your head. May you be like a rock!' and he cracks his counter-top hard with one knotted knuckle.

I know his life is boring: he never goes anywhere or does anything. The bread delivery is the highlight of his day. Certainly everybody and everything passes his door: schoolchildren, farmers, housewives, a few visitors from Athens, donkeys, tractors, buses. But it is a small world this, cabin'd, cribb'd and confined – not one easily lived in.

It is obvious then, why Spiro loves anything or anybody new and why my visitors are always received with the greatest courtesy, with Spiro immediately on his best behaviour and exuding an old-world, almost courtly charm. During their last visit, my parents, for example, were welcomed as old friends, as indeed they are, having now visited the village four times. There is always much back-slapping, hand-shaking and embracing for my father, and much bowing and proffering of chairs for my mother. In my role of interpreter I hover uneasily, but do not need to worry. Smiles, laughs and gestures say it all, or nearly all.

This time we even established our own pattern: up the street to call on Gregory and Panayioti at the Post Office, a stop at Spiro's to collect the bread and the morning tea supply of chocolate biscuits. A short conversation later, often conducted largely in mime, and we were on our way. We were comfortable, easy and secure, and pulled the swaddling-bands of routine more and more closely around us.

But Spiro proceeded to unwrap them. One May morn-

4

ing, he eyed me solemnly and issued an invitation.

'I would like it very much, would consider it an honour, if you three would come to eat at my house.'

He waited for an answer. I relayed the message, and could see that my parents were a little dismayed, rather uneasy at the prospect. So was I. But all they were worried about was the language barrier. Can we cope? What will we talk about? I regretted that language barrier too, for it is irksome being a less-than-competent interpreter: the shades of meaning that go wandering, the jokes that fall flat on their faces, the puns that are stillborn, all add up to a special kind of agony.

My dismay, however, cut a little deeper. I knew all about Spiro. The evening would be hard work, perhaps more than a trifle dull, and I would have to steer all parties clear of the thorny theme of politics, for on the political spectrum Spiro ranges somewhere to the right of Mussolini's ghost. Also, I told myself tiredly, I did not want a new dimension to our friendship: it was fine as it was, limited and safe. Almost at once, of course, I felt ashamed. Was I becoming infected by village snobbery? For this society is a rigid one, and Spiro, although a *symbetheros*, a connection by marriage, is definitely in an 'out' group, mainly, I gather, for reasons relating to politics. But I do not care about politics.

I took myself in hand. Spiro had no complicated thoughts, no ulterior motives, I was sure. This was hospitality pure and simple. He was making no excuses for the modesty of the suggested meal, either.

'Just plain village fare,' he stated. 'I hope you will like it.'

'Of course we will,' replied my mother, firmly.

'Just the thing,' declared my father, becoming hearty. And so it was arranged.

We met at the shop just before closing-time. Spiro was excited: an air of authority emanated from him.

5

'Your parents may not like the wine,' he announced. 'Off you go now, and bring a bottle of lemonade, just in case. Tell them I'll pay tomorrow.' I opened my mouth and shut it again. It was useless to protest: I trotted off meekly. I returned in time to witness the ritual of closing. It was, of necessity, very careful and slow. Each bright blue shutter was closed and then the windows were fastened. Outside, the old door was locked and bolted; then, with his one good leg, Spiro rolled a big stone against the door as well.

Off we set, down the street, round the police station corner and on almost to the end of the village. The lights of the main street faded behind us, the soft darkness clung, the olive trees stirred slightly. So we arrived at Spiro's house, where his wife, Maria, was waiting.

It is not appropriate, the adjective, but the house made the word *Dickensian* spring to mind, for it is tiny, perhaps almost as small as the smallest house Pip ever saw, Wemmick's at Walworth. Spiro's house perches on a narrow strip, a terrace built for olive trees. But the terrace was apparently never levelled, and so the house consists of three small boxes strung together by narrow passageways and little runs of steps. It seems, in a way, to hang in mid-air. Outside, in a sliver of yard, three goats live behind a brush fence.

Inside, the floors are covered with hand-woven rugs, the best room is crowded with photographs of family and smiling ex-royalty. That night, the kitchen table was set for our supper with crumbly *feta*, cubes of *pasto*, the rich smoked pork for which the local housewives are famous, salad, olives, creamy *tzatziki* and huge slices of fresh bread, hacked from the choice loaves Spiro reserves for himself every day.

Maria and Spiro plied us with food and drink, and Spiro need not have worried about buying lemonade. Everything went well enough. We relaxed and talked of this and that: relatives, villagers who now live in Australia, the village itself, how the March snow had ruined the olive, how it would be a tight year for everyone.

Spiro talked and ate constantly, his mouth almost seeming a Greek equivalent of Wemmick's post-box. Once he rose slowly, balanced carefully, and carved more slices of bread, clutching the loaf against his chest and sweeping the knife in great, dangerous arcs. Still standing, he made us clink glasses. *E viva. Chronia Polla. Stin iyea sas.* Good luck. Long life. Your health. He sat down again, slightly flushed. A silence fell, and we shifted our feet a little uncomfortably. What could we talk about next? Silence is hard to bear in these situations.

Suddenly, 'Open the window,' barked Spiro to Maria. She did so and we looked, a little wonderingly, at the rectangle of blackness.

'Listen,' instructed Spiro, and we did. Nothing. But then it started.

'The nightingale,' breathed Spiro, smiling softly, and in the same split second I registered both the sound of the song and the change in his face.

How to describe that change? I do not know. I suppose that hackneyed word *transformed* will have to do. I had never seen him look like that before. And I have never heard such a sound, either. It filled the blackness, the rectangle and the room. We still said nothing but now our silence had a different texture.

The bird was tireless. Later I tried to describe the song, and failed. Try as I might to fiddle about with gerunds like *trilling*, *warbling* and *jugging*, nouns like *grace-notes*, and adjectives like *throaty*, *liquid* and *ecstatic*, nothing worked. The song remained incorruptible, defying all attempts to dissect, analyse and label it.

Of course we could not resist leaning out of the window. We took it in turns. When my turn came, I could see nothing but blackness. It was almost like being blind, yet, for a few moments, this sensation, one of those I most dread, seemed not to matter at all. A light breeze touched my face, and the sound swelled, rose and fell about me. Inevitably, I suppose, I thought of the sad heart of Ruth.

While the nightingale sang, we did not speak. But after what seemed like hours, it stopped, and we three began to prattle immediately, our wholly inadequate *Ohs*, *Ahs*, *Wonderfuls* and *Magnificents* bouncing around the room. Then Spiro started.

'*Akou*,' he said. 'Listen.' And we did. His face was serious, but glowing still. Like the birdsong, it defied description.

'*Afto to poulaki*, that bird, sings all night. When it first came, it would stop singing, the way it has now, and I would be afraid.' His hand smote his chest. 'I would be afraid that it had gone. But then it would start singing again, and I would sigh with relief.' Sure enough, the `bird had started once more to sing.

'*Katalaves*? Did you understand? Listen. Often I can't sleep, and I lie in bed while the whole village is still. It seems that nothing is moving in the night, absolutely nothing. Everybody is sleeping but me. And then the bird sings – just for me. How can I tell you the way I feel? Nothing matters except the song. All pain, tiredness, anxiety, worry disappears. Sometimes I think I should pay for the privilege of listening, and the nightingale *chooses* to come and sit in our tree! I could die happily while it is singing. But I relax and go into a deep, sweet sleep. I get up in the morning and I think, 'another day, ugh!' but then I know that the bird will sing again for me at night.'

It was the longest speech I had ever heard him make. There was nothing we could say after it. But later I thought how strange it was that Spiro and I, having approached life from entirely different directions, should

8

meet in his tiny kitchen to listen to a nightingale. We were separated by almost every conceivable division, yet together we had been listening to a song which consoles exiles, comforts the weary, inspires poets and peasants alike, and which, finally, makes all differences and hardships seem irrelevant.

We left quite soon, with Spiro walking a little way with us. '*Akou*. Listen.' We did not need to be told. There came the song again. The stars were out. Tender was the night.

Now spring and summer have gone, my parents have returned to Australia, to their own seasons. In the autumn, the Little Summer of St Dimitrios deceives us all with its sunny days, cloudless skies, and the bursts of colour it produces in spikes of chrysanthemums and puffballs of alyssum. But there is a chill in the morning air and soon the rains come, changing everything, veiling the mountains in grey and making surfaces treacherous. Spiro slips on the road, and breaks his artificial leg.

It is not the first time this has happened. He is getting older and such falls seem to be occurring more frequently. He is in pain again; his stump hurts and he has skinned his arms. He is understandably bad-tempered, shouting and grumbling by turns at his customers, particularly young ones.

'He's off again,' announces Dimitri, gloomily.

'Well, he's got a lot to put up with,' I remark. 'We can't imagine what it must be like.'

'No, you're right,' answers Dimitri. 'He told me once that the phantom pain was awful, but someone else's pain, and a pain like that, anyway . . . it's hard to understand.' And he stands for a moment, all length and strength, before dashing off to the soccer ground. Pain is merely a label. Dimitri cannot understand Spiro's life, which has its own element of exile, its separation from

9

normality. Those in foreign lands ask the question: 'What if I were still at home?' Spiro must ask: 'What if I were whole, like other men?' Dimitri is too young yet to know that every person is an exile, cast adrift from the land of what might have been.

I go to collect the bread. Spiro does not mutter or grumble at me. Instead he says, 'Remember the nightingale?'

'Yes, of course,' I reply.

'She's gone away, *to poulaki*, the little bird,' he tells me. 'That's life. But she'll come again in spring. She always does. She'll come.'

'Yes, of course,' I say again, thinking that he needs the nightingale here now.

But, like Spiro, I have to believe that she will come again and again, for many springs and summers yet. And I have to believe that she will be here when he needs her most; that when the time is right, Spiro will lie listening to the nightingale's song and will cease upon the midnight with no pain.

Chapter 2

'IN the beginning was the Word,' wrote the saint, scratching away in a dank cave on his Greek island of exile, and he was right. Right about the beginning, all beginnings, right about mine.

It is part of our family lore that my sister began to speak at nine months, while I waited until after I had had my second birthday. My sister was adventurous, I cautious. Sound, words, conversation rippled round her in an ever-widening pool. She had always talked, or so it seemed, and her childish idiosyncrasies of speech, her *drawbobes* for wardrobes, *dinging downs* for dressing-gowns and her *Ging-a-nings* for Gillians are documented, quirky history.

Almost as compensation, my parents told me that I could pronounce *probably* and *antirrhinum* perfectly within a short time of deciding, at last, to speak. Nevertheless, my words, I believe now, had always been present, only stored in a mental file index of some sort, there to bide their time.

For words wrapped us round – our security blankets were stories, poems and songs.

'Once upon a time, in a faraway land, lived a sweet and pretty girl called Cinderalla,' intoned my mother at bedtime. Granny, deliberate and dramatic, recited end-lessly, but now only a few fragments of her monologues remain to tease my memory.

'Down came the mustang, and down came *we*, CL-L-inging together!'

'We gouged out a grave a few feet deep . . .'

The plot has gone, or was never there. But then, words were more powerful than meaning, very often; we, my sister and I, sang, 'Two little girls in blue *land*,' very cheerfully, never realizing that we had omitted a vital comma and had added an equally vital *n*. Yet perhaps it was significant that we sang *land*, after all.

Then there were the lists. The grocer arrived every Monday, seated himself on the tall kitchen stool and began briskly. 'Dried fruit? Peel? Raisins? Currants? Sultanas? Flour? Cream of Tartar? Biscuits? Milk Arrowroot? Morning Coffee? Chocolate Teddy Bears? Thin Captains? Tru-Bake? Uneedas? Well-baked Uneedas? Right you are.'

Granny and Grandfather patrolled the garden, hunting pests, checking, planning.

'Iceland poppies. Baby Royals. Peace. Mrs Herbert Davies. Masquerade.'

Ladies came for afternoon tea.

'PWMU today, Wednesday, Royal Doulton, Royal Albert, Worcester. Friday's Guild Day. Staffordshire and Wedgwood. We'll make butterflies, almond fingers, lamingtons – and we've got some Fruit Luncheons in the tin, haven't we?'

The words, the lists, created a world. The adults' past stretched back into the unknown territory, other lands. I thought they knew everything, controlled everything. Now I realize what words meant to them, accomplished for them too. Words were a link to another world, one they had never seen but knew to be important. Was there an idea that if the lists were long enough, they became a bridge, or at least a chain, which might do something to ease that perpetual sorrow of separation they felt, dimly, as being an integral part of their grandparents?

My mother learned lists from her grandfather. In 1852 he was born in Acle, near Great Yarmouth, near Norwich in Norfolk. Much later, when I read *David Copperfield*, Great Yarmouth was immediately mine. Acle's parish church was the church of St Edmund, King and Martyr. My mother's uncle was named after Sir Ralph de Norwich. I recited the lists without comprehending. King and Martyr. King and Martyr. De de de Norwich.

Other names were tucked around us, again the names of places. Redruth, Truro, Wendron, Dundee, Glasgow, Paisley, Inverness and Dublin were one list which had to be kept carefully separate from another; Rutherglen, Great Northern, Prentice Freehold, Cornishtown, Christmastown, Vaughan Springs, Taradale, the Buckland, Warrnambool, Kerang, Milne's Bridge. The lists marked stages on a continuum. The first represented my grandparents' spiritual homes; the places their minds and souls often seemed to dwell in, the second the actual homes of their youth.

Here and there exotic place names sprang up among the ordinary, evoking for us, as we grew older, scenes of high adventure, buckle and swash, death and glory in the midst of quiet suburban routine: Port Hedland, Paschendale, Vimy Ridge, Strath Creek, Broadford, Terang, Ascot Vale, West Geelong, Essendon.

Later we had lists of our own. Mine began: Melbourne, Mordialloc, Beechworth, Moonee Ponds, East Malvern, Eaglehawk, Nhill, Highton, Parkville, Lorne, Essendon, Moonee Ponds, South Yarra, St Kilda, Burwood, Camberwell – a long, slightly repetitious catalogue with sounds and meaning echoing each other. But then I added Arfara, Kalamata, Greece, the transforming power of which imparted the same air of unreality yet endlessly expanding possibility contained in the address I used to write in my school exercise books: 7 Roncliffe Road, Highton, Geelong, Victoria, Australia, Southern Hemisphere, The World, Galaxy, Universe, Space.

In another beginning, the blind old man of rocky Chios sang a song which became two songs and then many echoes, calling, calling, still calling, sounding and resounding through many worlds and words. He sang of war, blood, sacrifice, wanderings and exile, and was right. Right about those beginnings and endings, right about many things

But first there had been lists. For the masters of Knossos spoke Greek, and the mistresses and overseers made inventories of wheat, oil and figs, lists of workaday words. Now we can gaze at the neat lines, bends and squiggles, and see the long thread of history stretching onwards to Michael Ondaatje's Sinhalese alphabet, 'the self-portrait of language', Thomas Shapcott's 'entry through words into possession', Eliot's 'easy commerce of the old and the new', and to Seamus Heaney's *Alphabets*, the drawing of smoke, the forked sticks and swans' necks.

But further back along the thread, eight hundred years before Homer, individual pictograms linked, joined, formed a spiral; history, in the shape of the Phaistos Disk, is a circle, keeping its secrets close, tantalizing eager readers, making them realize the foreignness and exile of the past, teaching them the limitless power of language to divide, as well as to unite.

The boy only knew one book, the important one, *the book*, although there were some others upstairs in his father-priest's study. Other books stood on the revolving lectern in the dim light of church, and men with powerful voices translated the strange wavy lines, dips and dots into psalms sung for sixteen centuries. At home, in the cramped passage where six little children lay on a row of mattresses, there were no bedtime stories, no picture books to look at, thumb and tuck under the pillow. The children chattered until hushed, and fell asleep to the sound of murmured prayers a room away.

But lists gave shape and form to a routine, harsher and more monotonous than we, in another time, in another place, ever imagined. Important words like *olives*, *wheat*, *land*, *animals*, bifurcated, forked, split and layered into countless others: oil, *okathes*, not kilos, wind, threshing, *stremmata*, not acres, wells, water, donkeys, goats, cheese, milk, *pasto*, sausages. And always there was the word *work*; *thouleia*, heavy and dull and omnipresent. Only one word meant escape – *yiorti* means *celebration*, and the list of feast days lengthened and lengthened, sloping downwards from the Feast of Feasts, *Pascha*, to the Twelve Great Feasts and individual saints' days. A long list, this; today thick little books are issued, with as many as four or five saints for each day of the year. Then, people knew because their mothers had told them, as those mothers had learned in turn from their mothers. The word *feast* was balanced by the word *fast*: one seldom came without the other and *fast* immediately built two more lists, of forbidden and approved foods. Meat, eggs, cheese, milk; vegetables, fish, rice, gruel.

Then there were the words learned much later on; words which signalled progress, at least of a sort: matches, tap, water-pipes, running water, ice, electricity. Words sprang up, added themselves to lists slowly at first, and then multiplied rapidly, reflecting change: supermarket, soap powder, baking powder, detergent, steel wool, cornflakes, Seven-Up, Pullman, Scotch, plastic, nylon.

The boy and his parents did not need words as bridges, chains, to link themselves to a world thousands of miles away. Instead, words formed circles, resembling his life, his family's, his village life, snug, cocooned and compact, as was each community. Our village, and *not ours*. And that circle widened to include the ancestral ones, and stretched as far as The City, Constantinople. Later, much later, the boy would travel to The City, and be asked, *'Eiste apo kato?'* Are you from down there? Seas, mountains, hostile states, political barriers, meant nothing.

Constantinople was the significant name; after it came the name of Messenia, the Messenia mentioned in Tyrtaios's verses as Messene, a broad floor for dancing, Messene good for ploughing, good for growing. And these were the important things. The boy took for granted the ancient history of his land, which stretched back through generations, through Aphareus, Leukippos, Gorgophone, to Perseus. Within walking distance lay the river Pamisos, where in ancient times little children were taken to bathe, for its springs and marshes were sacred, and had curative powers; elsewhere the waters of the Pamisos had been broad and deep enough to permit ships to navigate it for a mile and a half. Further west lay the ancient city, shadowed by Mount Ithome, topped by its sanctuary of Zeus, for Zeus had been raised in the area and had been washed in the waters of the spring Klepsydra, which still gushes from a rock wall in the modern village of Mavromati.

I started school in Eaglehawk when I was four and a half. At school words rose up from the page and walked, moved, and had their being, and made new things, put flesh on bones, became flesh. Words meant power but needed to be triumphed over and subdued first. I had a tussle with the word *nephew*. I was five and words were obedient. *Tom was six. Dan was ill.* But *nephew*. I thought about it and its sounds. I spoke it but the p and h (puh and huh) were worrying. Daring was needed. Experiment took place. Suddenly, I had it. (Later, I understood Professor Higgins very well.) Suddenly I knew the word meant *neffyou*, and I knew what a *neffyou* was, for Granny had one of whom she was inordinately proud. 'My *neffyou* John is brilliant.' After the episode of nephew/ neffyou, I saw *Ralph de Norwich* written down for the first time, and immediately viewed him with new respect.

And then came Ronnie Elliott and his power of the word, a new list. I tried the lengthy catalogue out on my mother one day. The result was a careful question.

'Who taught you those words?'

'Ronnie Elliott,' I replied, pleased and proud. But suddenly, more suddenly than the resolution of *nephew* into *neffyou*, came the realization that Ronnie Elliott's list trailed, not clouds of glory, but clinging connotations, vines and jungle lianas of dirt, slime, darkness and dankness, the understanding that words could create all sorts of worlds and atmospheres.

I tried not to say the list again, although it exerted a horrible fascination. I thought it, nevertheless, over and over. The word was made fleshly indeed. My sister, more adventurous, as I have said, seized on new words, tossed them about in order to admire their sparkle, turned them in the light, the better to view each facet. She, too, felt the fascination of Ronnie Elliott's list, but needed the persuasion of soap and water, assiduously applied, before she stopped sporting with it.

Our names, too, helped create our safe, limited, small world. The same ones appeared again and again: William, Arthur, John, Robert, Eliza, Kate, Harriet and Doris. Here and there, however, two or three broke with convention: Wearne, Benjamin, Lindsay. Names were another indication of continuity – my father was the sixth of his name.

'The first is always called Percy, dear,' said Granny, quoting ironically from *The White Cliffs of Dover*. But she herself called her only daughter after a Zane Grey heroine. Did she envisage a life of romance and recklessness for Fay in the wide open spaces of another land? But when my aunt found such a life, or the Western District equivalent thereof, Granny was none too pleased.

Then there were very few names that were *foreign*. The tradesmen, doctors, dentists and ministers were a procession of Smiths, Wallaces, Thompsons, Naughtons, Reeds, Rules, Coles, Speedys and Ashmans. But there was Mr Biviano.

'Going down to Mr Biv's,' Granny sang, grabbing her raffia basket.

Mr Biv's dark little daughters peeped shyly from behind pyramids of oranges, or polished red Jonathan apples before nesting them in layers of green tissue paper. I envied the girls their olive complexions, flashing eyes and hooped gold earrings. Even the tiny ones had had their ears pierced. The ability to stand what I felt sure was excruciating pain enhanced their glamour, as did their names, now no longer recalled exactly. Angelica? Concetta? And was one called Claudia, pronounced *Cloud* and not *Clawed*? These were names which took wing and flew high above the earth-bound Dorises and Arthurs. Later there was Mr Leone's daughter, Serafina. *Serafina* was the most beautiful name I had ever heard. It dipped and soared whenever her mother called her: Sera-*fin*-a!

The new foreigners sold things. Louey Tong (always a Chinaman, never a Chinese) sat in a covered wagon and steered his horse around the dusty roads. It might take

Louey all day to sell a few vegetables, because he never whipped his horse and invariably let the animal go where it would. Louey was a living simile: skin like parchment, legs like sticks, eyes like slits. He was so thin that this face seemed to split and crack when he smiled; his horse though, was fat, and waddled and rolled.

The mysterious East was very mysterious then, and its images were regularly transmitted by frightening words. When he was a child, my father was routinely threatened.

'Bill, be a good boy or you know what'll happen. I'll sell you to the Chinaman.' (For every township had one.)

Poor Louey Tong was a much-tried individual. Even his name had been tampered with and pounded into a shape acceptable to Occidental tongues. He lived on the very edge of the town in a little tumbledown shanty which was almost genteel in its decrepitude, but which the local children had determined was a den of horrors. We seized words we hardly knew and fashioned a world out of them, for were not our mothers well-acquainted with the adventures and evil machinations of Fu Manchu?

So Louey's little shack was wreathed in opium smoke and hung with all manner of Oriental weapons of refined torture – even though we had never been close to the place. A radius of half a mile was our limit. The big boys said Louey had a curved sword four feet long (a scimitar in the Wimmera?) – but nobody had actually seen it.

'Poor old soul,' lamented my mother. 'People are so unkind. All that talk. All he wants is to go back to China. That's what he's working and saving for.'

A few years later, Louey vanished. Whether he ever found China, Formosa, Hong Kong or Singapore, which were all much the same place to us, no one ever knew. But I hope he died in a Chinese world. His horse, however, died in an Australian one, its death caused by a surfeit.

'See?' said Mum. 'He killed that animal with kindness, not with opium or swords.'

Mum had been to school with a Greek whose name she pronounced, wrongly, as George Kozzapoddiottis. Good old Kozza had been the only foreigner in the whole school. For me, his name provided a different music from St Edmund, King and Martyr and Sir Ralph de Norwich, Claudia and Serafina. Koz, Kozza, Kozza-poddiottis, I muttered, almost in a trance, feeling that his first name should have been Kon for purposes of harmony and euphony.

English names were prosy usually, but I had a favourite. Mrs Goldstraw was the name of a real live Englishwoman in England, with whom my grandmother corresponded. During the war, Granny had sent her copies of *The Australian Women's Weekly*, veritable cartwheels of boiled fruitcake and eggs, sealed in jam tins full of dripping. Mrs Goldstraw's was a magic name, almost a conceit, uniting the precious and the mundane, conjuring desperate princesses and wily Rumpelstiltskins. And Mrs Goldstraw dwelt in a faraway land.

So the boy lived in a circle, an O, a tiny one kept safe within larger ones. The Far East was not even an expression; the Middle and near East were blurred concepts. For then, as now, there was a sense of a line drawing itself down the middle of the blue Adriatic; anything west of that line was completely *xeno*, foreign, featuring a different lifestyle and mentality, unthought-of, undreamt-of.

But foreigners were any people outside the family and the in-group, so that the word *xeno* was first applied to people *not ours*, more than to people only vaguely heard of as living across the water. For out-groups could threaten, and the bitter lesson had been learned and would be taught and learned again, that the direst enemies were not necessarily invaders, but Greeks nourished by the same soil, even blood relatives, who were prepared to fight and die for the sake of hollow-sounding names, strings of initials. For civil war, that most unnatural of divisions, that most artificial of separations, stands language and logic on their heads, turns life, death and sacrifice about.

One name, however, although irrevocably *xeno*, took on a kind of familiarity over the years. *Ameriki*: the word swirled in clouds of adventures and romance for the young, but meant black foreboding, dire threat to the old. Many families had uncles who were mere names, gone to America. For the old, *Ameriki* spelled *finality*, and was connected with other words possessing terrible power: *xenitia*, foreign country, *exoria*, exile.

Panoukla and *sklavia* were older, still more powerful words, connected with old evils, old worlds. And always there was *To Mati*, the Evil Eye. Bad words, good words: old men read the lives of the saints in little booklets, weapons in the cause of good. Red thread marched down the slim spines of these little volumes, symbolizing, perhaps, the blood spilt as the saints gave up their lives in various terrible ways. But after the horrors of hangings, executions, boilings in oil and lead, such saints shone with glory, were transformed, became as twinkling stars in a brighter sky. And old and young alike satisfied needs for both drama and comfort in long lists of names, a wholly different communion from the saints Aidan, Cuthbert, and Columba we were familiar with. There is a different poetry in the names Paraskevi, Fanourious, Nektarios and John Chrysostom.

Books were for special occasions, for old men's Sunday afternoon reading. At other times the power of the word was transmitted through dreams, spells, magic, witches' incantations, for every village had a witch, who listed ingredients for concoctions bound to influence the path of love, or to restore health. For cures, certain grasses and roots were to be eaten at certain places on the second last night of the moon. But witches were not needed to interpret dreams in which huge bulls wrestled each other to the death. War was clearly indicated.

One word, the family name, was a bright thread running through generations without change. The boy had the same name as both his grandfathers; neither his mother nor his grandmothers had changed their name on marriage. Even when one or two maverick ancestors changed the name to Bourathanassopoulos, son of Atha- nasios, or Lafazanos, he who talks too much, the thread continued in lists of names drawn up for national service. Boys were assured of an immortality in print because of the commands and demands of the State; girls, unregistered, gave up even their christian names on marriage and lived their lives fenced in by the names of their in-laws, surrounded by *syggeneithes*, relatives, and *symbetheroi*, relatives by marriage. There are two separate words for sister-in-law, two for brother-in-law, and another word to denote the relationship of those married to siblings. Yet there are no separate words for great-uncle and great-aunt, so that a child may have a multitude of grandfathers and grandmothers; similarly all his parents' cousins are called *aunt* and *uncle*: words waver and swing between the minutely particular and the widely general. And names belonged and belong to a family, not to an individual. Whose are you? was and is the question, and he gave and still gives his father's name, not his own. *Tou Papadimitri eimai*, even though Papadimitri has been dead seventeen years.

The saint sat shut away from the light he no longer needed, anyway, and wrote on. 'And the word was with God.' Right again, naturally. Every Sunday during the

1950s, the modest weatherboard with its wooden lace, blue fleur-de-lis carpet and crimson and purple stained glass, proved this. God was there, surrounded by words as offerings but words which also created something comprehensible out of the incomprehensible.

Mighty Protestant hymns spoke of the supernatural in terms of the natural, using a strength and concrete imagery which have never faded in the memory. A shape was imposed and a vision provided. Every Sunday morning, the saints cast down their golden crowns around the glassy sea and the cherubim and seraphim fell down before the Holy, Holy, Holy, which wert, and art, and evermore would be. Punctuation, syntax and imagery combined instantly to convey God's triple nature and His immortality.

God, an invincible force, reigned far above us frail children of dust. His chariots of wrath the deep thunder-clouds formed, and dark was his path on the wings of the storm. His justice was like mountains high soaring above, while we, standing in our pews, were anchored, bound, powerless indeed.

But the minister had some sort of pseudo-power, it seemed, for he aimed words at God regularly during Prayers of Intercession. Free from the confining influences of Prayer Books, burdens carried by less fortunate denominations, *he* chose the words, designed the strategy, planned the bombardment. We listened for God's answer. His precise words never came to me, I must confess. But, as He knew the secrets of every heart, why was there any need to comment? Far better to keep His own counsel, to keep the Word with Him. Thus I reasoned.

Later, in anger, I hurled a few words, feeble enough darts, at God myself, and waited, tremblingly, for the reply. A thunderbolt? A call in the night, with myself a substitute for the infant Samuel? A stern telegram? None came. I wondered whether God collected all these words and turned them into an everlasting dictionary. Did I have a prophetic vision of floppy disks in Heaven, a God as Omnipotent Word-Processor?

Again there were lists and names, lists of names: we had to learn the names of the books of the Bible by heart. We sang them, chanted them, muttered them softly, transforming them into a rosary we were otherwise denied. The Old Testament list was by far the more interesting, even if it did start with a heavy plod over Genesis, Exodus, Leviticus, taking a while to reach the satisfying run of First-and-Second Samuel, First-and-Second Kings, First-and-Second Chronicles. Then there was another dip until Psalms, when a march-like rhythm took over with each name getting longer. But after the Song of Solomon, I used to lose my way, wandering like a lost soul from Isaiah to Nahum, finding myself at last with the triumphant vowels of Habakkuk, then coasting home with the *i's* and *ah's* of Zephaniah, Zechariah and company.

The New Testament list was dull until we came to the letters of St Paul. This saint never showed the remotest sign of suffering from writer's block, it seemed to me; nor did he worry about the inflated cost of postage. It was a long while before I connected the measured syllables of *Corinthians*, *Ephesians* and *Philippians* with actual places, however. Even when I did, I could not imagine the places. They were so far removed in time that I felt sure they were equally removed in space, could not be quite real. Constant repetition could not alter that feeling of inaccessibility.

I was learning about words. They could change some things but not others. They could not change the surrounding landscape, for example. You could stand near the Adelaide highway, close your eyes, command *hills, valleys, mountains*, all to no avail. Your eyes would open a

24

crack, hoping, then pop wide in a resigned way at seeing the flatness stretching away on every side. Here and there a silo stuck up like a little finger, here and there a cloud of dust swirled and altered appearances, but only briefly. Obviously, God kept words like *mountain* and *sea* with Him, and set them down in other places.

You could not say Sundays were *fun*, either, and know it to be true. *Play* was a dirty word, almost, on Sunday. The local lads (louts, people said, labelling them and changing them automatically) lounged outside the Commercial Hotel. Listless with boredom, they combed their oiled hair and thought about Monday and the pub being open and about next Saturday night's dance at the Mechanics' Institute Hall.

Women sat in lounge-rooms with blinds drawn against the heat and against prying eyes which might discover that they were doing fancy-work. Now it is called embroidery; then, its very name had a slightly shady allure, at least to me and, like Goldstraw, carried a suggestion of wit and a conceit. Could anything as dour as work ever be *fancy*? The instant a doorbell rang, the fancy-work disappeared into box, bag or basket.

What did children do? This one sucked on lollies carefully hoarded in a paper bag with pinked edges: threepenn'orth of mixed, bought in Coles on Saturday morning. You got a lot for threepence then: black cats, buddies, aniseed balls and conversations. The conversations hinted at an adult world of assignations and flirtations. Heart or rosette-shaped, they wasted their messages on juvenile taste-buds. Be mine. See you soon. What's cookin'? This child read endlessly, often from stuff that did no harm, but did not do much good, either. *The Testing of Tansy* and *A Quiet Time for Molly* were Sunday School prizes, as one could tell by the titles alone. Such reading matter abounded. Enid Blyton had not yet fallen under a cloud; nor had Capt. W. E. Johns.

The stories I remember were read at school, re-read at home, and dealt with pain, grief and horror of separation and isolation. In Grade 3, I sat on the rug with thirty other children and wept silently while our teacher, a heartless young thing who wore Purple Passion lipstick and chewed Wrigley's PK even while she was reading, went through *Lassie Come Home* chapter by agonizing chapter. In a later year, I lay awake at night reliving the terror of *Lost in the Bush*. The whole drama had taken place not far from our town, and the heroine, Jane, by now very old, was living nearby. The fear and apparent hopelessness of the children's plight haunted me continually. Thirty years later, I thought I had forgotten all about this tale – until it appeared in my son's correspondence set. I began to read it aloud. Then I began to shake.

We also read *The Drover's Wife* at school. Now I understand that mother, but even then I felt a constriction of the throat when the little bush boy flung his arms round her neck and declared, 'Mother, I'll never go droving.' The closing sentence, completely satisfying in its simplicity, has been at the back of my mind forever. 'And she hugs him to her breast, and kisses him, and they sit thus together while the sickly daylight breaks over the bush.'

You could read on Sundays, but children also engaged in other rituals whenever possible: fishing for yabbies in the storm-water drains or in the fringed waters of the swamp, half-heartedly playing with dolls or swapping marbles, playing alleys under the tankstands. I went regularly to a grove of birches and self-dramatized determinedly for two months after reading L. M. Montgomery's *Pat of Silver Birch*. There I sometimes caught a glimpse of an old woman who always wore black, who always walked with a stick, poking and prodding, and who never said anything. As in the case of Louey Tong, it was almost possible to see a sign hanging round her neck: *Outcast*.

Once we came face to face. She stared. I swallowed hard. No words came and we shuffled off in different directions.

There are words which were alive then, and are dead now. Or with God and History? The ice-man came. There was a gap though, between the vision and the reality. He ought to have been a hybrid Jack-Frost-Snow-Queen figure, stiff with icicles, frozen and glittering, like a hard and sparkling rock, quartz or diamond. Instead, draped in hessian, he loped into the kitchen every Tuesday morning and slid the blue-white block off his shoulder into the top compartment of the wooden ice-chest with one easy, fluid movement. 'See yez next week,' he said, without fail, and he did see us next week and the week after that and every week until, eventually, we bought a refrigerator, and the words *ice-man* and *ice-chest* disappeared.

They disappeared before the word night-man did. The night-man, I thought when very young, was simply a man who inhabited the darkness and looked something like a witch, with the moon and stars embroidered on his clothing. Later, he deteriorated into a prosaic figure who came and went with his burden, not always at night. He was an object of pity mingled with awe. What work! But picture the humiliation if you were actually seated when the exchange, full can out, empty can in, took place. The possibility often loomed large in our conversations and so did Ronnie Elliott's list.

Columns, pages, whole collections and categories of words and phrases seem to have vanished, in fact, to be replaced by a tintinnabulum of high-tech new ones. Children no longer *run messages* or *wear pinnies*, there are no longer *back bedrooms*, no more *wigwams for a goose's* (geeses'?) *bridles*, no more *travelling in dolls' eyes* and *slate pencils*, and y is no longer *a crooked letter which can't be made straight*.

27

'And a butcher's farewell to you!' screeched my grandmother, on one occasion. 'God loves Ireland!' sighed my mother in a mixture of irritation, exasperation and despair.

Do people play with words as they used to before this visual age? I do not know, but remember well my sister's puzzlement which resulted when, aged four, she gravely asked our uncle:

'Why do you call my daddy George?'

(Our daddy's name is actually Bill.)

'Because his name is Fred,' replied Uncle, grinning.

Even Grandfather, a sedate, dignified man, used to play mischievous games with words. If a female wore a flimsy dress, she was wearing 'ninon over none-on'; if she wore a tight sweater, she was 'pulling the eyes over the wool'. My brother's name has a silent p in it.

'A silent pee as in surf-bathing,' Grandfather would announce, chuckling quietly, thinking himself greatly daring, and we would titter as we were meant to do.

And all the while we never dreamed, not really, that there were other languages, other Sundays elsewhere, other ways of doing things. We knew about the Tower of Babel, of course, but surely God spoke English, the King James version?

Language, like land, has layers. Top soil, clay, bedrock; narrative, legend, epic, myth. In the last decades of the twentieth century, tourists prowl the site of Troy, with its own nine layers, and know that the famous conflict was a straight-out war of commerce, for the Achaeans needed access to the Bosphorus. But it is the bedrock of myth that is remembered. 'An angry man – there is my story,' sang the blind man, telling us of war and longer exile, of heroes and villains, gods and mortals, names and places: Nestor of sandy Pylos, Odysseus, with his proud Kefallonians in vermilion-cheeked ships. Now such names are familiar, for in half a day we can reach Ithaca, in two hours Pylos, where Nestor's 'ninety ships could ride at ease'. Nearby lies his Palace, discovered as recently as 1939, rich in Linear B tablets – so rich that the first ones were found within twenty-four hours, as the excavators' spades (surely guided by Providence?) drove straight into the Archive Room. At the end of the first season, six hundred precious pieces of clay had surfaced.

Yet another name is familiar, for ten minutes' drive away from our village is a village mentioned in Book 9 of *The Iliad*, as one of the gifts Agamemnon was prepared to bestow on Achilles. Then the village was a city inhabited by 'men rich in flocks and rich in cattle'.

Here in this village, the boy's earliest memory is of a sea of hats and heads. Held high in his mother's arms, he gazes about the crowd in the *plateia* and wonders. As a big boy he learns that he has been at a *yiorti*, perhaps for the *Aghioi Theothoroi*, twin-named saints of the village church. Their name means *gift of God*, and their day is a present indeed, falling as it does in Lent. It is significant that his first memory is of a crowd, of people, for this is the way Greeks like to be.

A slightly later memory is again of a crowd. It is October, 1940, and the Greeks have uttered a word defiant and inspiring. The child hears it, but does not quite understand, even though it is a word soon learned by every child: *OXI*, NO. But he had the experience, even if the meaning had to come later. This word would endure; it was not a case of last year's words belonging to last year's language.

And in November the crowds gather again and wait for news of the Greek army's struggle against the Italians. That month a proud people added more names to its list of battle honours: Korytsa, Aghioi Saranda and Argyro-kastro. But the boy's memories are not of those names, but of the man on the bicycle, bringing newspapers and calling out the headlines, riding slowly up the street and shouting, '*Tous fagame. Tous rokanisame.*' We ate them. We crunched them up. Primal imagery, with its direct appeal to a child's imagination, has lingered in the mind forever.

Another word which endures is fear, *fovos*. The boy and his sister are alone in the house. They are tiny children. Four years old, five? The boy is a year younger than his sister, but he, naturally, is the one who goes outside to the wooden door when he hears it rattle. He leaves it locked, as he has been instructed to do, but carefully puts his eye to the large keyhole. He freezes: another eye gazes into his through the hole, which seems to grow larger and larger, more threatening, as if it will open into a space big enough to admit the stranger. The boy cannot move, but continues to stare. There is a slow movement and the eye disappears. Still he cannot move, but watches, waits, watches, and sees a uniform walk across the street. He has never seen a uniform before, but knows, is absolutely certain, that the person he has seen is a German soldier.

The words *war* and *fear* wove their threads through his life. He sat on a window-sill in a large, draughty schoolroom and listened and watched. Here was no instantaneous learning of shapes, practising the drawing of pot-hooks, swans' necks, little spades, for books, paper, pens, slates and pencils did not exist. Instead, there was much reciting of what the teacher wrote on the board: Alpha, Veeta, Gamma, Thelta, Epsilon . . . through to the satisfying sound of Omega.

And when books finally came, the poring over them under the watchful eye of the teacher. More recitation. Mi-mi-Mimi-mi. Gabbling, followed by the teacher's careful question: 'Where does it say *Mimi*?' Floundering, and then comprehension that syllables joined together make words which we speak. A flash of memory reveals the bead frame, a giant square; recitation while he moves the beads. He does this too quickly, not realizing the connection between the recitation and the counting, and his elder brother mouths at him. *Siga. Siga.* Slowly Slowly.

But big boys laid their guns on their desks, and did not come to school every day. And once the boy had to leave the room, lay down the pencil he had recently acquired, pick up a shovel instead, and go with his class-mates to dig for bodies trapped in rubble after a battle between the Communists and Rightists. As well as their alphabets, children learned lists of initials during those years: *EAM, ELAS, EDES, EKKA*. They had the experience of war, witnessing death, feeling fear, but missed the meaning; now this boy wonders if there ever was any.

The saint continued to write, extending the sentence for the benefit and mystification of posterity. 'And the Word was God.' A couple of millennia later, inspiration came to another poet who sat in rather more comfort. He set down this, as I learned in 1963:

> 'Every phrase and every sentence is an end and a beginning.
> Every poem an epitaph.'

– and revealed what I had somehow always known: the supreme power of words. No wonder the Word was God; the Omnipotent and the Word flowed together, joined, overlapped.

Throughout the fifties we saw it all, the exercise of that power, the capacity of words to praise and uplift, or to wound and destroy. 'THE KING IS DEAD' proclaimed the banner headlines of the *Sun*. I gazed in awe at the four-inch-high words of solid black. They announced a fact: an apparently blameless life was at an end. Other words, many, many of them, were more ambiguous, filling column after column of newspaper space, entering people's hearts and minds. The name *Petrov*, so very foreign, hung heavily in the air and then vanished.

The leader of the land was a silver-haired, silver-tongued orator, given to casting artificial pearls of poetry before the population. '*I did but see her passing by*,' he announced, later, '*and I will love her 'til I die*.' We were meant to have the same feeling but some people were not persuaded. 'Pig-iron Bob,' muttered my father, making poetry of his own. 'Plausible coot.'

The leader even came to our town on his way to visit his birthplace in the Mallee. The high school choir sang 'God Save The Queen' and 'Men of Harlech' at the reception centre, the local picture theatre. 'Here he comes!' people called in great excitement. 'Plausible coot!' muttered my father again, among a great many other phrases. But the leader endured unchanging on for an awfully long time, while other mortals rose and perished.

Another white-haired man became the centre of attention and then disappeared quite quickly. 'The Doc's destroyed. They've destroyed him. *He's* destroyed him. A smear, the whole bloody thing.' Again my father muttered, when he wasn't roaring with rage. I understood little, but long remembered for their sound, two sets of initials: RGM and HVE.

Swirling rumour, snide words decided another fate. I cannot remember precisely when it appeared and disappeared but again, I was fascinated by a name: Sidney Sparkes Orr, an SOS in the wrong order and so doomed? And yet again, my father lamented, mourned, raged and bellowed. 'Poor old Sidney Sparkes. That wonderful mind. Bloody Hell. How *dare* they? *Immorality!* Humph!' My mother too, was indignant; she mentioned the eleventh commandment and held forth about people casting the first stone, the presence of motes in their brothers' eyes and beams in their own.

Words, God, God, words – interchangeable? It seemed so, very often. Words, like God, held the power of life and death, could create and destroy; they could project an aura of charm or give off the fumes of decay. The Word made the world, and the flesh, and the Devil.

The adults at home knew well the sway of words. Granny doted on her youngest brother. 'She worships that man,' the rest of the family stated as a matter of fact. 'Thinks the sun, moon and stars shine out of him.' Instantly Great-uncle Bill was ranged alongside the saints. Did he, too, cast down his golden crown beside the glassy sea? My father used to sing, loudly, enthusiastically but erratically. 'Ramona. When deep purple falls over da–dum castle walls. Smi-ile for me, my Diane. I wonder who's kissing her now, an Aussie, a Yankee, a Chow . . .?'

'Bill!' my mother would warn. 'That's enough. No army versions in front of the children.'

And still those missing words of the forbidden parody are a tantalizing blank in the memory.

The boy lived his life while men fought, and while other men worked, as soon as they were able, to unlock the mysteries of the land and language. Scholars worked on the puzzle of Linear B, on those tablets discovered under the earth at sandy Pylos, tablets bearing groups of signs separated by small vertical bars, bearing even erased signs which are still just visible and legible. By 1951, a list of 159 words had been painstakingly compiled, and would soon give clues to a way of life lived more than three thousand years before.

Other men, living more modest lives, wrote histories of their own small region, listed the foreign names of Don

Pierre Antonio Pacifico, Colonel Leake, Pouqueville, Fourmont, brave travellers and explorers of hundreds, rather than thousands of years before. The explorers had written books in Italian, English and French, in which they told old and new stories of plague, conquest and exile. In the eighteenth and nineteenth centuries plague ravaged Messinia; the Albanians forced whole villages to convert to Islam, and sold thousands of people into slavery, so that, now, to call a Greek an Albanian is still an insult. One Englishman, John Thornbull, rescued many Messinians from such hardships, taking the makings of a community, priests and all, to Florida, weaving yet another thread in an old, old pattern.

And the word *thanatos* came closer. Little Anna died. She was two years old, she had measles and there was no doctor. The priest-father arrived home from his olive-groves and vegetable garden and turned away, weeping. *Pethane? Pethane?* he kept asking in disbelief. She died? Nothing could comfort him. He felt, with the poet Zalokostas, who wrote a famous poem about the death of a child, that words were useless. *Loyia hamena*.

The word *plague* was replaced by others possessed of terrible power in the fifties: measles, diphtheria, meningitis. Another sister tosses and turns on a narrow pallet in the coolest spot in the house. Her throat closes and she fights, rages and struggles for breath. The mother readies herself. *Tha pethanei tora. Tora.* She will die now. Now. The *now* is repeated, but the tortured breaths continue in their fashion, and this time *o thanatos* retreats. Pipitsa does not die.

Instead she lives to run about the streets with her older brothers and sisters while they hear and learn of life and death elsewhere. New strings of initials, new words come across the water. *EOKA. Enosis. En-o-sis!* the children chant, aping their elders, but not really understanding. Union, union for Cypriot Greeks. But the Cypriots remain separate, apart, and for them much worse is to come.

The word exile, *exoria*, has layers ready for the excavators' tools. In ancient times, wearied by war against the Lakonians, racked by sickness and deserted by their slaves, the Messinians had exiled themselves, leaving their inland towns and seeking a fertile valley and the fastnesses of Mount Ithome. Yet eventually, Ithome, too, had to be abandoned, and the Lakonians razed it to its foundations. For three hundred years the Messinians lived outside Messinia; Pausanias records that divine power scattered them to the ends of the earth. Some migrated across the narrow waters to Nafpaktos, others sailed further away to Sicily and Libya, taking olive cuttings and establishing great cities as well as an agricultural way of life like the one they had always known.

And during three hundred years they practised the art; with grammar, oratory and speech they kept their Doric dialect intact. While other Peloponnesian speech patterns had changed, theirs was pure. Finally their dream of return came true, and the city of Messene rose again, with its statue of Zeus Saviour, its divine sanctuaries of Poseidon and Aphrodite, and its iron statue of Epaminondas, the Theban who caused the city to be rebuilt as a permanent check to Sparta. His walls still rear above the slopes as they did then. We can imagine, seeing them, how they helped Bakis's 'strong-coloured flower of Sparta to wither'. The Messinians had come home.

Yet they would continue to wander. The boy knew of two uncles in Chicago. Only one ever returned. The boy himself would become a man and wander, taking with him a stone from the pebbled shores of Kalamata, a precious piece of *homa elliniko*, and eventually bringing it safely back again. Yet perhaps his is a permanent exile, for he does not know where he belongs. Another Greece, another community elsewhere, is always in his mind. And now his sons, too, have Janus faces.

The boy was sent into exile when he was twelve. Twenty kilometres might well have been twenty thousand. So he felt, as he went to the only secondary school in the large town and returned every afternoon to a room he shared with his brother; they cooked, studied, and battled home-sickness together. They could not go home very often; instead, with other boys, they waited at the bus stop. The bus would lumber in, its roof luggage-rack crammed with cane baskets, each one covered with a tea towel. Each boy, and there were many, recognized his own mother's weaving and use of dyes: no printed names and labels were ever necessary.

At twelve, he realized that there were other worlds. Town boys, more sophisticated, articulate, sat in desks alongside boys who had walked down mountainsides, who were quiet, shy and spoke with distinct country accents and their own words, even though they lived only short distances away. By boat they came from the Mani, that land of vendetta tradition, harsh justice, wild poetry, different vocabulary. They all came, carrying more than their bundles and parcels, because their parents wanted a different life for them. At school they would learn to slough off their peasant layers, would hear and learn *katharevousa* and French with which to dazzle their often illiterate parents. The syllabus itself was another world, other words: Latin, mathematics, physics, chemistry, art and the laws of perspective, music and the tonic sol-fa.

At school pride in their past, their commitment to freedom, would be reinforced. The Greek flag fluttered over the building, the pupils learned patriotic poems, sang songs, and re-enacted episodes from the life of

Kolokotronis. So we, too, a world away, swore the solemn patriotic oath every Monday morning. My mother informs me that a whole generation of Australian schoolchildren regularly chorused: 'I love God and my Country, I honour the Flag, I will serve the King and *Chifley* obey my parents, teachers, and the laws,' but that was before my time.

And we, too, learned poems. What feelings did twenty-five little girls have, in fact, that night as they stood stiffly in red-and-white crêpe paper and recited: 'They shall not grow old, as we that are left grow old . . .'?

At least one was a war orphan; I could not imagine how she felt. How did we feel when we sang the Recessional, as we did so many times?

> God of our fathers, known of old,
> Lord of our far-flung battle line,
> Beneath whose awful hand we hold
> Dominion over palm and pine.
> Lord God of hosts, be with us yet,
> Lest we forget, – lest we forget.

Did we feel proud, complacent, indifferent? Perhaps we felt nothing and thought nothing, even when we came to the reference to 'lesser breeds without the law'. It is hard to remember. What seems fairly certain is that such words gave form and shape to something which had a definite presence, and which needed to be understood, needed to be manageable. So the words recreated, made acceptable, that experience, that background: war, colonialism, Empire, dominion.

So we play God. And sometimes we have to, in order to stay sane. Sometimes it is essential to use words as therapy, to give shape and meaning to lumpy experience, to dull pain, to make a home out of strangeness. 'Home is childhood recreated,' writes John le Carré, and so I sit and write endlessly about my childhood, setting it all down, recreating it, seeking a home, playing God, doing it all in middle-life before it is too late. Deafness already looms. Words blur and fuse, lose their meaning. What is next? I do not know, but know only that a life without the 'air and harmony of shape' is not to be borne. Read, write, build a fence, moat, castle walls, against the possiblity. But make sure the drawbridge is working, for words, and the study of them, can isolate as well as connect.

And now George, too, plays God, and tries, at least, to recreate his childhood, to go home to the past. He tries to build a bridge, as I do, for our children. Bridges of sighs. In a sense our sons form their own island, with connecting spans to very different worlds. Which one will they choose to cross? And is there any necessity to choose only one? Or any?

If my world is alien to them, then George's, paradoxically, can often seem more alien still, frozen in time, far from their own reality. George talks of routine, endless routine, as part of his parents' struggle to keep six children fed. Clothing was another matter; there are many stories involving shoes, those twin symbols of respectability. During Yiayia's childhood, donkey-hide shoes used sometimes to be soaked so they would be soft enough to wear once a week. When George was a boy, a family of ten children had only two pairs of shoes, so that the children took it week about to go to church.

'Weren't you bored out of your mind?' Dimitri, Niko and Alexander ask, after recitals about the interminable round of weeding, gardening, watering, running messages, supervising goats, collecting eggs.

'Boredom comes only to the affluent,' instructs their father. 'We knew no other way; nobody was any better off, and many were worse off. Resentment. Now that is different. I was often resentful. We all were. We didn't want to leave our games of poison ball, hopscotch and knuckle-bones to wander along the ditches with the goats. Of course we didn't. But there were compensations.'

He laughs nostalgically and breaks into a story about a playmate of his who did not take the family goat to the right place, with the result that the goat ate nothing. In order to disguise its hollow flanks, Pavlos spent half the journey home fluffing out the goat's fine hair. His parents, however, were not deceived, and Pavlos learned, somewhat painfully, that the individual's wishes counted for nothing when a family had to be maintained.

'We were learning all the time,' adds George, 'even when we didn't realize it. We learned what grasses and plants sheep, goats and donkeys would and wouldn't eat. We knew how to tie all sorts of different knots; we had to know, so that we could load the donkey correctly. We knew far more about the natural environment than children do today. At least that's how it seems to me. I can still tell, simply by tapping it, if a watermelon is ripe or not. *You* can't do that. Ours was a small world all right, but we knew it well. Sometimes I think I've stubbed every one of my toes on every rock around here!'

And the boys listen yet again to tales of barefoot hopping races along the stony paths to school. They like hearing all this, hearing about the *specialness* of Feast days, about summers way back then. They like hearing about makeshift toys: tops made by boring a hole in a ten-drachma piece, and attaching a piece of string, balls fashioned out of old rags. They like hearing about hazardous sports like that of making hot-air balloons out of paper, wire, bamboo and petrol-soaked sponges, and about the launching of them over outdoor fires. They find it hard to believe that no soccer was played in the village before 1955, and that then, practically the whole village became addicted to it: mothers, fathers, *yia-yathes* and *papouthes* would all be there, with the women anxiously counting how many times their sons bit the Peloponnesian dust.

These are the light-hearted recollections. Through others run a thread of fear. Walking through the olive-groves at dusk during the civil war years, because the bus only went a certain distance along the Athens road, George used to hear every slight movement, every grassy rustle, every flutter of wings, see a guerilla behind every tree, sense an ambush in every ditch. It took a long time to reach home on such evenings.

Another journey he was too young to make, but speaks of in tones which suggest the tension and fear felt by his family, tension and fear which, although nearly fifty years old, still seems fresh and sharp. When the Germans entered the valley, the inhabitants, true to age-old tradition, retreated up the mountains to their ancestral villages. Once there, lack of food became a problem, and George recalls his mother sending the two eldest children home, down to the valley, to bring back some cheese. Because they were mere children, then about ten and eleven, there was less risk. So the parents reasoned. But I do not like to think about the fear both children and parents felt, children as they went into danger probably made worse for it being linked to familiar territory, parents as they waited for hours for boy and girl to return, as they eventually did, from a fourteen-kilometre journey along mountain tracks.

Returning. Going home. Going back. So much of the migrant's life seems constructed around these phrases. Only a generation ago, poverty and danger were forms of exile, an exile from opportunity. Many people chose a more literal form of exile in order to escape both, and the consequences of both. But then, having made the choice, all they could think of was going back.

I turn to my Greek dictionary to search for *logos*. The large dictionary contains thirty-five entries. I baulk at these, and turn to the smaller, more manageable one. *Logos:* speech, sermon, word, reason, account. Inspiration was ambiguous and protean on Patmos. Does it matter? Probably not. Interchange, substitute as you will, the results will be much the same: attempts at communication, dialogue, comprehension and coherence.

A summer memory of an evening service drifts back. The congregation, sweating slightly in suits, hats, gloves, sings:

> Lord, speak to me, that I may speak
> In living echoes of Thy tone . . .

Did the reply come during the anthem when John Smythe's bass voice proclaimed, '"I am Alpha and Omega," saith the Lord.'?

Chapter 3

GOING back is easy. One blink and I am there, seeing not rocks, tufted mountains, olive trees and cypresses, but a maze of suburban streets edged by clipped nature strips, each of which had a prunus planted in its centre. At the heart of the maze is a wide bitumen road along which the milkman's and the baker's horses still clopped when I first went there, and where Nana, five feet nothing and in her night clothes, once held the milkman's horse, which had bolted, leaving a dawn trail of splintered glass and greasy milk.

At the end of the bitumen road was another, threaded by tram track, an indicator of a different world. Every morning Uncle Lionel walked to the Number 57 tram. We heard its faint rattle as it bore him away to The Shop. We heard its clack as it brought him back again to the same greeting every evening.

'You're late, Lionel.'

'Am I, Harriett?'

Nana and Uncle Lionel, both widowed, lived together in Number 7. Number 7 had a cyclone-wired front fence, a wire gate with a latch which never quite shut, and a long tin letter-box. A semi-circle of buffalo grass bristled in the front yard; straggly rows of hollyhocks stood by the enclosed part of the verandah. Into this space Nana's window always gaped open; fine white curtaining flapped, billowed or dropped over the cane chaise-longue, the elegant name of which belied its thoroughly battered condition. Near the open window rested a brass plate which said WALLACE – why, I never discovered. Brass also gleamed on the front door, and the knocker, when lifted and let fall, sent its sounds reverberating eerily down a long, dark passage, much as memory calls now, from a great distance.

Uncle Lionel's room was at the back. To get there, you stepped along the mossed concrete path at the side and came first to Rory's Sleep-out. Rory was Uncle Lionel's son, at least ten years older than we were, and a mysterious, remote figure who took judo lessons and rode a racing bike and who was rarely actually in Rory's Sleep-out. Next to this sanctum, to which we were forbidden entrance, was the washhouse (not the laundry), and the lavatory (not the loo and never the toilet), and then there was the Shed, which housed pile upon pile of tattered magazines: *People*, the *Australasian Post* and *Woman's Day*, and the overflow from the shop.

The shed was an avenue of escape when the pressure to listen to Christian broadcasts became too great. So was the pear tree, which produced fruit unfailingly ridden with codlin. We ate the woody, unholey bits anyway, always making sure we were sitting in a good light, and entertained ourselves.

'What's worse than a worm in a pear?'

''Alf a worm, stupid!'

Outhouses and garden were agreeably ramshackle and messy, for suburban living then was not the competitive house and garden affair it is now. Lilac and lavender, never the tidiest of plants, bloomed profusely, creepers curled and twined insidiously in and out rusted piping, ferns brushed and dripped against worn weatherboards. Potplants cluttered the back steps and part of the kitchen near where the Kooka stove resided. You staggered slightly as you entered the kitchen because the floor needed re-blocking; but the back window, a square of stained glass window through which crimson and blue light filtered gently, softened the shabbiness of worn lino and faded wallpaper.

Many, and more affluent, years later, that weather-board house in suburban Melbourne seemed basic, worn, run-down, but above all basic. It did not have the stand-ard of comfort we had grown used to. In her old age Nana did not possess an automatic washing-machine, dryer or freezer. What heating there was came from a woodstove, the like of which is now back in fashion.

But in 1975 I met another house, a house completely functional, a house which called for a new definition of the word *basic*. It was built of stone, bamboo and terracotta tiles, and the wood used in its construction still resembled the tree-trunks it had been. Upstairs the minimal furniture was draped in dull stuff which cast an air of gloom, as it was meant to do. All white eye-let work and delicate crochet covers had been banished upon the death of George's father.

Nor was there any clutter. Clutter, I realized, had been an essential part of Nana's house, of Uncle Lionel's shop. Here, in another world, clutter was, and is, dealt with ruthlessly. Any presents (ornaments, place-mats, pairs of gloves, snapshots, most things) are admired briefly and then stored in one of numerous trunks. Very few things are on display. Austerity reigns, and now seems to me to be an indication of a different, but equally compelling kind of Puritanism: there is no sense of pleasure in things, no real sense of the endless possibilities in life, no real grasp of lives different from the ones lived for more than a hundred years in this house. I still cannot decide about this austerity, whether it is good, bad, or immune from this sort of judgement.

All I knew then was that this house was, to me, an alien, harsh environment, not comfortable, not exuding an air of welcome. The house reflected the struggle that life had always been, and part of me was reluctant to learn about this struggle, for I felt guilty enough about the privileges which had always been mine.

One of those privileges, taken for granted, was a bathroom. The Greek house had none; to take any sort of overall wash you had to retire to the floor above the animals' quarters, bolt the far from draught-proof double doors with their metal bar and hook, and then turn blue and shivering while you stood or sat in a shallow-sided wooden tub which doubled as a laundry trough. The water for this cold ritual had first to be heated in a copper-lined cauldron which sat on a trivet over an open fire which blazed either in the courtyard or on the raised hearth in the kitchen.

Uncle Lionel's home life was austere in a different way and for different reasons. The first evidence of his presence was in that bathroom inconveniently situated next to the kitchen. The bath itself had a permanent green stain trickling downwards, and clawed feet, and was filled by means of a lethal weapon – a gas heater. Then, matches held in trembling fingers, and mini-explosions, were an inevitable part of cleanliness. Uncle Lionel's razor strop, worn black with use, hung on the towel rail. We were allowed to stand in the bathroom doorway and watch him shave. The cut-throat razor, ivory-handled, whished and swished along the leather and then carved tracks through the foam on that white-skinned, bony face. We held our breath as the blade, wickedly sharp, passed smoothly over his prominent Adam's apple. But nothing ever happened, for Uncle Lionel's hands, like a team guiding blade and flesh, plucking, easing, pulling, smoothing, worked perfectly always.

Then we trotted past the tall kitchen-dresser where the

45

blue picture plates of Burns and Dickens gazed from the top shelf, and found ourselves at the entrance to his room. His room was an austere place, containing his bed, a cupboard and little else. He was rarely to be found there, for most of his life was lived at The Shop, yet a mere push of the door evoked his presence. But on Sunday mornings we were allowed to climb on his bed and watch while he fashioned mouse's ears out of handkerchiefs or made sixpences appear and disappear in the blanket folds. Once I found a money spider instead.

'Let it go,' he instructed. 'Harmless little thing.'

He permitted us to arrange his six strands of hair over his domed skull.

Later, in much the same way, my children would finger and poke at Yiayia's bun, admiring the tight ball that was pinned so efficiently to the back of her neck.

We counted the strands carefully and wondered, but did not presume to ask about his bumps, for in his youth, so our mother said, he had consulted a phrenologist. Before Sunday dinner, we sat and listened while Uncle and our father talked of Evatt and Santamaria and used strings of initials which we did not understand and more or less assumed were much like the nonsense language we babbled while walking up Maribyrnong Road – designed to impress, but meaningless.

Very occasionally, we visited the shop, which occupied two floors in a building next to the railway track near East Richmond station. Our mother always took us, and squabbled amiably with Uncle Lionel when he bought us ice-creams, which he always did.

'You can't afford it, Uncle.'

'But Marjie, it's only fivepence!'

And so we entered, taking care not to drip Toppa strawberry or Sennitt's vanilla or Peters' chocolate on shining walnut and mahogany surfaces, for Uncle Lionel was an antique dealer, who spent his time shuttling endlessly back and forth between the shop and the city's auction rooms. Periodically a relative would set the shop to rights, clear out the junk and create some space for more saleable pieces. In what seemed like the twinkling of an eye, however, the entire premises would be full to overflowing once more with all sorts of *objets*, artefacts and items, good, bad and indifferent, for Uncle could resist nothing that went under the auctioneer's hammer.

Uncle was one of the most charming men I have ever known, but utterly hopeless at business – and now my mind makes the connection between these facts. He could never decide on a price for anything, gave trinkets, ink-wells and book-ends as presents to people he liked, and would not charge for the French polishing ordered by his clients, many of whom were wealthy Toorak residents and did not need his charity. Small wonder that John, the French polisher, looked thin.

John inhabited the top floor, a dark Dickensian haunt packed to the ceiling with crazy piles of furniture, all shapes and sizes, which loomed in shadowy outline against the dim light of a bare globe. Clouds of chalk dust and gluey vapours hung in the air. A tiny barred window gave a view of roofs and of the railway lines snaking away towards the City. John's domain was a dismal place but he stayed because he loved Uncle.

We all did. He enchanted everybody, constantly creating the illusion that you were the only person who mattered. But now I realize that he never gave too much of himself and gave least where he was most needed. His great pleasure was to give us and our friends impromptu tea parties with treats like jelly-cakes and cream, but I cannot remember Rory and Uncle in conversation, ever. It is hard to recall them ever being in the same room.

Perhaps he was a hollow man. Perhaps. For most people the thought, the doubt, made no difference. 'He's still the one I miss,' sighed my aunt, long, long after his death. I think, myself, that the hollow was the result of hurt, that his was essentially a free spirit which had been taught by Fate not to trust to deep involvement – of which Rory was a constant reminder. For in that bare room at Number 7 there was one photograph and only one. The faces of his dead wife and child were the first Uncle Lionel saw each morning and the last he saw at night.

In Nana's room there were two photographs; nor was her room austere. The place suggested the tension in her, a dual nature, the clash between worldliness and other-worldliness. On her chest of drawers resided her tortoise-shell vanity set: brush, comb and hand-mirror with matching tray, home to real hair-pins, 'not those new-fangled bobby things'. In the corner stood a cheval mirror which had the effect of twisting your mouth to the right when you looked in it, as if it understood your secret spite and malice and immediately betrayed them to the world. And on a satin pouffe next to the mirror sat a most magnificent doll, dressed like Marie Antoinette down to the last detail of fake powdered wig and glittering high-heeled slippers.

In 1973 Yiayia saw this room, but made no comment. Her own room, as I discovered later, contained a bed, her ancient treadle sewing-machine, three or four icons on the wall, and the *kandili* burning beneath them.

But above the evidence of frivolity in Nana's room ('after all, girls, that doll *was* a present') a print of Durer's *Hands of an Apostle* hung, all ascetic fine lines, and near it was another, much larger picture, beloved of the Victorians. A tall Christ, be-robed and wearing a spiky crown of thorns, carried a shining lantern held low. His hand knocked, tentatively I always thought, at an ivy-mantled door (or window?). Beneath his feet a scroll unfurled itself and proclaimed the appropriate message: '*I am the Light of the World.*' Years later, I learned a little about Holman Hunt and wondered which version Nana's print was. And now I no longer know where the picture is.

A fat black Bible lay on the bedside table. Its frayed silk bookmark showed that this book was in constant use. We often watched while Nana's gnarled forefinger accompanied her reading, moving steadily down the column of references which divided each page into two. Pages were turned, cross-references were consulted, and other makeshift cardboard bookmarks were inserted.

A square, innocent-looking radio also rested on the table. But we were not deceived, and viewed it as an instrument of torture, for it transmitted the dreaded Christian broadcasts. Try as we might to escape (the pear tree, the narrow space behind the verandah wall, the bluestone lane at the back), we were always captured, hauled in and made to sit in a meek twosome on the bed. The content of the broadcasts now escapes me, but I can still squirm and summon up vague feelings of horror which settled, at least on me, when Nana took our hands in hers and announced that she wanted to save us for the Lord Jesus. At eight and seven years old, we did not see the necessity for salvation. But there we sat, trapped, resisting the mental and emotional assault, the determined take-over bid for our souls which we felt, even then, were our own property and not as yet, for sale, not even for love. I fixed my thoughts on the prospect of play with the Promise Box, which I could not take seriously, but thought a beautiful toy. There it waited, with each tiny pink roll snug in its minute compartment. You picked up the tasselled tweezers, selected your target, squeezed and pinched and lifted out the little piece of paper, spread it out and read it: 'Behold, I am with you

49

always. Ye shall eat of the fat of the land. As thy days, so shall thy strength be. Underneath are the everlasting arms.' And so on, one for every day of the year.

Or I looked at the photographs. One was very large, a glassed, wooden-framed, tinted picture of the grandfather we never knew. For us, his was merely a patient face staring from the wall. We knew his story, comprehended the facts (the farm, drought, flood, ruin, death from pneumonia at forty-six) but could feel nothing. Nana would sigh, '*Oh, Will*' or, when the children were present, '*Oh, Daddy*'. Her recollections of the past always started with clasped hands and a wistful 'When Will was alive,' or 'Oh, Marjie, when your Daddy was with us,' and we would titter, cruelly, as children do, knowing nothing of love, separation, death or grief. She had loved him greatly and had broken an engagement and defied her father to prove it.

For her, Will lived on, although her imagination had given him a halo and her memories swirled in roseate clouds. He had become a saint; but every so often we sensed a slight ambivalence, a resentment. (Why did he leave me?) But there was also a vague sense of the pattern of life, the idea, never really acknowledged, the thought, quickly banished, that it might have been *All for the Best*, for Will had been deeply old-fashioned and had abhorred dancing, vaccinations and education for women. Had he lived, my mother and aunt would have been condemned to A Little Millinery, the only permissible paid occupation for ladies. Nana, however, struggled to give them the education she always wanted and never had.

The other photograph, oval, and much smaller, was just faintly recognizable as Nana herself. She stood (reclined?) in a favourite Edwardian pose, her face resting on one hand, her waist-length hair ('Your Daddy asked me never to cut it, Marjie') cascading down her back and on to her striped skirt, falling forward and softening the jaw that had become set with steel determination and wilful old age. The picture had a tenderness and beauty we admired but it was quite different from the reality of the tiny old woman who seemed as fragile as her own porcelain and who was, in fact, as strong and unbending as her own antique fire-tongs. How the grown-ups worried about pleurisy in winter (for she was a Christian Scientist and would not seek medical attention) and heat exhaustion in summer, blindness, senility and a dozen other possibilities. She lived for ninety-three years and two months precisely, and to the end of her days read the daily newspaper and, reminded no doubt by other headlines, never failed to tell us how she remembered the relief of Ladysmith. Thus she linked us firmly with a past that we, in the self-conscious 1970s, preferred not to think about.

In the Greek house where George was born, there are, again, only two photographs on display. One is of the priest father-in-law I never met. His face, too, stares from the wall, for villagers have always had an uneasy relationship with the camera. (Will this machine steal my soul, or not?) His steady gaze is framed by his black beard and stove-pipe hat. He is as unlike my unknown grandfather Will as he can be, yet he, too, seems to have been almost canonized. His name, when it is mentioned, is spoken in whispers. Indeed George hardly speaks of him at all. He will answer questions, but the sense of separation, loss, death as that final exile are all too keen, even now.

The other photograph is of Yiayia's parents, who died too soon for George to remember them. This *papas*, Papayeorgi, sits, while his wife, Panayota, stands. As a concession to the occasion her headscarf trails loose, but she could never be described as being relaxed. Nana wooed the camera, but they face it, this couple, I fancy, as they faced life: prepared for the worst, but also prepared to meet it squarely.

Both priests were, by village standards, highly literate, their wives illiterate. Now I think of Yiayia and Nana, who met in 1973, and consider how lost Nana would have been without her Bible and her books, and how Yiayia has never known the consolation of the written word. 'No one who can read,' stated Dickens, 'ever looks at a book, even unopened on a shelf, like one who cannot.' Yiayia looks at books and bookshelves warily, as her husband and parents faced the camera. Often she picks a book up upside-down.

Papayeorgi was born in 1865, Panayota in 1877, Nana in 1886. With some connection in time, their certainties in life, their frameworks of existence were almost totally separate, lives led along different roads.

Panayota probably knew nothing of life beyond the village. It seems highly unlikely that Papayeorgi ever knew of the relief of Ladysmith. Despite the suspense preceding the latter event, Nana knew herself, in her youth, to be part of a secure, ordered world, part of that Empire on which the sun never set. Everyone, with the possible exception of the colour-blind, knew which parts of the map of the world were pink. There was no such security in the Greece whose boundaries were not yet set. In the uncertainty of Balkan lives, the only real safety was bolted, barricaded home. Greece dreamed of the union of all Greeks and of the recapture of Constantinople, of the Great Idea. But the gap between the dream and the reality would continue to be all too large.

With ten morning newspapers and three afternoon ones serving the population of Athens alone at that time, it is very probable the Papayeorgi knew something of the outside world, even if only as it affected Greece. He may have known of the existence of Queen Victoria, but his sense of reality, urgency, would have been pinned much more to information concerning the 1878 Treaty of San Stefano which threatened Greece because of its provision for the creation of a 'greater Bulgaria', Greece's defeat by Turkey in 1897, the Balkan wars of 1912 and 1913. Then it was war, *polemos*, which took young men away.

I suppose Nana did remember the relief of Ladysmith. I remember her, the photographs, the room. And I remember yet another scene, far away from Number 7. Recall wavers and blurs around the edges, for I was very young. We were in the country, in the heat of summer, for the grass was yellow, short and sunburnt. Other people must have been there, but I remember only Nana, my mother and a child, myself.

In my memory we stand, we three, in a paddock of scorched stubble, and Nana is already old, older than my mother is now. There are two or three twisted, blackened trees, an impression of a straggling wire fence, and a stronger picture of rusting railings. And then she says 'Oh, Marjie, it's gone, all gone,' and she does not cry, for Nana never cries, but I hear the tears in her voice and I cannot understand.

'Yes,' soothes my mother, gently, 'but you knew it had. You knew about the fire.' The reply comes, 'Yes, I knew,' and then, dimly, I become aware, for the first time, that knowing is never the same as feeling.

The house, the orchard, the well, the dairy had disappeared, taking with them all outward signs of eight years of her life, the most important years, the ones she never forgot, the ones that set up a pattern of acceptance and rejection, the ones which let the iron enter her soul, the ones she always talked about. She left and never returned, and it is only now that I feel for her, that I understand that vision of something lost forever, that empty space, that sense that you are, and yet are not the same person who walked through those years. And now I know why and can understand as I could not then, why she stood and stared at the gap in her life and cried, 'Oh, Marjie'.

And cried as every person does sooner or later, for we are all migrants, at the spectre of loss, separation, finality. We all carry a vision of home, an important time as well as an important place, within us. Christo, our friend from this village who lives in Melbourne, has a vision of the Peloponnesian spring constantly in his mental landscape: pink, purple, white and yellow flowers carpeting the olive-groves, light, warm breezes, cotton-wool clouds drifting across an azure sky. All this is still the same; he, however, is not.

Yet now too, traitor memory being what it is, I am not sure that we went to the Buckland Valley, we three, to look at the past, that we ever saw the railings and the graves of Robert and Harriett, which the fire had not touched. But surely I did not dream it all?

But for bad temper, so the story goes, that branch of the family might still be in Acle, near Yarmouth, near Norwich in Norfolk. Nana's grandfather Robert was to have inherited the mill but quarrelled violently with his father. The son threatened to emigrate; the father disinherited him and, adding insult to injury in inspired fashion, paid his passage to Australia.

The story continues, resembling in its ingredients, plot and characters, nothing so much as the historical novels and television mini-series on which strong-minded critics like to pour scorn. Grandfather Robert married Grandmother Harriett before he left, but in a secret ceremony. The redoubtable Harriett was soon beset by problems for scarcely had her husband sailed away, leaving her pregnant, than his brother began courting her. One imagines that the secret did not remain so very long.

What were the characters in this saga really like? Grandfather Robert remains a shadowy figure, a successful farmer who suffered from gold-fever, and a rescuer of Chinese during the Buckland riots. There are vague tales of a feud in that narrow valley, and of his life being saved in the nick of time by a Chinese who pushed him into a side-passage of a mine on sighting the Enemy, armed with a hefty boulder, poised for action at the mouth of the shaft. Did Grandfather Robert have any regrets about Norfolk, the mill, his father, family, England, emigration? I do not know.

Grandmother Harriett comes down to us through the rueful recollections of our own Harriett, as a much more definite personality. One wonders about the effect of her new environment on her character; she had consented to leave Norfolk only on the condition that she could return. The promise was kept. She sailed home, as she thought, hated the place and left it forever. The reasons for this emotional and physical volte-face were never passed on to us. Perhaps she did not, could not explain. Now that I am a migrant myself, I can guess that she realized that the Norfolk Harriett was gone, irrevocably lost, that the Australian Harriett was a different person, a foreigner, that she had seen things, had had visions that her family and friends would never understand. Best to get on with the new life, with no repining.

She did get on with her new life, running a large farmhouse with great efficiency. She was a Christadelphian and mindful of her duty, helped all her neighbours, including the Chinese women, whose midwife she was. But she was stern.

I picture the young Harriett, high-spirited in that valley of pure air and haunting beauty, but able to enjoy few of its freedoms, bound as she was by hampering clothes and discipline. I suspect that Grandmother Harriett saw her own implacable will reflected in her grand-daughter and could not bear the sight. They clashed. Nana was forbidden to go near the well, tried to work the bucket regardless and received a great blow to the forehead when the windlass handle tore out of her grasp. Nana was forbidden to ride horses, but was always sneaking away to do so. One bolted. Nana was forbidden to go near the river for she could not swim and swimming was, according to Grandmother, too dangerous a skill to acquire. Nana played truant, went bathing and was caught out when Grandmother felt the dampness of her clothes. No school picnic, was the edict, and even though nine months were to elapse between crime and punishment, the punishment stood. Clemency was not a word included in Grandmother's vocabulary.

Nana was a beautiful child, but ran no risk of becoming vain. If people commented on her looks, Grandmother sniffed (with the nineteenth-century attitude towards race relations) 'Fair as Phyllis, and she was a black,' or 'Maybe, but she's got a head like a forty-shilling pot.'

'But how big was that, Nan?' we used to ask.

'Very,' she would reply wryly, and we could see how the wounds still opened a little, even in old age. Like Mary Tudor, she had certain words graven on her heart.

One incident she did recount with satisfaction. A ceremonial visit was once paid by some neighbours, the Snells, who lived miles away. Great were the preparations, lavish was the food. In the middle of dinner, young Nana gravely enquired of Grandmother Harriett, 'Grandmother, what did you mean when you said that Mrs Snell came from Takington and not from Givington?' And the old Nana would chuckle with pleasure at the memory. 'What a naughty girl I was.'

She had been taken from her family when she was six years old, so that her grandmother would have company in the remote, isolated valley. She did not see her mother, sister and brothers again until she was fourteen. She saw her father twice in those eight years, when he came to fetch her back. On each occasion, stern Grandmother Harriett dissolved into tears and begged her son to leave his daughter. He capitulated to his mother, as grown men so often do.

When Nana was finally reunited with her immediate family, she found a mother who was a stranger, six brothers and a sister who were immediately jealous and suspicious of the petted interloper who was being made much of after her long absence. For the rest of her life, she was inclined to monopolize, inclined to cope badly with separations and absences. 'They all went away and left me,' she remarked once, when discussing her children and their marriages.

All this, surely, was the effect of that early separation from home and family, not as physically violent, but certainly as reluctant as that forced upon George's great-grandmother. I try to imagine the scene, to choose appropriate words with which to describe it, but words are not up to the task.

The match is arranged, the male ancestor has travelled forty kilometres on mule-back across mountains and valleys to a place called Alagonia, the name of which derives from Greek words meaning *other corner*. Originally the inhabitants of this area, too, had been strangers in a strange land. The groom is nearer sixty than fifty, the bride very much younger. He is so old that he is a veteran of the 1821 struggle against the Turks at Tripoli. A man of the wider world, he does not trust the bride's family, and so stations his brothers and cousins, who have accompanied him, in strategic positions in and around this tiny foreign village.

The groom arrives, but the bride's father emerges from his low stone cottage, and with scarcely a greeting, tells the party that the marriage is off, the contract null and void, they have changed their minds. Nothing is said, but, covered by his brothers, the outraged bridegroom dismounts, pulls out his pistol, seizes his betrothed, places her on his mule, and defies her family to follow them.

Words sketch the bare bones of the story, but cannot guess at the girl's feelings. There was no return; her trousseau, a village girl's pride, was borne to her new village by the groom's relatives. There was no choice but to settle down to marriage in a strange place with a much older stranger. Perhaps her children were her solace; they, at least, did not leave this village when they married. And she herself led a pampered life, so the story goes: she was fair and fat and was never expected to work in the fields.

Another scene I remember. It is a stormy night. The rain is drumming on the iron roof, lightning flashes intermittently and a branch of a tree taps in relentless rhythm against the verandah lace. I know that next door the elderly Salvationist is dying.

'He's very near the end,' I have heard the neighbours say, earlier in the day. Suddenly it is all too much. The darkness clings like a shroud; the tapping inexorably measures minutes and seconds. Panic sets in and horror overwhelms. I wail and bawl, thrashing about in the double bed, burying my head in the huge, kapocky pillow, smothering and sobbing by turns.

And a crack of light appears under the door, widens, and then Nana appears, clutching her dressing-gown, her wispy pig-tail hanging down her back, her striped pyjama-legs flapping above her slippers. She is all concern. Whatever is the matter, dear? A bad dream? – and I gasp out something about being worried about, sorry for, the old man next door. She is sympathetic, but instantly assured and firm. But it's nothing, dear, really, to be afraid of. He's quite happy and contented. He *knows* he's going to our Saviour, don't you see? He *knows* that this is not really an end, but a beginning of something better.

But her confidence was not enough for me, and how could it be, in view of what I had failed to communicate? My only concern with the old man's dying, I know now and surely felt then, was that it forced on me an appalled recognition of an end. For the first time I felt the dreadful dislocation of being only a speck in the vastness of the universe, felt the grim sadness of impotence, of brevity, of human limitation. Such things I could not express.

Few children can. It is only recently that George has recalled and talked about his constant terror at night, the recurring feeling of being crushed, reduced to nothing by the darkness, his sleepwalking, and his very conscious crawling into his parents' bed in the early hours of the morning.

Towards the end of Nana's life, her Bible lay unopened and religion, her Saviour, her prayers and all matters theological previously discussed at length went unmentioned. Instead she wandered the valley again, not in childish senility, never that, but because she chose to remember those years. Perhaps, I thought, the Great Search had been abandoned because the lost had been found, because all the questions had been answered. But there was always a curtain of reserve between us and Nana and so we never knew.

The reserve between Yiayia and myself is more like a wall. Occasionally, usually accidently, I poke a chink in it. One day I was showing an English friend various items from Yiayia's dowry. This, by now, is a set ritual. Her trousseau night-dresses, pillowcases, sheets, and voluminous bloomers are all hand-woven; her crochet and embroidery, now slightly creamy with age, are truly exquisite. My friends come to applaud and admire; she remains to be gracious, flattered and complimented.

On this occasion, my mind not really on the contents of the cupboard, I lifted the lid of the box and saw a bolt of some very expensive damask material, all white.

'What's this?' I murmured, absently, taking it for a tablecloth. Yiayia drew herself up, gave a rueful half-smile.

'That is for the *teleftaio taxithi*, for my final journey.' I stared and did not know what to say, thoughts crowding of that exile from which there is no return. What I held was a winding-sheet.

Once, in a rare moment of self-revelation, the curtain flicked aside: Nana clutched my mother's hand and said, 'Marjie, I don't want to die.'

'Well, I understand that completely,' replied my mother, floundering a little. 'But you've never worried about death before. You've always had faith in the life everlasting.'

'Oh, it's not all that life and living business that worries me,' she retorted impatiently. 'It's just that I don't want to say goodbye to you all.'

And Yiayia has said the same thing. Once I told her what Nana said. 'Ah, *i kakomira*, ill-fated one, how right she was! Now I, I want to dance at Dimitri's wedding.' For Dimitri is her godson as well as her grandson. Lately she has changed her mind about the dancing; mere attendance will be sufficient.

'It'll be a long wait, Yiayia,' says our seventeen-year-old sworn bachelor.

Now I look back on Nana's long span, which stretched from well before the relief of Ladysmith to the fall of Saigon and further, and I ponder the pattern. It is one of tensions. Here is no kaleidoscopic random shifting and falling, but a constant pulling, a balancing, an habitual adjustment of weights with an uneasy equilibrium sometimes being achieved, for the constraints had come early to a spirited and sensuous nature.

As children, we noticed only the constraints, the discipline, the solemn pronouncements about the human condition (Oh, the sin in this wicked world), the injunctions about goodness and virtue, the horror of alcohol. It was only later that we remembered the pots of face cream and rouge, the shopping expeditions, the hats and dresses, the recollected delight in dancing (while Will glowered!), the enjoyment of food, the sense of humour, the jokes told against herself, the delight in language. It was only later that we recalled the morning story sessions in her bed. Her fingers flashed and wove her plaits. She began, 'Tell me a story about Jack-a-nory. I'll tell you one and then my story's done.' The 'Three Little Pigs', before the dull Disney version, was ours and the rhythms of 'Fire, fire, burn, stick, stick won't beat dog, dog won't bite pig, pig won't jump over the stile, and I shan't get home tonight,' haunt the memory still – thirty-five years on. She had a perception of language as a living, changing thing.

'Your great-great-grandmother never used the word *broom*, girls. She always called a broom a *besom*.' We pronounced the word solemnly; there was our link with Old English, had we but known it.

Hers was a deep love of life, but a love kept firmly reined. Literature was the Bible and Church of Christ hymns. Creativity, love of language, the desire to communicate, spirituality, all focused on the weekly prayer meeting which she often led in extemporaneous petition and praise.

Space dwindled. The valley was replaced by suburban Melbourne, her room and a cluttered community life in which the same names and routines recurred. Canterbury Street, Eglinton Street, Puckle Street (just slipping up Puckle). Maribyrnong and Holmes Road, The Parade, Ascot Vale, Moonee West. Once a year the family took the suburban train to Sandringham where another of Nana's brothers had a shop which was far more successful than Uncle Lionel's.

Almost to the end of her life Nana loved to go out, loved to read, garden, to do things, to be busy. She never mentioned her age, for fear that others might expect her to do less, to fit into a mould she was not ready for. Only other women were old.

Since her illness last Christmas, Yiayia goes nowhere and does nothing, she who could once do anything. Instead she shuttles restlessly between her daughter's house and her son's, stays briefly and wonders why she has nothing to talk about. Still clad in the black she has worn ever since I have known her, she seems to me to be slipping away, slowly and surely, to join that dark she has been imitating and anticipating for so many years. For her there is no raging against the dying of the light.

She seems unutterably weary, although the doctor says there is nothing wrong. Worn out by worry, fear, and work, perhaps she now simply wants the luxury of waiting. Perhaps doing nothing has been a lifetime's ambition. Whereas in Western culture the old build up accretions, things, activities, in Greece the ideal is bareness, simplicity, with everything stripped away. In *Blood Wedding*, Lorca wrote that marriage, to an Andalusian peasant woman, meant 'a man and his children and a thick stone wall to keep the rest of the world out.' At eighty-two, it seems too late for Yiayia to hack a hole in the wall, too much for her to confront her fear of the new.

The father who had left Nana in the valley and who had tried, until the very last minute, to prevent the marriage, denied her an education and a career. She had longed to be a nurse and would have made a good one. Instead, widowed early in the Great Depression, she ran a boarding-house.

Like Grandmother Harriett, she was a strong-minded survivor. Like her, she tried to help others. Through those years, we heard, a procession of shadowy men trooped into the back yard, chopped a pile of wood and ate a meal on the side verandah. 'There was never any money but I always had some extra food and Marjie always took two lunches to school, one for her and one for the teachers to give away.'

In Nana's heart, she was always the lonely child, despite three children, eleven grandchildren, nineteen great-grandchildren, brothers, cousins, in-laws, nieces, nephews, friends and acquaintances. There was a sense of the inconsolable about her, as there is, indeed, about George. When he left home at the age of twelve in order to go to school, he spent much of his time, he says, crying, and was often not even aware *why* he was crying. As the grown man mourns the mother of his childhood, the exile mourns a lost land, a home. Nana mourned, and George mourns, all of these. In middle and old age the question repeats itself: What if? What if?

In Nana's heart, she brooded on the loneliness, never, it seemed, valuing the independence, the freedom that was hers. Widowhood was an unsought liberation, but liberation it was nonetheless, and she never realized it, or if she did, dared not express the traitorous thought.

Her siblings died one by one – rejecting her again? She nursed the brothers who had resented her homecoming. Uncle Lionel, a gaunt shadow, was propped on pillows and fed thin porridge carefully prepared. Strange now, that it is easier to remember the steaming bowl with sugared islands of gruel, surmounted by sprinklings of nutmeg and knobs of butter appearing in pools of milk and cream, rather than the person's suffering.

Long afterwards, it was Nana's turn. In April, 1979, she started to fail. 'She will die at Easter,' predicted a cousin, who is, more than most people, aware of life's patterns. On the night of 11 April, her only son returned to his own home several miles away. Feeling worn and tense from waiting, he took a sleeping pill. At two o'clock the next morning, Maundy Thursday, he awoke with jolting suddenness from heavy sleep. It was the precise moment of Nana's death. One goodbye, at least, had been said.

Chapter 4

IT takes several blinks to catch up with Granny and Grandfather, for they were wanderers. It would be romantically satisfying to see them traipsing down the corridors of memory, one carrying a swag and the other a spotted, knotted handkerchief on the end of a stick, but they were respectable nomads. Every few years, having been twin pillars of organizations such as the Bowling Club, the RSL, the Masonic Lodge, the PWMU, the Ladies' Guild, the Presbyterian Board of Management and the Church Choir, they would move on in search of another god: Promotion. Every few years, before the move, sheets of paper, copies of the *Education Gazette*, and the map of Victoria, the one showing railway lines, appeared on the dining-room table, and the air would become thick with talk of mysterious things like transfers, third-class male assistance, and consequentials. There were grim jokes, cracked in an atmosphere of suspense, about the desolation of places like Nullawarre, Salt Lake and Yanac South.

When news of promotion, or occasionally an unwelcome transfer, came through, Granny would sigh resignedly and begin the hard work of packing and wondering how the furniture and ornaments would look in the next house and whether the piano would fit through the doors and passageways. It was an article of faith with her that she and Grandfather, travelling in the Little Standard with the dicky seat, should always arrive first at the new school residence, so that she could supervise the unloading and placement of the furniture. She was a formidable supervisor and organizer, our grandmother, and now I see that her efforts went into continually recreating *home*, into clinging to the core of things, in spite of change.

Within a day, she would be gibbering with exhaustion, but the house would be *right*: the furniture, the piano, the blackwood sideboard with bowed, spindly legs, the wardrobes with the oval mirrors, the painted cane chairs, the bookcase with the leadlight doors, the oak desk, having all been cajoled into their new positions and told to like them.

But the cloth-fronted radio always had to stand out a little from one wall so that Toby, the dog, could have his refuge, chosen in infancy, from Grandfather's violin playing. Grandfather had perfect pitch and played well but Toby was not a musical canine, found *Humoresque* particularly grating, and yelped his protests from behind the wireless.

Toby was definitely an insecure animal, but then he had had an early identity crisis. Grandfather bought him for ten shillings; shortly afterwards the dog inspector called, licence form at the ready, and looked at the tiny puppy.

'What breed d'ya reckon he is?' he asked, eyeing him doubtfully.

'Your guess is as good as mine,' replied Grandfather, 'but I'd say he was a brown retriever.'

'H'm,' came back the voice of authority, 'I can't spell retriever; he's a brown setter.' And the relevant piece of paper changed hands: Toby was labelled for life.

Toby cried. He was always crying. Granny took him everywhere with her, with the result that, years later, nobody could go to the loo alone. Toby always followed.

As little children we were allowed to peep through the white trellis at Granny enthroned with Toby sitting beside her, for that particular outdoor structure had a wall-to-wall seat. Is there always one animal recalled? George remembers his grandfather's donkey, Petros, who was pratically unique because he had a name: most working animals, still, are never named. Perhaps our children will think fondly of Ozzie, our golden mongrel, and of the symbolic value of his name?

With each move of house the new garden had to be checked, lamented over and assessed as to potentialities. This was done very early. Sighs over glories necessarily left behind were few and firmly controlled; plans were hatched, involving Sunday afternoon walks, which were in truth plant-snatching expeditions. No trail, vine, creeper or venturesome plant was safe from Granny: if it showed as much as a frond of green over a fence, she considered it rightfully hers.

It took longer for trunks and tea-chests to be unpacked, but there were certain items in those containers which we considered almost essential parts of our grandparents: the spiky shell that always held flower arrangements featuring asparagus fern; the six pieces of crystal in various sizes being saved, one each, for all the grand-daughters; the cream penguin lamp with its dipping shade of gold-threaded net; the crocheted doyleys which, freshly laundered, had to be slipped under glass tops in the nest of tables; and the red china pixies who sat demurely, their pointed faces becoming a little chipped and cracked with the passing of time, their folded wings acting as bookends for innocent volumes of Zane Grey and E. V. Timms. Both our grandparents loved good yarns, history, adventure and romance. Serious works like *The Ring and The Book*, *Sesame and Lilies*, morocco-bound volumes of Keats and Shelley, and books not for Little Pitchers, like *The Tribe that Lost its Head*, *The Cruel*

Sea, and the various writings by Colette, were imprisoned in the bookcase with the leadlight doors.

But it was not until two photographs were in place that the new house became a home. One was a large diamond-shaped frame which always hung on the wall above the double bed. My father and his sister, trapped forever in a sepia and white childhood, gazed solemnly down on their parents. Bill was plump and clad in rompers; Fay was ethereal and pinafored, but the camera lied, according to Granny, for Fay was a *fizgigs*. The plural, Granny's own invention, of course, made the fizgiggery seem worse. The picture was always called Half-Each-Bill-and-Fay, and life could not be imagined without it.

The Bombardier too, was always there, coming to rest on the left-hand-side bedroom wall, secured by a 'V' of wire to the picture-rail. If you clambered on a chair you could see him in close-up: the buttoned-down pockets, the metal *Australia* on his shoulder-tab, the stripes on sleeve and cuff, and on his collar the rising sun badge with its three scrolls.

But I did not bother with the chair very often. Usually I viewed him from my vantage-point, snug between Granny and Grandfather as they lay luxuriating in those thank-heaven-it's-Saturday mornings.

From that distance the details faded and the face became everything. It was a young face. Even I, who was so much younger, could tell that. It gazed, serious and serene, into the room and apparently beyond it, seeing something that nobody else saw. I could hardly connect the handsome young face with Grandfather, who was still handsome, in my opinion, but decidedly different. And my grandparents always talked as if the photograph had no connection with them.

'There he is,' one or the other would say with a laugh that was half a sigh, 'the Bombardier.' Of course they were right; there was no connection. By then they were nearly sixty years old and had few illusions left. Frozen in youth, the Bombardier still had his intact.

But the word *illusion* was not in my vocabulary; nor did I know what a bombardier was. It was a lovely word to say, though. In my dreadful innocence, back then in the 1950s, I capered in the passage and chanted 'bomb-bomb-bombardier', savouring the sound and knowing next to nothing. I knew the word *war*, however. But even though I knew the word, war itself was a shadow, an insubstantial thing, a shadow with symbols like the photo of the Bombardier, and my father's Japanese sword hidden in a cupboard. And I basked in the sunlight of ignorance.

Occasionally though, the shadows lengthened a little. There were other photographs, snapshots tucked into a battered album. One showed the Bombardier with his hat askew and his lips lop-sided in a foolish grin.

'Why does he look so funny?' I asked Granny.

'Because he was as drunk as forty cats,' she replied, tersely, flipping the page over. This was strange: Grandfather's idea of a spree was a weak shandy during a heatwave.

As I grew, the word *war* became just another part of a pattern. I remember my first school Anzac Day. I was four and a half. My mother made me a cross of white chrysanthemums; I held my partner's hand as the long crocodile wound towards the town's memorial; I deposited the cross below the list of names I could barely read. The words 'Lest We Forget' meant nothing. Later we listened to broadcasts from the Shrine of Remembrance in Melbourne, with Professor Browne telling the story of Simpson and his donkey for the umpteenth time. Surely it was only a story?

The shadows deepened and darkened during the 1960s against the background of the Bay of Pigs and Vietnam. There was a friend of Grandfather's, a geography teacher, a sweet, gentle man who carried his charts and maps about, and kept his coloured chalks in a Pibroch tobacco tin. But he was old, old and deaf, and we gave him hell; the smart alecks said he had a plate in his head.

And then, one 25 April, I saw him on television: he was marching bravely, carrying a banner at the head of a thin line of equally old men. 'He's MC (Military Cross) and MID (mentioned in dispatches) you know,' remarked my father, comfortably.

Later, when the teachers lent their early photos for a guessing competition, he shyly unwrapped a sepia print. The Pyramids were in the background; in the foreground, he and a few companions perched on camels. His face beamed under the slouch hat; once he had been young, eager and alive.

'Hard to believe, eh?' he said, reading my mind. I could not reply. Years later, I read his death notice, 'So dearly loved, so greatly missed . . .' and felt deeply ashamed we had not been kinder.

Grandfather never talked much about the four years. To be sure, we knew the bits that made a good yarn: how he asked his best friend to write to his favourite sister and how friend and sister married after the war; how disappointing it was, half-way through training at Langwarrin, to discover that he would not be going to Gallipoli after all; how bitter-sweet it was when the ship pulled away from the berth at the Port Melbourne quay; how boring it was in Egypt, with all those camels and all that foot-slogging and sand; how utterly thrilling it was to be welcomed by dozens of French girls on every railway station as the troop train moved slowly towards the front lines. 'They gave us cups of cocoa and their names and addresses, and by the time the journey was over, we had not a badge left!'

It all seemed like a successful adventure story, nothing more. Even the list of battles inscribed on two spent shells, always kept highly polished, meant little to us in terms of reality. It was, after all, only another list of place-names: Dickebusch, Flers, Bullecourt, Messines, Nieuport, Passchendaele, Vimy, Robecq, Hamel and St Souplet.

It was a long time before we heard the dark bits, and some of those we learned only by reading his diary and letters after he died in 1970. The best friend, who had been awarded the Military Medal, was dead by 1930: he had been gassed too often to live longer.

Grandfather suffered agonies of homesickness. Whenever he received a letter, he read it so often that it almost fell apart. In France he was demoted for drunkenness one winter: he could not bear the cold and took to rum in self-defence. There was virtually no water for washing and no possibility of a bath for weeks on end. One of the lads 'went off the deep end' as a result of shell-shock, was hospitalized and never returned.

One story he did tell, occasionally, in sheepish fashion. He saw action much sooner than he had expected to. As the shells rained down, he flung himself into the dirt. From a distance he could hear, through all the noise, a high-pitched scream, a voice calling 'Mother! Mother!'. When all was quiet, he realized that the voice had been his own. 'I was scared bloody stiff,' he would say, grinning ruefully.

Interspersed with terror were fatigue, boredom, depression, disillusionment, and still more fatigue. By 1918, he had had enough, and wrote to tell a friend not to enlist: 'In the long run, who thinks any more of you? A satisfied conscience is the only reward.' Yet when it was all over, he often seemed glad that he had had the experience, although *glad* is too simple and slight a word to describe his feelings. Perhaps, being of a rather diffident, nervous disposition, he realized that he had known intensity, felt he had won his own battle against fear and death.

Grandfather always had a sneaking regret that he had

71

'missed out' on Gallipoli. This was a view I could understand yet still consider a great mystery. It is always desirable to be among the first and famous, particularly when people like Sir Ian Hamilton considered that the Anzacs would 'hardly fade away until the sun fades out of the sky and the earth sinks into the universal blackness'.

Yet Gallipoli was, from all accounts, a hell on Earth, a place of unspeakable horror. A. B. Facey collected the pieces of his brother's body for burial, was wounded twice, and invalided out after four months, 'the worst four months' of his life. He later wrote that he would not have enlisted had he known about Gallipoli.

But they went to war, that first lot, for all sorts of reasons: from a desire for glamour, for a lark, but also from a sense of duty and a feeling for others. Times, motives, people, were all different then. Hamilton considered that war deserved 'the credit of being the only exercise in devotion on the large scale existing in this world'. Such sentiments can never be ours. Did anybody ever believe such words? Now we can only read them and think of them with an appalled wonder.

Yet in 1915 the Bombardier wrote to the woman who became his wife: 'I know you think I have done right. I enlisted because I could not bear to think that you might consider me a shirker'. So the thought persists, at least for me, that many men all those long years ago *did* enlist because they believed themselves moved by the spirit of love and devotion. For this reason, above all others, the Bombardier will be with me always. I cannot let him fade away.

In Greek the word *war* is *polemos*. The power of that word. In a way it caused Yiayia's mother's death. On hearing of the outbreak of *polemos* in 1940 she had an immediate stroke, so great was her fear that her only remaining son would be conscripted. *Pethane noris.* She died young, my mother, says Yiayia.

Solid, old-fashioned patriotism, of the sort expressed by Australian Prime Minister Andrew Fisher in 1914, still flourishes in Greece. Fisher declared that Australia would stand behind Britain to 'the last man, the last shilling,' and young men flocked to enlist. The head teacher of our village high school, a woman, interestingly enough, recently exhorted her charges: *Paithia*, you must be ready to defend your *patritha* to the bitter end. Be prepared to shed your last drop of blood for *Ellatha*.

In Greece nobody is confused. Certain areas on certain maps are, or should be, Greek. So says collective opinion, and this opinion is inculcated in the tiniest child. 'How are you going to take Constantinople? How are you going to go to the City?' grown-ups ask when crises occur over eating vegetables or drinking milk.

Before Alexander was even four years old he had to recite a poem, *Long Live 1940*, at the celebration of OXI day, 28 October. Parents had been invited to the kindergarten for the occasion. I was amazed to see the place transformed: flags were everywhere, a stage had been erected, and posters depicting a sword-waving Liberty vanquishing the invaders were prominently displayed.

Twenty small children sat while the teacher told the dramatic story of 1940. It came out rather like the tale of David and Goliath, but it was difficult to guess how much the obedient pupils understood.

Soon it was time for the poems. Alexander recited his brief verse, his enunciation rather blurred because of a comforting finger stuck in the corner of his mouth. Everything was very serious. However, one little boy would only recite if the rest of the group shut their eyes. He launched into his poem, but stopped indignantly after five lines, pointed an accusing finger and roared, 'Maria's peeping!' A gale of laughter swept the room and it was rather difficult, then, for the teacher to recapture the attention of parents and children.

We thought Granny and Grandfather were like every-body else's grandparents on the whole, although we could certainly observe the difference between them and Nana. They were more sensible and temperate about religion, for one thing. But their lives were ordinary and they had always known each other. How boring, we thought: none of that seeing-a-stranger-across-a-crowded-room romance or adventure. Even the drama in their lives, like the war, we took for granted. And, with the indifference of childhood, we never asked Granny the questions we should have asked.

While Grandfather was in France and Belgium for four years, Granny was in Port Hedland. It took weeks to get there by boat from Victoria, and life, once there, must have consisted largely of a struggle against heat and flies. Forty years later, Granny would chuckle at the thought of butter muslin, cheesecloth and Coolgardie safes. And there was apparently no compromise, no concession made to conditions in this outpost, for a photograph extant from this period shows Granny and her sister-in-law in light ankle-length dressing featuring insets of broderie anglaise and pin-tucking, wearing white shoes, and with their abundant hair piled high in elaborate coiffures.

Granny had accompanied her brother, the Reverend Jack, a Presbyterian minister who was then working for the Australian Inland Mission. We were not particularly interested. We laughed over the photo of Granny seated on a camel, but were more impressed to learn that she had actually met Mrs Aeneas Gunn, author of *We of the Never Never* and *Little Black Princess*, two of our favourite books. References to Daisy Bates floated past us, and, with the wastefulness of childhood, we never thought of catching at one and asking.

Yet the Aboriginal chant remains, and I can still say it for my children, although I fear it is sadly garbled by years of disuse and neglect in the mental-filing system, the recesses of the memory. Granny would recite it with great emphasis, tapping out the rhythms until we could almost hear the didgeridoo and almost see black feet slapping and stamping red dust.

> Moondi-ah-*dah*
> Moondi-ah-*dah*
> Moondi-ah-*dah*
> Kar*lah*-loo.

For the next verse she would pitch her voice high, almost to a rhythmic wail:

> Ninny-ninny-ninny
> Woodja *mah*-ah-nah-ta
> Ma-ah loo-oo.

And her voice would die away. We never laughed. It seemed too ceremonial and dignified for that, although memory whispers that it was a simple little tale about a man carving wood. We would try to reproduce it and Granny coached us patiently. Then she would sigh and mutter, 'Lovely people. Magnificent sense of humour'. And once again we never thought to ask.

And what about Granny herself? She had, I think, imbibed a sense of exile and loss, of a people inconsolable, but did she ever ask questions of herself, her brother, of the church and mission? I suppose not. But now every time I play Granny and recite the mysterious words, attempt to catch the rhythms, while my sons sputter with laughter at the thought of an Antipodean tribal chant being sung in the Peloponnese, I feel a sharp pang of regret for a past that is irrevocably lost. We could have reached out for it, salvaged some of it, but, heedless as ever, we did not. A failure.

Their lives were ruled by routine and order. Every week day morning, Grandfather would walk across the road to school, enter the building, pause to open the time-book in which he would occasionally write salutary messages in red ink, step from bluestone flags on to brown linoleum and take up residence in the office. Before I started school the office was my playground. I enjoyed everything: swivel chairs and typewriters, ink pads and rubber stamps, magnets and paper clips, the smell of the spirit duplicator and new paper, and the sound of Dick Cranbourne and community singing on the wireless.

At 12.25 precisely, he would walk home again for lunch at 12.30 precisely. Lunch was always served on a stiff-starched white tablecloth. An equally stiff napkin was bent and pushed into a chased silver serviette ring. The meal was always two courses, the second of which was a thin white custard until the day when, after thirty years, Grandfather announced bleakly, 'I think I'm off custard'. Consternation. Upheaval. The menu had to be changed – and was.

Little else changed, however. At 7 p.m. a deep hush fell immediately the opening bars of *Hearts of Oak* announced the ABC news. Some nights there were meetings; other nights there were music sessions or a sedate hand or two of bridge. Saturday meant either bowls or golf according to season, Sunday was church, a roast dinner and gardening. Monday was the start of the same routine all over again.

It took me years to realize that this ordered life was their comfort, their insurance against fear and insecurity. The drama of their youth had been enough, apparently. It was almost as if, for them, their youthful worlds had expanded too fast; as if, though descended from daring

76

individuals who had forced the world to grow larger, they had not had the same power, or had only had it temporarily.

Years ago I found two old snapshots in Yiayia's cupboard drawer. One shows a very thin old woman standing awkwardly in a vegetable garden. She is looking away, either unaware of the camera or afraid to face it. The other is of her husband, George's father's father. He is seated and wearing a fustanella. Beneath his bristling moustache a half-smile can be discerned. It is no accident, surely, that in these old photographs the men always look more robust, have much more presence than the women. No accident, either, that the photographs of the women could almost be interchangeable. Men then were priests, farmers, teachers, shop-owners; women were always women, working endlessly for husbands and families, trapped in an endless routine, with individual quirks and the nuances of relationships being the only variations.

Now Yiayia says, '*Ti thimamai. Ti thimamai.* The things I remember.' I ask, 'What *do* you remember?' She gives a rueful grin, then, and replies, 'I remember everything always being the same, summer, winter, war or peace. Work, work, work, house, children, olive-groves, garden, *routina, routina, routina.*'

That skinny old woman, her mother-in-law, and that fatter one, her mother Panayota, were probably gripped in an even tighter routine, going nowhere but to church or perhaps to a neighbouring village for a name-day or *panegyri*. When the routine finishes, there is nothing to take its place. Now Yiayia sits outside on the step, as George remembers his grandmother sitting, keeping in touch with life, chatting to the neighbours, being entertained by the passing parade, saying a few well-chosen words to transgressing schoolchildren. Security is a familiar street, familiar faces and, above all, a familiar home. One *routina* replaces another, it seems, but perhaps this is what the very young and the very old need.

Grandfather had had his early security jolted a number of times. His father lost two fortunes, and Grandfather, who had been used to servants and a soft life, returned from France and Belgium to a life of genteel, school-teaching poverty. He was jealous: an enraged, one-sided correspondence details my grandmother's flirtation with one or more pearl-fishers from Broome; he arrived home, a warrior from the wars returning, to find my grandmother playing the piano and singing for another man. But the marriage of the publican's son and the mine-carpenter's daughter took place almost immediately, and off they went, my grandparents, to the first of their many school residences, a cottage which had a separate kitchen with a clay floor, a vegetable garden and chooks scratching in the dirt. Houses in the Strath Creek of the 1920s were probably not much different from the traditional cottages of the Peloponnese.

Later salaries were cut during the Depression, and Grandfather never quite recovered from his second shock involving money. As a child I dreaded hearing the word. It brooded over two households and the women never had any money of their own.

When Granny died we found a row of one-pound notes carefully concealed under the layers of newspaper on the floor of the wardrobe. 'That's her cache, with savings from the housekeeping,' said my mother, who was the only one who knew about it.

They were, like a great many other people then, a curious mixture of earthiness and restraint. They knew the power of passion and were often fearful of its consequences. It did not take much to translate Granny's supposedly cryptic messages. 'That girl,' she would say, naming a name, 'is a high stepper. She'll be in the family way soon, mark my words.' It was continually impressed on us that certain impulses were natural but that moderation and discipline were prime requirements for a happy, peaceful life. We were, in short, ever to beware of brief delight and lasting shame, and religious training and fear of disapproval were every bit as effective as the walls and chaperones still forced upon some Greek village girls.

Our grandparents were also believers in the value of leisure well-spent. They were always doing something. Every morning, Granny, propped up in bed by a long bolster, cocooned in a puffy eiderdown, ate toast, drank tea and plied her crochet hook. During the war she could knit a sock, she claimed, during a double feature at the pictures, carefully munching on Mackintosh's Minties, chewing Rowntree's jubes and drinking Kia-ora 50-50 cordial. At other times cardboard milk-bottle tops were covered in raffia and transformed into baskets, or moccasins were made from thonged and threaded leather. Granny lived vicariously through music and drama: in her sixties she adored dressing up in sheets and towels to become a singing shepherd in the Country Women's nativity play, and was highly commended for her acting in another play in which her role was that of a sinister housekeeper in the Mrs Danvers mould.

As we grew we gradually became aware of the frustrations and limitations of her life. Like Nana, she had been forbidden to have a career or a job. But she had never hoped for a career, she told us; she wasn't the academic type. Hadn't she even failed her Merit Certificate, having fallen short of gaining the required number of marks in the Arithmetic examination? And she would laugh. 'What's it matter? It's only a bitta paper.' But Grandfather had two degrees and was Head Teacher of Higher Elementary schools. If this difference was a source of tension between them, we never noticed it, but then we did not know about the early years, or about her first efforts at playing hostess to District Inspectors who, at that time, enjoyed a status roughly equivalent to God's.

Yet Granny never stopped reading and learning, and while in later life her taste veered from the novels of E. V. Timms to things like Catherine Marshall's strongly Presbyterian biography, *A Man Called Peter*, her presents to us were always of a solid, classical turn, and now I come to think of them, surprisingly masculine. Thanks to Granny we read R. M. Ballantyne and were acquainted early with the *Swiss Family Robinson*. Her own favourite was *White Fang*, and she encouraged us to read Australiana such as *Ralph Rashleigh*, *Sara Dane*, and *My Love Must Wait*, over the last of which I wept copious tears.

Picture another life. One Saturday morning I walked past the Kalamata newsagent's. Outside the shop various editions of the nation's numerous dailies are pinned up so that many people read the headlines and sports pages there, it seems, rather than go to the extravagance of buying a paper of their own. On this Saturday I paused. An old woman was standing by a pillar, reading a paper. Many, many Greek women of her age are illiterate; she wore the black clothes and knotted headscarf of a country widow. But she stood and spelled out the words, reading aloud slowly, with great emphasis and determination; her gnarled, brown forefinger pointed the way. For that space of time she needed to read and that need was paramount. And so she stood, oblivious to the passersby, and quite unconscious of my sympathetic gaze. For that moment there was only the trying; the rest was not her business.

I wondered at what stage the written word had entered her life, how the magic, that seduction by symbols, had first affected her, whether she had drawn Seamus Heaney's smoke with chalk and then the forked stick, calling it *Ipsilon*, not Y. But perhaps, like Heaney's father, she had

had to be content with digging with a spade, not with a 'squat pen'. For reading is easier to learn than writing. In any case, reading, that day, was enough.

Granny loved the theatre and the cinema, and was not afraid of creating controversy. 'That Laurence Olivier,' she sighed, disgustedly, after seeing the famed film version of *Hamlet*. 'Can't stand him. Chews up his words.' In the early fifties this was akin to blasphemy, yet now I read that in Richard Burton's notebooks Olivier's voice was only a 'machine-gun rattle with an occasional shout', which Olivier threw in as he himself said, 'to keep the bastards awake'.

But if Granny loved the theatre, she adored the ballet: her proudest boast was that she had seen Pavlova dance. She collected ballet books and seemed to know all there was to know about Moira Shearer and Margot Fonteyn. Daryl Lindsay ballet prints hung on the lounge-room walls. In 1964 I queued for long hours in Myer's, Melbourne, in order to get her tickets for the Fonteyn–Nureyev *Swan Lake*. At times I nearly gave up in despair at the tedium of standing. Something made me persist. Granny came to the performance and pronounced it one of the great nights of her life. Four months later she was dead.

Of our three grandparents she was the first to die and the youngest. With her death we learned bitter lessons about life's injustices. It is ironic, now, to consider that the best-loved are sometimes the hardest to recall, almost as if friction scores and scars the memory. There is an injustice, surely, in the fact that Granny and Grandfather made us secure, never *worried* us, were always there, and yet now specifics go missing. Yet Nana is always there, in sharp, very sharp relief. It was unjust, too, that she, the eldest, died last. So we felt.

And yet, and yet. If the effort is made, the details start to creep back, bringing a wave of grief as fresh and as painful as ever, but also the knowledge of what positive personalities they were, the memory of the individual worlds they created. Granny taught generations of schoolchildren to dance dances the very names of which conjured romance: *The Pride of Erin*, *The Evening Three-Step*, *The Parma Waltz*. She told us about dances, long ago, in the township on the Murray, where ladies wore egg-shells on the heels of their dancing slippers and competed to see who was the lightest of foot.

She had no cooling Anglo-Saxon blood, being a mixture of Scottish and Irish. She was enthusiastic, illogical, noisy, a passionate gardener and craftswoman. She was a woman of deep prejudices, but loved life and faced it with great humour and spirit. She was one for making extravagant statements and her own rules. She loved words, anecdotes and an audience. We neared collapse from hysteria, horror and mirth every time she told the tale which ended with her shrieking dramatically, 'Maggie, Maggie, I've got a snake up me drawers!' We all delighted in finding new names for people: the monastery on the hill was inhabited not by the Passionist Fathers but by the Passionate ones; the local store-keeper, of whom Granny disapproved, was privately called *fish-face* by her, much to our delight.

If we laughed at all these things, we used to snigger quietly over Granny's highly idiosyncratic vocabularly and her mispronunciations. Venetian blinds were transformed into *Fenetian*, with every syllable sounded; a pillar was always a *pillow*; the words boon and swoon mysteriously acquired an *m* in place of their final *n*; she pronounced vase the American way, and sink, the West Country way, as *zink*. Once again we never asked. But then, children would have found it very difficult indeed to say, 'That word sounds wrong. Why do you say it that way?' It never occurred to us that the words may not have been wrong, but merely different, that they may have been part of a parent's or grandparent's speech, were, perhaps, an echo, even, of a dialect. We were only dimly aware that language was living and thus changing, even though we particularly noticed that Grandfather said *et*, while the rest of us said *ate*. My teacher said that Grandfather was right and we were wrong.

It never occurred to us then that the language of the past is also a foreign one and can have a distancing, even alienating effect; nor did it strike us then that the old sometimes use their own distinctive language as a weapon. Now, much later, I notice that Yiayia seems, consciously or unconsciously, to choose and use the most obscure words, those unknown to children and foreigners. Seamus Heaney's poem *Clearances* records how his mother refused to use his 'new' language, thus forcing him to use the *naws* and *ayes* of the past. But one's own idiolect is a basic liberty, and the old have as much right to cling to theirs as to cling to life.

Granny was even positive about the prospect of death, facing it without flinching while the rest of the family was strenuously denying it. But she felt cheated. 'There are so many things I still want to do,' she told my mother. 'I'm so disappointed.' Early in her illness she fretted to Fay, her daughter, about the garden.

'I suppose it'll be a while before I can dig it over and get it all to rights.'

'I think you'd better give up the idea of digging,' replied Fay. Granny fixed her with eyes the colour of flecked steel. 'If I can't dig, I don't want to live.'

After her death, Grandfather was bewildered and quieter than ever. He had always known her, could not remember a time without her, nor a time when she had not been important to him. Once more he clutched at the supports of routine and order: he kept a little bundle of notes about the stages of her illness, her death, funeral and anniversaries, as though the scale of the crisis could be reduced by careful documentation.

When his own turn came, he sent for my father. 'I may not make it through this operation,' he said, calmly. 'But everything's in order. Here's an envelope containing funeral instructions.' He did survive the operation, but not for long. For a week he fought silently and tenaciously for his life, but on the eighth day the struggle became too much and he drifted gently away. There were no famous last words. Even then, as he slipped in and out of consciousness, routine kept claiming him. 'Must put the kettle on,' was one of the last things I ever heard him say.

Now they lie together, my grandparents, in a grave over which are inscribed the first words of the Presbyterian benediction, Number 727: 'The Lord bless thee and keep thee'. They had no doubt that the Lord would make His face to shine upon them. Words as a talisman: how I envy them their Greek *phylacto*.

Chapter 5

My sister went on a sentimental journey, becoming a tourist in a place we once called home. She took snapshots in Kodachrome, and once again I saw the lantana bushes against the wooden fence, the Black Boy rose spilling dark petals by the gate, the flowering gum standing sentinel. I could just see the telephone box on the corner, scene of a memorable row between Bluey, the builder's labourer and Lil, the local good-time girl.

'You've bashed me, Blue,' she wailed, 'I'm gonna call the p'lice.' She lurched into the box, then lurched out again. 'Gimme tuppence.'

I stared at the coloured prints and compared them with old black and white ones. I have never been back. Now the scenes resemble a stage backdrop, a setting, with figures, viewed through memory's telescope, moving in stylized fashion against it. Into this set piece our nomadic parents blundered and eventually learned, painfully, that they could never join the lead players because they were too new, and had perforce to be content with bit parts, suited to wandering minstrels.

I see the backdrop and hear the dialogue and monologue. My father stands, dressed only in pyjama pants, and gazes through a square of hot light down on a dusty street. I join him. We are in a hotel room in our new town. I see a brick building and two straggly gums. At eight o'clock in the morning the cicadas are shrilling deafeningly and the heat already presses like a weight. He speaks his lines, a despairing question: 'My God, what have I done?'

What he has done, in fact, is to manage promotion to a school a long way down his application list, repeating the pattern of recurrent small exiles set for him by his parents. At the end of four years in this township he realizes the truth of the Kazantzakis statement he has never read, that he is « στο φυσικό κλίμα του ανθρώπου, στη μοναξιά. »

How childhood prepares us. Now I, too, am new, from another world, and will never be anything but a bit player in this theatre. I even find it hard to learn my lines, but often hear myself, particularly during winters of discontent, mouthing the old question 'My God, what have I done?'

We leave the Commercial Hotel and lug our suitcases for four blocks through the January morning. More dust, heat and cicadas. We pass the shops: Coles, Snadden's on the other side, and then Buzzeau's, where I will buy, later, copies of *Hopalong Cassidy*, *Phantom* and *Chucklers' Weekly*. I will not be permitted to purchase *True Confessions*, but will be encouraged to spend my birthday presents of ten-shilling notes on yet more volumes by Enid Blyton. We enter the unknown, remembered garden to Number 50, and explore the house. But we know how it will be, for the Education Department of Victoria builds houses which are always the same. The backyard, however, stretches away for half an acre. 'My God!' moans my father yet again. 'We'll grow canteloupes,' comforts my mother, and we do. In the garage my sister and I find fifty empty jars labelled *Ponds Cold Cream*. 'Good idea to have *cold* cream,' we say, and our mother laughs. 'She was looking after her complexion, her skin,' she explains.

The name of the township fascinates me, for we have never before lived in a town with an Aboriginal name. There are various translations, no longer recalled exactly. One is dull. Is it *Red Clay*? I prefer *Mists Over the Waters* and *The Spirits' Abode*. There is a swamp on the edge of settlement, fringed by reeds, bordered by gum trees, where a teacher from the high school sits and paints in watercolour every Saturday afternoon, and where hundreds of ducks die horribly in the dawn of the first day of the shooting season. A boy younger than I sees two nuns on the swamp road and yells, 'Where're ya goin'? Off to get some holy water?' We admire his daring, but know he is right, for then we are all taught that Catholics were, are, will be deceivers ever. But in any case, the swamp is not for nuns, painters or duck-shooters. It is easier to think of it as it is in the morning, with the vapour rising, a mist from another time, an untouchable home of the Spirits, with black people wandering and returning, knowing it, loving it, using it wisely.

My father is not fascinated. The name, he announces, translates as a big, round O. I know he means a nought, a nothing, but he could just as easily mean the roundness of the world, I think. For it is the only world I know for quite a long time. But I at least have seen the sea. The name of the village where I now live also has its roots deep in history, connected, it would appear, with ancient Pharai. It is a different world from the one I lived in as a child, with borders of mountains, and a main road which links some of the most ancient cities in Europe. But still, here, there are children who have never seen the sea, and the sea is only twenty kilometres, or a forty-minute bus-ride, away.

Some of my class-mates have seen the flat salt lake, miles away, but others know only the swamp. The notion of roundness, circularity, takes over. Perhaps this is a theatre in the round? Certainly there is a circle, around the edges of which my parents skate uneasily. In the magic circle live the old settlers, German names predominating. A few post-World War I settlers, with Anglo-Saxon names, are in it, too. The bank managers, although nomads like us, are always admitted, because they have to be: they know all about the overdrafts. Doctors are automatically included, too, one for the Catholics, one for the Protestants, in practice, if not by design. But teachers and ministers resemble the little satellites we do not even know about then. They are noticed first and then settle into orbit, forming around the magic circle, becoming an accepted part of things remote from real life and action. And, as later there is a succession of Sputniks, teachers and ministers are always replaceable: plenty more where they come from. If they become threatening, use new words, have different ideas, it is easy to blink them away. Shut your eyes and they are gone.

Settlers, doctors, bank managers roll all their strength up into one ball, a marble on a very flat plate. The huge continent, space and light, climate and vagaries of the seasons, are all threatening. Is there sweetness to roll up, too? I do not know. They shun outsiders, protecting their vision of Australia. Do they know this vision to be as artificial as the map-shaped goldfish pond in at least one garden? Again, I do not know, but they punish people who flee the received life of the magic circle. I hear whispers about unmarried mothers, wealthy widowers who know more than their prayers, a black sheep, a drinker in a famous family. But I never see these individuals. Where do they hide? Where have they gone? I ask the questions and receive no answers. The magic circle has all the answers, keeps them close, and asks no questions of itself. It keeps its world, its O tight, small and still, fearing that one movement might send it hurtling across the endless plain which stretches away to nowhere, towards the very edge of the huge, flat plate.

The village, too, is a closed circle, guarding its secrets jealously. Once again I ask questions and receive no answers. Once again there are rumours of love affairs, ruination through drink and cards, of people hiding from others who are seeking them. And once again this place, at least as far as I can judge, asks no questions of itself.

My father taught at the high school, taught English, history and junior maths. Those were the days when Proficiency and Intermediate Certificates meant something. For Dad they meant a continuing struggle to teach Shakespeare and the rudiments of expression in a population which had little feeling for either. Once the owner of the local picture theatre made a grave error of judgement and hired Olivier's *Hamlet* for the Saturday night showing. Dad took a seat in the lounge and sat on while the seats banged around him. The noise from the stalls was deafening. But after half an hour Olivier's voice could at last be heard, speaking to an audience of one.

Bluey, the builder's labourer, would not have liked *Hamlet*. But Bluey's appearance gave the opportunity for selection and practice of adjectives and similes. He was huge, enormous, colossal; his skin was brick-red, his fingers were like sausages, his hair like mouldy hay, resembling that of Tim, the ostler in *The Highwayman*. His eyes were not hollows of madness, although Lil might have disputed this fact on their drunken Saturday nights.

Bluey was illiterate. On a building site one day, somebody twitted him about this. Whoever it was must have been a brave man. There was, however, no reaction from Bluey. Instead the master builder leapt to his defence.

'Aw, leave 'im alone,' he said. 'He can lay bricks like a beaut, can't he? Anyhow, if he couldn't do that, he'd be far better off scratchin' than pennin'.' It had to be admitted that most of the pennin' undertaken in the area involved sheep.

By now these circumstances and attitudes must have changed. Surely Bluey is dead and surely there are no other Blueys, or none at least quite like him. Here, too, change is starting to chip away at the scenes I first observed fifteen years ago and have been living with for nearly a decade. In another decade, people say, agriculture will be fully mechanized. I find this hard to believe, but fear it is an unfortunate fact that those who cannot do anything else will be the ones to maintain an almost mediaeval strip system, to keep little flocks of sheep and goats, and to have a donkey as an essential working tool.

Fortunately for my father, he was a superb sportsman. During the four years he played tennis, cricket and table-tennis, and swam and fished for redfin in the salt lake. He had been a nifty little rover for the Borough, but advancing age had forced his retirement before we moved to this township. It was then that my mother was able to give up measuring out her life in blued bootlaces and crêpe bandages. Later he was a sports reporter of a kind, and wrote up the local match for the main paper in the area. The necessity to count marks and present an unbiased account of matches in no way impaired his enjoyment of the game and its accompanying rhetoric. He revelled in both.

As tiny children we had liked watching our father play for the Borough. 'Carn the Borough,' we chanted, slurping at our PK or Juicy Fruit chewing gum, and rearing back in alarm if a huge, sweaty man-monster came too close to the boundary fence. So many of them were frightening sights without their false teeth; their lips hung damply slack, saliva glistened and shone, their whole bodies convulsed as they panted desperately.

As we grew we enjoyed our father's career as a spectator even more. We realized that his men friends regarded Saturday arvo as a type of double feature. There was the match and there was Bill's reaction to it. He was occasionally seen to trample on his flat cap, and any resemblance between his Saturday persona and the correct, dignified, schoolteaching one was coincidental indeed. But the love of language was still there – even if love of fair play and umpires had completely disappeared. And now memory's ear plays the phrases back:

'Open y'r glass eye! Open y'r other eye! Go home and get y'r little dog, Umpy. Another decision like that and y'ought t'go out and cut y'r throat! *I'll* put ya out of y'r misery, Ump!'

Instructions, declarations, proclamations, uttered in an inimitable, full-throated bellow, punctuated play. Sometimes he would turn, eye his family angrily and yell, 'The man's a raving idiot; he oughta be shot!'

The reading of *Love in a Cold Climate* came as a considerable relief to me. Nancy Mitford had Uncle Matthew; we had Dad. My mother felt uncomfortable, but was always mild. 'Oh, dear,' she would say, or 'Keep *calm*, Bill.' 'How *can* I keep calm in the face of such arrant idiocy?' he would retort.

George said very early on that my father is not a 'cold, hard, Anglo-Saxon'. His blood boils. *Vrazi to emma tou!* But it was pugnacious Irish blood presumably, which seethed uppermost during football matches, for Grandfather, an agreeable mixture of Cornwall and Scotland, was always very dignified. His comments ran as a weak counterpoint: 'Goodness to me. What a sausage of a kick. Do better meself.' (For he, too, had been a nifty little rover.) 'Bad decision, right enough. Rotten football, I say.'

Granny was there with her knitting and picnic hamper. If it rained, we sat in our ancient cars which had their bonnets pressed against the boundary fence. We were so used to country matches that we felt a sneaking sympathy for the family we heard of who had taken their picnic tarpaulin to the MCG, and had been mildly surprised to find that they couldn't use it. 'Would ya believe it? Not a skerrick of space to spread the old tarp?'

My career as a spectator did little to prepare me for Greek soccer matches. The first one I ever attended was a country match at a neighbouring village. The soccer pitch, itself lapped in mud, afforded a magnificent view of the surrounding snow-capped mountains, but watchers of match or scenery were very few. Yet six policemen were in attendance.

'What on earth are they here for?' I asked. 'There's no crowd to control.'

George grinned. 'You'll see.'

Sure enough, after a mere ten minutes' play, soccer was transformed into gladiatorial combat. One of our men thought he had been wronged and started yelling at his opposite number, who started yelling back. Suddenly our man's right arm shot out, and just as suddenly opposite number fell flat on his back in the mud. Three policemen marched out and escorted our man off the ground. The other three glared at the spectators who, though few in number, had become vociferous in the extreme.

'See?' said George. I nodded. I did see.

Mum and Granny came into their own at home. They lived very ordinary lives, but continually pushed at the edges of the world, forcing it bigger for us. Just the names of the songs they played on the piano made that O expand, anyway. It seems strange now, but we seldom sang Australian songs. Occasionally we managed a chorus of 'Gundagai' or 'Croajingalong', but usually we worked our way through a list consisting of numbers like 'The Rose of Tralee', 'My Pretty Jane', 'Drink to me Only with Thine Eyes', 'On the Banks of Allan Water', 'Early One Morning', and 'The Vicar of Bray'. The adults believed, rightly, that the children 'liked a good tune', but never seemed to realize how seriously we took the words. Uncle Lionel's party-piece was a pleading 'Speak to me, Thora'; as a small child my mother's sister was heard to remark in exasperated tones, '*Speak* to Uncle Lionel, Thora'. I, for one, puzzled over the words, never quite understanding the notion of 'drinking with eyes', and worrying slightly over the last line of 'Allan Water': 'There a corse lay she'. A feeling of weighty inevitability dragged the whole line down.

Another list marked yet another expansion of the O, for Mum liked to listen to radio soap operas while she did the housework. On school mornings our hair-ribbons were tied in place and anchored with bobby-pins while Brockhoff Biscuits announced further adventures in the lives of *The Markhams of Four Winds*. This serial seemed interminable, but was so successful that it was followed by *Delia of Four Winds*. 'Oooh, she's a scheming wretch,' said Mum. *Dr Paul* slotted in somewhere, too.

No one is immune from the contagion of soap, it appears. Recently Yiayia came to call and we proceeded to chat in our usual desultory fashion. My attention was caught when she said, 'And did you see the old man?'

'Which old man?'

'The one with the three daughters.'

'No, I don't think so. What's his name?'

'Oh, I don't know his name.' This in itself was strange, but then she launched into a tale which I had the utmost difficulty in following. After a great struggle, light dawned. She was giving me a resumé of a television soap opera. It just so happens that it has a Portuguese soundtrack and Greek subtitles which she is quite unable to read. No wonder both of us were confused. Yiayia, anyway, does not draw a clear line between television and life.

'When it's election time', she told me once, comfortably, 'and I'm tired and have to switch some politician off, I always apologize as I'm doing it. It's polite, isn't it? *I* wouldn't like to see someone switching *me* off!'

On frosty afternoons and evenings long ago we listened to *The Argonauts*. How we prepared ourselves. I knew nothing about Ancient Greece but eagerly joined the Argonauts, becoming Hippoclides 35, sending in feeble watercolours to Pheidias, who never awarded them any points. How I listened and listened in vain for the name Hippoclides 35 to come bouncing along the air-waves. The story was much the same with Corinella: I amassed piles of red and blue certificates, but no postal notes marked ⅔ ever winged my way.

The Argonauts was fairly serious stuff. Afterwards we listened to *Smoky Dawson, Lavender Grove, No Holiday for Halliday* and *When a Girl Marries* . . . for all those who are in love, or can remember-r-r. On Sunday nights we listened to the unforgettable team in *Take It From Here*: ''Ullo, 'ullo, 'ullo' and 'Haow, Ron', became part of our daily vocabulary. But undoubtedly our favourite programme belonged to a world only too familiar. We listened avidly to *Yes, What?* and hooted with glee as Greenbottle drove his teacher slowly insane – at the rate of fifteen minutes a day.

Mum took us to the productions of the Elizabethan Theatre Trust. *The Gondoliers* and *Iolanthe* bore us away for brief snatches of time; life would never be quite the same again. It changed too, after we saw the matchless Gene Kelly's sparkle and dazzle in *Singin' in the Rain*, our first motion picture. *Hollywood* became a magic word and I soaked up anything I heard and read about that world and its inhabitants.

'Mrs Brown says Marilyn Monroe's a dumb blonde,' I remarked to Mum.

'Blonde she may be, but dumb she certainly is *not*,' replied my mother sagely, adding, as an afterthought, an exhortation to use the word correctly.

Before too long we were permitted to go to the Saturday afternoon matinées at the local picture theatre, where the stalls seemed to generate a life of their own. Queen Elizabeth sat on her chestnut horse, Winston, and stared through scratched celluloid while *God Save* was drowned out by yells and roars. Jaffas and Fantales flew through the air, and silence only fell when the serial came on, for we were all agog to learn whether the hero had escaped the burning car, the rolling boulder or the deadly ray-gun wielded by hostile alien life.

As far as I know Yiayia made her first acquaintance with Hollywood when George and I took her to the Toorak drive-in in January, 1974. She was then sixty-five. What she really thought of Barbra Streisand and Ryan O'Neal in *What's Up, Doc?* I have never discovered.

And now I tease my mother. Riddles and song for all occasions, I tell her. 'You'll be propped up in the old people's home, singing and reciting.' 'Better than crying,' she retorts, frowning slightly because I have interrupted her at play with Alexander.

'Alexander, why did the owl 'owl?' He grins happily, because he has learnt this one.

'Because the woodpecker would peck 'er,' he yells, Greek accent and all.

'Very good,' and then come the harder ones for the older boys. Even I have forgotten 'What noise annoys an oyster most?' Blank looks from the teenagers. 'A noisy noise annoys an oyster most, of course.' Loud moans.

'Don't go. Listen. Why did they call the rooster Robinson?'

'Dunno.'

'Because he *crew* so.' A note of triumph.

'That's good,' says Dimitri, admiringly, while Niko imbibes a rapid lesson on the past tense of the verb *to crow*.

'Last one for now. What did Neptune say when all the seas ran dry?' They struggle to no avail. 'I haven't a notion.'

'Aw-w!'

Later, for their entertainment, she tells them about her grandfather, that redoubtable Robert who was born in 1852, retired in 1892 and died in 1945. 'Now then, Marjie, spell Constantinople.' The young Marjie sat and tried. C-O-N-S-T-A-N-T-I . . .

'No!' he roared every time, and then chuckled irritatingly.

'It was *years*, boys, before I realized that N-O. were the next letters!'

'Mean ole beast!' they cry, in a burst of retrospective indignation.

'Oh, he was kinder with other games. I enjoyed them. Try this one. Three-fourths of a cross, a circle complete, two semi-circles perpendicular meet. Set a triangle upon its two feet. Two semi-circles, a circle complete. What does the above spell?'

Grabbing at pencils and scraps of paper. Furrowing and knitting of brows. But it doesn't take too long. 'Got it!' Triumphant cry.

'TOBACCO.'

'Right. Good boys.'

But the *piéce de résistance* is too much for them. 'Mum can work it out,' they decide and drift away. And who can blame them? They are completely separated from this sort of English, and Greek, even at word-play, does not sound like this; the texture is different. But I listened and am pleased by the sonorous roll:

In order to extract the semi-fluid matter from the product of a domestic race of gallinaceous birds it is necessary to make an incision in the apex and a corresponding aperture at the base. Then, by creating a vacuum in close juxtaposition at either extremity, the calcareous outer covering will rapidly become devoid of its contents.

Blowing eggs. Across the road from Number 50, our independent-minded neighbour lived. She had belonged to a wealthy Establishment family but had married out; now she sniggered often about the airs and graces assumed by the inhabitants of that magic circle. She herself was shaped like a dumpling and was as warm and comforting. Our brother practically grew up in Bee's kitchen, an enchanted place. The wall between the kitchen and the yard often seemed a mere architectural whim; in the yard itself was a well, heaps of scrap metal and a battered T-model Ford. In the kitchen anything might happen, and usually did, for Bee was endlessly tolerant and indulgent. Her youngest son bred white Leghorns. 'Chooks!' we thought, disgustedly, not being used to aristocrats, but rather to the smelly, cantankerous bundles of feathers that picked and pecked in everybody's backyard.

But before a show, Grantley's birds were bathed, blued and then powdered with Johnson's baby talc. They were brushed, petted and cajoled into a good temper and kept in the kitchen, lest, like Tom Kitten *et al*, they spoil their sartorial elegance before the appointed time. They roosted in rows on the kitchen table, clucked, rustled and waited. They knew they would win prizes and they did.

Another neighbour also practised for Shows. A member of the local Pipe Band, he played the bagpipes while walking up and down his front verandah. Some people complained about the wail and moan, as they called it. Perhaps they preferred the hurdy-gurdy sound of the

mouth-organ and the bump, bump, bump of the Pastor's
square dancers in the local Lutheran Hall. But this was
McPherson Street, after all. And we glimpsed yet another
world – the land of the shining river, as John played 'The
Bluebells of Scotland', 'Loch Lomond', 'Scotland the
Brave', 'Caller Herrin' and 'Bonnie Dundee'. Mum sang,
'To the Lords of Convention, 'twas Claverhouse spoke
. . .', and we sang, too, totally ignorant of history but
spellbound by the words and music. More than thirty
years were to pass before I saw Killiecrankie from a train
window.

Granny, irreverent as ever, taught us:

Auntie Mary, Auntie Mary, lost the leg of me drawers,
Auntie Mary, Auntie Mary, won't you lend me yours?

We had a vague idea that other people knew this tune as
Cock o' the North but nothing can banish Auntie Mary and
her supplicant from the memory.

Agricultural Shows were one of the year's highlights
way back then. At least they were regular occurrences,
unlike Coronations, Royal Tours and Prime Ministerial
visits. Now all the details merge in the mind: spangled
kewpie dolls glittering on sticks, furry monkeys and
tinselled balls bouncing on elastic, mists of fairy floss, red
globes of toffee apples, and the gaping clowns disapproved of by our grandmothers. Gambling! We were not
allowed to play them; nor were we allowed to see the
various horrors like the two-headed lamb. We were,
however, permitted to view the large, august figure of
Big Chief Little Wolf as he sat outside the wrestlers' tent.
Painted and wearing his feathered head-dress, he smiled
benignly, immediately nourishing our suspicion of
Hopalong Cassidy comics.

From there we were taken on an inspection of handicrafts and food: in the case of marmalade-making and
cake-decoration, these categories merged. Rows and

rows of jars, filled with translucent orange and neatly tied bows of rind stood, mute testimony to hours, endless hours of work. The fruit cakes were sliced through to reveal the texture and the layers of marzipan icing. Embroidered tablecloths, cross-stitched napkins, dressed dolls and soft knitted toys filled case after case. We looked, admired, but were not inspired.

But I still love to go to the Greek equivalent of Australian agricultural shows. These are *panegyria*, which are, even now, associated with saints' feast days. Our own is held on 23 May, the Feast Day of Saints Konstantine and Helen. But it is a trifling affair compared with the huge one held at neighbouring Messini every October. An icon is brought down from a hillside monastery to be venerated; elsewhere, for acres around, it is the turn of Mammon. Anything and everything, from donkeys to dusters, from goats to gridirons, can be bought at the Messinia *panegyri*.

One year I was entranced by the sight of a huge stall selling nothing but bras. All shapes, sizes, constructions; blue, white, pink, black and mauve; made of lycra, cotton, wire, sponge-rubber; tied to long poles, they fluttered and danced in the breeze. A suitably buxom saleswoman peered out from behind rows and stacks of similar products.

Nearby a man was selling nothing but vegetable-peelers, while another specialized in selling icons which featured flashing lights in various colours. Gipsies, beggars, tourists, villagers, everybody descends on the *panegyri*. There are dodgem cars and ferris wheels, souvlakia and fairy floss, which in Greek is called, cruelly, *old woman's hair*. But there are no handicrafts or food competitions, though Greek women excel in both spheres.

Somewhat strangely for the fifties we were not encouraged to excel in the domestic arts. 'If you can read, you can cook,' stated our mother, grimly. Our grandmothers, on the other hand, elevated jam-making to the level of an arcane mystery (all that jelling, setting and fussing with thermometers) so that we were too awed to try. Needlework was agony; every week I clutched a blood-spotted piece of green cesarine, wrestled with a row of satin-stitch for *My Sampler*, and wondered what would happen in the next chapter of *Lorna Doone*. While wondering and anticipating, I would prick my finger yet again.

Life there and then was much like life here and now, even though there might seem to be little resemblance between Wimmera townships and Greek villages. There were various headings: birth, marriage, death, money and scandal, and the threat of nature in flood, fire and drought. People were still preoccupied by the war and were wondering about the prospect of another. The name *Korea* hung heavily in the air, and even that same air could pose a threat: we were supposed to be careful about over-exertion or running about in the open *air*, for the dread *Polio* was thought to be present in the atmosphere itself; the miasma theory was still popular.

Gossip was almost as dread a word. Teachers and ministers never gave females lifts in their cars, and ruthlessly shot past housewives laden with shopping, for fear of prating tongues. And here in the village a lone man will never come further than my front gate, and will roar his questions, 'Where's George?' 'When will he be back?' for all the world to hear and register propriety.

There were no dinner parties; afternoon teas were the thing. People either drank a lot or not at all: the taking of a Pimm's or a dry sherry once a month marked you down as a drunk, or at least a *drinker*. 'Oh, yes, he likes a drink,' was a damning statement and produced immediate visions of the six o'clock swill, unshaven men and heaps of vomit on street corners. The idea of drinking at meals was foreign in the extreme, and wicked. I've been drinking wine since I was two, said George when I first knew him, and I can still remember the thrill of shock this announcement produced. Tea was the universal beverage and panacea. All milk coffee, made with essence from a tall black bottle, was an almost sinful luxury. Food was regimented too: shredded lettuce wilting under a mantle of mayonnaise, lamb in gravy on Monday after Sunday's roast, lamingtons and *butterflies*, topped with cream and sprinkled with icing sugar. Soups, stews, and shepherd's pies. Occasionally there was bright yellow smoked cod for tea or German sausage . . . only there it had to be called *Paloni*.

Those who say Australia has no vendetta tradition and Australians are free of the inherited fears and hates of Europe, never lived in an Australian township during the fifties. There had been no invading armies or oppressive overlords, but a harsh environment, years of physical labour and the triumph of survival produced clannishness and suspicion. Then people had long memories and too little to think about. The breath of scandal could pursue one through time and distance; many years later in a city, a chance meeting and the mere mention of a name exhumed an episode long buried, and once again I was a child watching, and speculating from a distance on a pain I could not understand. Words had the power to destroy, and did. In the same way, the whole of Greece seems to be a big village: there is no escape from scandal here.

We were not apathetic. Violence was a part of school life. We played noisy war games, and fist-fights were common. On more than one occasion I was informed that the most popular girl in the school was determined to fight me. 'She's gunna bash ya up for sure, this time! She's waiting for ya at the gate.' But each time I managed, following the good example of Joseph and Mary, to depart into my own country by another way. I had not yet learned any Shakespeare but knew instinctively that discretion was the better part of valour.

And now my words chip away at this world. Like a theatre critic I sit, passing judgement on the play and players, listing words on scraps of paper, peering up at the footlights, remaining detached, trying to bridge the gap between stalls and stage, between past and present, recall and reality. I frown; no imperfections pass me by. Am I a brusher of noblemen's clothes? Or a cut-throat bandit in the path of fame? Neither, as it happens. I am a list-maker instead, weighing up the pros and cons, measuring the good and bad on paper.

For there is a great deal of good, a great many pros, wide scope for criticism of the constructive sort, ample opportunity to accentuate the positive. For there is much to be said in favour of being fenced in by slogans. 'I love God and my Country,' we recited every Monday morning with our hands placed approximately on our hearts, 'I honour the Flag, I will serve the Queen and cheerfully obey my parents, teachers and the laws'. That was the way things were.

We never thought about the concepts of security and freedom. We were too young; in any case, it was, perhaps, a measure of our situation that, even later, we did not need to think about them. As in Greek villages still, the outlines between church, school and town life and home were blurred. The reality may have been a constricted one, but we had the freedom to investigate its area and perimeter at will. We wandered where we liked, went to the swimming pool unattended, climbed trees, rode our bicycles, played cricket under the gum trees. That same curbing curiosity, found still today in Greek villages, meant that we were unwittingly protected: eyes followed us wherever we went, observing, checking; tongues were always ready to report, ready to save us from others and ourselves. And we at least were in a privileged position. We escaped from that small O every three months, to Geelong, to Melbourne, to the South-west coast.

I was eight years old when we drove straight down from the Wimmera to the Western District that first time. I ticked off the names which were to become familiar over the years: Horsham, Stawell, Ballarat, Terang. Through the desert we came, the Moses basket holding our new baby brother sitting between my sister and myself on the back seat of the huge 1936 Pontiac. It was a recalcitrant car which had to wear a hessian bag over its engine in wet weather, and which used to boil regularly in hot weather in sheer pique at the demands made on it; once, in the desert, we small girls had to balance on a lever of sapling while our father sweated and groaned over changing a wheel. But we always arrived safely.

We topped the crest of a hill and there it was, the Southern Ocean, a vast expanse of greeny-blue, flecked and foaming, sweeping and pounding on to curves of golden sand where it had gouged beaches for itself. Jagged, ochre-coloured rocks reared everywhere; we learned that in the past they had caused the death of at least one ship. And the sea stretched away to Antarctica and the bottom end of the world. Here was space vastly different from the waving wheat-fields; it beckoned and threatened simultaneously.

For George as a child, the sea was something quite different. The summer sea at Kalamata is like a huge bolt of blue silk, changing occasionally to taffeta shot with green and white. People swim for what seems like miles, bobbing up and down on the pond-like surface. The water is warm, sometimes like soup, I think discontentedly. And George as a schoolboy knew that across the water there lay Crete, Cyprus, Israel, Egypt, Africa, a host of inhabited places. When we stared at the Southern

Ocean we knew that only frozen wastes lay beyond it.

At Childers Cove the words *security* and *freedom* took on a new meaning: the exhilaration and fear we felt in the tumbling surf, the exploring that went just so far and no further, the watching of water boiling over knobby kelp and fringed seaweed in repetitious, regular movement, the comfort of being safe in bed while the wind howled and the waves crashed all night.

But the adult world began to loom. I went fishing with Grandfather who was then in his sixties. Rock-fishing can be dangerous; Granny gave me firm instructions: 'If he falls in the sea, *leave* him there. Do you understand? No point in both of you drowning? Is that clear?' I nodded. It was clear, very. Cray-fishing was safer. He sank nets, smoked the Rothman's Filter Tips which Granny was not supposed to know about, and talked. 'See the silhouette of that cliff over there, just now when it's getting dark? Looks like Queen Victoria in bed. What d'you think?' And yes, the portly shape, the matronly bosom, the beaky profile were all obvious. But 'She's still got her crown on,' I remarked, critically. 'H'm, well. From what I know of *her*, she probably never took it off.' The explanation was satisfactory.

Here was a world of history, and now, much later, I can see how this place is for me, Australia. It conforms to the pattern. There we were, a family drawn by wild water and rocky landscape: calls from Scotland, Ireland, Cornwall stirred in the blood. We perched, like most Australian families, on an edge, with vast space pressing behind and enticing in front.

Ancient and modern threads began to interweave, here in the world resembling the inside of those balls on strings we bought at shows: peel the paper off and see strips of raffia criss-crossing, overlapping, intermeshing, lacing, plaiting, each part inseparable from the other. Grandfather took us to the badlands where little white button shells were scattered, the remains of an Aboriginal kitchen-midden. From there the beach was clearly visible; from there the black people must have seen the 1839 shipwreck, must have seen people of another colour stagger from the sea. I imagined *fear* . . . and wondered who felt the greater terror.

Away from the sea we discovered city life. Now, decades later, I crane my neck as the Geelong–Melbourne V-Line train moves slowly through South Geelong station, under the bridge Granny and I walked across many times on our way to a not very satisfactory beach; there it is, still, the small square of grass which marks O'Connell Street. Half-way up lived an old man who played the button accordion. But Number 69, the school residence, is at the other end, up near Pakington Street, the *Packo* of our childhood.

Packo was a threatening, crowded, dangerous thoroughfare. We raced to the corner to watch the green trams going up and down. While we watched, our nostrils twitched at the yeasty scents emanating from Mrs Hill's bakery. Standing there we could tick off the names we knew: Ashby for Grandfather's school, for Geelong West was always Ashby to older people; aristocratic Newtown, home of Geelong College and the Hermitage; gracious, leafy Shannon Avenue, not-so-classy Chilwell, and, back in our direction, Manifold Heights, the tucks and pleats of which were now covered by countless Californian bungalows. Later we would live on the other side of the Barwon, and discover new names: Highton, Belmont, Ceres, Barrabool and Mt Pleasant for places; Batman, Gellibrand, Flinders, Hume for explorers and school houses.

We could only stand on Packo's corner in the mornings, for opposite brooded an ugly red-brick building the name of which I have long forgotten. But it was a *hotel*, a place in which one only stayed at a time of dire need, as when leaving a town or arriving on the Overland train at three o'clock in the morning. For gone to the hotel read gone to hell. More slogans: wine is a mocker, strong drink is raging, Demon Drink, Lips that touch Liquor shall never touch mine, are only some from a list from Bible and popular culture, a list that once seemed endless.

Nana and Uncle Lionel once debated whether they could stretch a point and buy us lollies from the licensed grocer in a much more remote area where the next shop was a mile away.

'Should we? I don't like it, Lionel,' sighed Nana.

'I know, Harriett. I don't like it, either, but the children . . .' We heaved a sigh of relief.

Granny was not as extreme; nevertheless, we were forbidden the street, even the front garden, during the late afternoon. All respectable families spoke in fear and loathing of the six o'clock swill, implying its piggish connotation at every breath. Of course we crept out to the front at the first opportunity: in the afternoons the baker's aroma had been replaced by the rank smells of stale beer and staler perspiration. The very fumes seemed visible, curling wraith-like around the Foster's Lager and Victoria Bitter signs. Lines of men trotted back and forth behind a wall of corrugated iron: the conveniences, the facilities, the WC, even – oh, vulgarity! – the dunny. And we chortled, quietly of necessity, over the joke we had heard about the chap who spent an hour opening bottles of beer and pouring the contents straight into the lavatory. Aghast, his fellow drinkers demanded to know the reason for his lunacy.

'Simple,' he replied, with grim logic, 'I'm sick and tired of being the go-between.'

Around the corner and further up Pakington Street was Scots Church, where Grandfather, four times a year, dispensed the communion wine, in reality two small bottles of grape juice. There Granny sang alto in the choir and thus added to her repertoire of psalms. Anthems would ripple out from behind the dahlias or the fruit trees as she practised in a tremolo which we always called 'singing like a big lady'. 'Lift thine eyes, O lift thine eyes to the moun–tains, whence come–th, whence co–o–ometh help!' The only vaguely mountainous structure visible was the hotel, but that did not seem to matter. Sometimes the tremolo was transformed and militant verses trumpeted forth from the rose-bushes: 'Some trust in *chariots*, some trust in horses, but I will remember the name of the Lord!' It seemed absolutely certain then, that the Lord preserved the faithful, and would always do so. Now her old Scottish psalter has found a home on my Peloponnesian bookshelf. To travel back thirty years all I have to do is turn to 'That Man hath perfect blessedness who walketh not astray' or to 'Ye gates, lift up your heads on high'.

Sometimes we visited Drumcondra Bowling Club, watching while Granny and Grandfather played tensely: rhythmic movements, swing, balance, trip forward, slip back as the heavy black ball rolled away in search of the elusive white kitty. Now again, as memory, speaks, orders, rearranges, the globes and the endless smooth green, the stylized white figures moving silently, all take on symbolic value. So much control and no more. All too often the big black ball would speed and crash into the gutter, and a collective sigh would rise and fall among the players. We were always slightly bored, but admired Sir Francis Drake, so that even Saturday afternoon suburbia had its tinge of history.

Sometimes we went to the city, driving first along Latrobe Terrace, then into Ryrie Street, Malop, Gheringhap, Bellarine. Some names linger, others have gone forever. But Griffiths' bookshop is, as far as I know, still there, reminding me of the day when I exercised power undreamed-of and handed Mr Griffiths himself a note from Grandfather. The two men were on first-name terms, a fact which dazzled me. '*Dear ******,*' and the note went on in crabbed handwriting, 'Please supply my granddaughter with a Parker 50 fountain pen, and charge the purchase to my account'.

'Which would you like?' Mr Griffiths asked, smiling benignly in the manner of those who bestow gifts and make money at the same time. 'The gold or the silver?'

'Um, ah, the silver, please,' although my heart longed for, coveted desperately, the flashier and more expensive gold one. But we had been taught to be modest. Somewhere, probably in a shoe-box a hemisphere away that pen lies still, exhausted after mountains of book-summaries, hills of lecture-notes and bumps and rises of examination papers, after millions of words. Here in the village, pens and even the humble Bic are thought of as small luxuries. Old shopkeepers make do, often, with licked stubs of pencil, reminding me of George's own recollections of his schooldays, when he and his brother had to saw a pencil in half in order to share it.

We remembered everything when we went back to the O. Grandfather's letters came every fortnight, anyway, in case we needed any reminding. But we were rarely bored by our daily round, and were busily accumulating furniture of the mind, designing stage-sets for future drama and major roles. I kept guinea-pigs, collected stamps, took photos and piano lessons, sang in the church choir, and read a book a day, although tomes like *Lorna Doone* slowed me down. I was hopelessly addicted to Louisa M. Alcott and had read *Little Women* and *Good Wives* fourteen times before I was twelve. These books, leafed in gold and illustrated with engravings, provided a glimpse into yet another world: we muttered words like *Yankee, Marmee, Genius Burns* and wondered vaguely about the American Civil War. Jo, of course, was a doughty heroine, and even more interesting (how impossible that sounds!) than Norah of Billabong. We loved Norah, but Jo had the pull of the slightly strange and exotic.

Ours *was* a small world, but at least we had glimpses of others. George, as a child, knew there were other lands elsewhere, but had no contact at all with them. Even as late as the mid-1960s, for example, the radio programmes came from as far away as Pirgos. If the weather was bad, such contact was reduced to a crackle of static, before usually dying away completely.

We played endlessly, and our patient mother never let us know that she penetrated our disguises with a single glance when we turned up at the back door drooping feathers and fringes, weighed down by old hand-bags and a moulting fox-fur which had one eye still gazing balefully, dirt rubbed on our cheeks, lipstick slashed across our mouths.

'How nice of you to call, Mrs Kilphobycat,' she would say, gallantly. 'And what can I do for you today?' Invariably the answer in this struggling dialogue froze on our lips. The disguise was all; no energy had gone into the script. We retreated to re-think and re-write.

And then there were the farms. How different they were. Sometimes we spent a weekend at one, and the sense of space and untrammelled freedom is with me still. At home I could not look out the bedroom louvres without seeing the Head Teacher's buffalo-grass lawn, the beds of lantana and roses. Occasionally I could see him prowling the garden, still gazing over his spectacles, this time at the heads of flowers. It was a slight relief to see him relaxed and touching petals gently, for at school he struck terror into every heart.

On the farms wheat waved in every direction, and it is only now that I understand the effect of seeing an endless horizon. Recently a young relative of George's came to call. He had to wait half an hour for George's return, and, very unusually, said yes, he would come in. Dionysos is twenty-five, tall and handsome, and lives in George's ancestral village, seven kilometres up the mountain. He was very happy to chat, but our store of small talk was soon exhausted. I cast about somewhat desperately for something to go on with, and found, by great good luck, a Sunday paper magazine sent from Australia. One of the features was based on Philip Quirk's collection of photographs, *The People and the Paddocks*. I opened the magazine at the double-page spread of Junee's wheat crop for 1988. And waited. Dionysos's mouth opened, shut, then opened again. He flashed his shy grin, incredulous this time.

'That's never *all* wheat?'

'All wheat,' I affirmed.

'Will y' look at that?' he muttered, shaking his head. 'So big. Such a lot of it.' And he gazed at the mass of textured gold, at the completely flat, knife-sharp horizon, and the sky brought lower by great puffs of shadowed white clouds.

After that I showed him the picture of the ploughed paddock at Woomelang in the Mallee, with its furrows curving in stylized fashion, a pattern on a gigantic scale, towards that same ruled horizon. And then the picture of the Parkes Grain Terminal. It seemed minutes before he lifted his head.

'What a pity,' he said, 'that all the writing is in *ta xenna*. I'd really like to read all about these photos.'

In Dionysos's village a big piece of land measures a *stremma*, or a quarter of an acre. Farmers still wait for windy days so that they can winnow.

Our eyes were used to the vast expanse. There was little else to see except a few sheds and a few animals. A silver lozenge meant the dam; we could, if we were careful, and equipped with rubber boots, fish for yabbies, tying lumps of ripe meat to lengths of cotton. We could bottle-feed lambs and see words like *slobber, gobble, slurp* and *slaver* leap into action. We were invited to plunge our fists deep into merino fleece. 'See? Up t'y' wrist, easily, eh? And this feller's not one of me best!'

The feel of crinkles and grease and the matted texture on the top was second only to the feel of a calf's tongue rasping on fingers. Both produced shivers, tingles, goose-pimples, physical reactions we did not really understand. The farmers often read books, had Player Pianos and sent their children to boarding-school. For their children they, too, pressed the edges of the O ever outwards, forcing it larger.

One day, I, too, must make a sentimental journey.

Love of a Country

Chapter 6

LET me tell you about my friend Seamus. He was a slight, short man in his early seventies, with a bald head, sharp features and lively eyes. Once I held him in his chair while he had an epileptic fit. It was the first time I had seen such a thing; while he thrashed, mouthed and moaned, time seemed frozen. Towards the end of what seemed like half an hour but could only have been two minutes, I felt as if I were holding some sort of self-willed puppet, with its limbs jerking stiffly in a rhythm of their own.

I remember that I heard a voice shrieking: it was mine, calling for the landlady.

'It happens all the time,' she said, resignedly. Eventually, the spasms stopped and Seamus spoke in a muffled, confused voice. Every attack does a little damage, I'm told. But perhaps the damage was done long before the epileptic fits started.

We met in the street during my first summer here. I trotted out my basic Greek greetings, but he cut me short.

'I'm not Greek,' he announced, firmly. I eyed him warily.

'Oh,' I said, and waited.

'My name's Seamus, and I'm Irish,' and he all but twinkled at me. A leprechaun, or just an average Irishman in a small Greek village seemed to stretch credibility too far, even here where it stretches easily and often. There was nothing for it but to consult the twin oracles: husband and mother-in-law.

George laughed; Yiayia chuckled and sighed. 'Poor thing. See what too much book-learning can do?' and she threw me a warning glance as she waggled her fingers near her head.

'You mean he's not quite right? Rather eccentric?' I guessed at the unfamiliar gesture.

'More or less,' replied George. 'He was born here, he's as Greek as we are, and his name's not Seamus,' and he mentioned a name as Greek as Panayiotis Papadopoulous.

'But what about his accent?' I asked, for Seamus spoke perfect English with, yes, just a hint of brogue.

'People say he lived in Boston for years, so perhaps he picked it up from Irish immigrants. Perhaps it's a New England accent, rather than anything else,' hazarded George in reply. People, blunter than George and Yiayia, also said that Seamus was as mad as a hatter. Somehow I didn't think so.

We met infrequently after that, but always in the street, for then Seamus neither paid nor received visits. Conversations always came straight to the point.

'Who is your favourite author?' he asked me abruptly, early in our acquaintance. I felt reluctant to announce that I hated that sort of question, and equally reluctant to think aloud: John le Carré? Isaac Bashevis Singer? Barbara Pym? None of these?

'Jane Austen,' I answered, mentally ticking what I snobbishly hoped was the right box.

'Ah, yes,' he replied. 'The immortal Jane. My own favourites, however, are Homer, Chaucer and James Joyce.' A deep hush followed.

'Wide range,' I mumbled, and the foolish comment sank without a ripple into the well of silence. This was only the beginning, however. With mingled awe and dread I listened to Seamus hold forth at regular intervals on James Joyce and *Ulysses*, a work which he apparently knew inside out. He had even read *Finnegan's Wake*.

'The great unread,' he remarked, complacently.

As well as having a thorough knowledge of his favourites, he was very widely read in literature and history generally, so that I came to fear his questions, feeling my own small learning like a drop in the proverbial ocean. The villagers, I think, thought he was mad because he knew too much, thought too much, was one of them, but refused to be like them. He was a vegetarian and an animal-lover; he fasted periodically and thought nothing of walking twenty kilometres or more; he boasted that he ate only 250 grams of sugar a year and that he spent money only on the bare necessities; he had visited Istanbul ten times and had travelled extensively in what he always referred to as Asia Minor, never Turkey; he spoke Turkish and had made a study of the Koran; he had spent 280 hours in Aghia Sophia. He was firm in his opinions and could be ruthless.

'Joe Blow's not a philosopher's bootlace,' he would say, or, 'You watch yourself among these Greeks – some of them are *tarrible* larrikins!'

And all the while he insisted on his Irishness. 'Your parents should have called you Maura. I was ill last month and I swear to God I heard the banshee wail forty times. Forty times, begorrah, but I'm still here. What d'ye mean, I've kissed the Blarney stone? Ye look younger every day! Bye, mavourneen.' He would grin, raise a hand, and disappear. It became a sort of grave game. We both knew it was a game, but we never admitted we were playing. We stuck to the rules.

We enjoyed playing with English, too.

'I nearly forgot the word *skillet* this morning,' he said once. 'Do Australians use this word?'

'I think it's used more in America,' I replied, cautiously.

'What about the expression *as right as a trivet*, then?' he asked.

I laughed. 'My grandparents used to use that,' I said, 'but it's a long time since I've heard it.'

He thought I was careless. When I referred to the name *Sacha* as an abbreviation of *Alexander*, he grew stern.

'You mean *diminutive*,' he reproved. 'Now tell me the derivation of the word *antipodes*.' This was an appropriate punishment. 'Good girl,' and he patted me on the back as I erased the blot from my copybook.

I never learned his whole story. He left here when he was six and returned fifty years later, after, people said, some sort of breakdown. He had been a professor, they went on, but he came back here and was unpopular. There was talk of quarrels and enemies. It became obvious to me that he led his own life, refused to waste time in idle chatter and remained his own man.

There was a sadness, a deep loneliness, *something*, and he had the kind of strength that comes through suffering. Perhaps the *something* was a sense of inconsolable loss? It almost seemed, sometimes, as if his identification with Ireland and obsession with Asia Minor were substitutes of a sort, an attempt to fill the gap wrenched in the child whose parents had taken to him to . . . America, to great opportunities, to a new life, which, as it happened, went awry.

But self-indulgence was a sin, he believed. Once I said it was difficult living here. He paused.

'Yes,' he answered, and almost added something. But then he changed his mind. 'A person with intellectual resources can live *anywhere*, though – and don't you forget it.' And so he put a stop to my self-pity that day.

He was staunchly independent and would not be told.

'I'm getting a bit dizzy lately,' he remarked one day. 'I can only read for six hours at a stretch; that's not much for me.'

'Go to the doctor,' I urged.

'I *am* a doctor,' he grinned. 'I don't need anybody else's opinion.' I discovered later that he *was* a doctor – of philosophy.

He had a stroke. In hospital, feeling shocked and helpless, I patted his bald head and held his hand, and could not imagine how he felt. I talked, inconsequential nonsense mostly, but he could not reply. Later he seemed to recover. A landlady was found and he began to have visitors. He learned to speak again, and he walked with a tripod walking-stick.

'Look,' he laughed, 'I'm as right as a trivet.' And we applauded.

But his right hand was paralysed. I wrote letters to America. They were guarded in one way, desperate in another. *A, I have written to T, but have had no answer. Please tell him to write – or come.* I took dictation obediently, but never dared to tell him that I knew how he felt, that I understood.

'What were the letters about?' whispered the landlady, curiously, at the front door.

'Oh, nothing much,' I lied, suspecting all the while that the letters were Seamus' story: he was alone, but wanted, had always wanted, someone or a way of life to come. Neither ever did. All that came were the quarterly magazines from a very distinguished Ivy League university.

'My Alma Mater,' he said, with just a trace of pride.

Towards the end I visited him and found him quite alert, apparently, but initiating no conversation. He answered my questions but that was all. No, he wasn't reading much. Yes, he was thinking and remembering.

Yes, he had a lot to think about, and a great many memories.

'He's neither dead nor alive,' said the landlady. The epileptic fits continued.

Not long afterwards, Nikolaos, my second son, came rushing home.

'Sit down,' he commanded, trying to prepare me. 'Seamus has just died.' But I felt relieved, rather than sad. The sadness came later, as I began, slowly, to comprehend how the shape of my life was altered by his absence. Only after a visit to Australia, did I finally understand how much he had helped me through what had seemed like five interminable years of exile.

I could not go to the funeral. Yiayia went instead. 'A respectable gathering,' she told me. (I heard later that even his enemies were there and I laughed to think of it.) The day they buried him I was in the garden, listening to the cracked note of the knell. Unbidden, the thought came that he and I were the only ones in the village who knew the appropriate English reference:

> Never send to know for whom the bell tolls;
> It tolls for thee.

It tolled for both of us that day, for our vanished hopes, our fragile friendship, the similarity of our feelings, and for the deep reserve we had had about expressing them.

And so I stood and wept.

Chapter 7
1986

It is back again, that leaden weight on my chest, just when I thought I was safe. Of course, I ignored the warning sign that bleeped at me as the aeroplane swooped earthwards in the Athenian dawn: one moment of almost complete despair, like a knife-thrust in its intensity. Fatigue, I told myself, briskly. Enough of that. Prepare for battle.

And battle there was. A customs man of the officious and disgruntled variety, the long curving nail on his little finger betraying his peasant origins, threw his weight and my luggage around to such effect that I was last out of the airport. Infuriated to discover that the Singaporean Chinese ahead of me knew no Greek, and thinking himself hot on the scent of illicit videos, he fumbled and fossicked among dressing-gowns, underwear, bags of Violet Crumbles and Cherry Ripes, broke an ornament and peevishly demanded my help in wrecking the neat order of my own suitcases. I grudgingly complied, glowering at him and thinking how his search would never have discovered drugs, smuggled birds or firearms cunningly concealed. But at least the adrenaline started to flow, and chased the black dog of despair away.

And then the euphoria of welcome and family reunion took over. Alexander was glad, glad, glad to be back and chortled and giggled with glee over his father and brothers, who all announced with heartfelt sighs that we two had been away for *simply ages*. Yiayia embraced us as we stood hock-deep in Australian bounty. I went up the street to Spiro's shop and received a blindingly beautiful smile, a hug and a command. 'Sit down, *paithaki mou*, and tell me everything.' 'Good to see you back,' said Gregory and Panayioti, 'You've been gone a long time.' Alexander trotted off to kindergarten, where his teacher made a great fuss of him.

But I had been back (home?) two days when my sister's card arrived. I skimmed it once, then hastily stuffed it behind a pile of books. I'll read it again tomorrow, I promised myself, playing my favourite Scarlett O'Hara role yet again. Words, communication, are not always a consolation.

Tomorrow came with its usual inexorability and brought with it an aerogram from my mother. Clearly I was in a bad way: it is very seldom that grey paper and the print of Brisbane's Gateway Bridge reduce me to tears. Within ten minutes both aero and I were small sodden heaps. Action was needed. I flailed about and shoved the first cassette to hand into the player. I gritted my teeth through the stream of lemonade which is Mantovani and even endured the heartless gaiety of 'The Happy Wanderer' taking me back to carefree school choruses circa 1960. But by the time Mrs Mills (remember her?) started pumping out 'Faraway Places' followed by 'Melancholy Baby', I had had enough. The tape recorder is still intact, but the relentless tinkling of Mrs M.'s piano may never be quite the same again.

What you need, I told myself, sternly, is a good lecture on the sins of self-indulgence. Something Victorian. Alas, the effects of this attempt at discipline were not quite as planned. Why did I have to find 'The Lotus-

Eaters'? And why did my eye light *first* on those despairing lines:

> What is it that will last?
> All things are taken from us, and become
> Portions and parcels of the dreadful Past.

It became obvious that I had to have a crying jag, so I gave in ungracefully and had one.

The next thing was a head cold, a real humdinger, followed by a cough, a new ache in the chest. All this, after five weeks of perfect health in Melbourne. Now we were into really dark, dank psychological stuff, myself and me. This meant, surely, that one of us, at least, thrives on a life of self-indulgence, loves being pampered and petted, spoiled by Mummy and Daddy, actually *prefers* being an infant . . . at the age of forty-one? The minute we are replaced in an adult role, the old body cracks up. The mind threatens to follow suit, dwelling irresistibly on the nasty thought that the past is the most important thing in life. (I have always felt that I understand Jay Gatsby completely.) Expatriates have parallel lives which can periodically leave the rails and collide with each other, leaving a trail of wreckage in their wake. However, the really significant expatriate delusion is that the parallel lives are not like trains, but like reels of films which can be replayed at will. (What if I went back?)

George does not often talk about how he felt while living in Australia. The occasional anecdote and some random recollections are threads I have picked over the years and woven into a somewhat untidy piece. His first feeling, after nearly a month aboard the ship *Patris*, was one of relief, even thankfulness, on making a brief visit to Perth. Perth lay in the autumn sun and looked, he thought, very Mediterranean. Melbourne, however, did not.

In Melbourne, a much wider and more threatening world than the one he had known, he missed the gatherings, the celebrations, the special days, but, he remarked ruefully once, just once, 'going back doesn't necessarily mean that you find what you missed'.

Migration was one thing, migration to Australia quite another. The latter involved a tremendous sense of finality, comparable, even, with that of transportation, because of the distance, the slowness of voyages, and the fact that very few migrants in the fifties and sixties had ever returned to their own countries. Migrants to America, on the other hand, were always coming and going, or that was how it seemed. But the sense of finality often made young migrants to Australia old before their time, becoming set in their ways, because they could not see a future they wanted.

Memories of such individuals form the main pattern. George once asked a man from Ithaca whether he had ever been back there. No, he said, he had been in Australia so long that he had Australian-born grandchildren. Did he think he ever *would* go back? The answer came in a sigh. 'No,' he replied once again, 'the anchor of my boat is grassed and covered with weeds.' There would be no more journeys.

On another occasion George overheard two acquaintances of his talking. Both men in their thirties, they had been in Australia about ten years. The first man was homesick.

'Are we going to stay here?' he asked.

'Of course we are,' replied his friend. 'What else can we do now?'

'You mean we are going to die here, leave our bones here?'

George walked away, not wanting to hear more. That same year the homesick one died.

Other people lived out their childhood fantasies, at least for a while. George worked with a man who had, very early on, bought twelve pairs of shoes, because as a child he had had none. He later bought a white Valiant car, because at home his family had had only a donkey. But such consolations are only temporary.

Kalamata was George's first place of exile. He remembers his pain and tears, but remembers, too, that he eventually came to love it, that it added another layer to the meaning of the word *Home*.

Now that the native has returned, he loves and remembers Kalamata as a piece of his past, part of his early life, a lost idyll of orange blossoms and horse-drawn cabs. People love places, particular places, even if such places exist, ultimately, only in the mind. What is important in middle life is your own landscape and setting, the feelings you have for them, the imaginative response to them.

Alas, I did not find Kalamata instantly loveable. How could I? Crammed full of middle-class Western notions about cleanliness, tidiness, organization, suburban shopping centres, space and traffic-flow as I was, I found sections of the town distressingly run-down. Potholes studded the roads; paint lifted off walls; a tide of rubbish ebbed and flowed in drains. *Tacky* and *seedy* were adjectives which constantly sprang to mind, and, just as constantly, I caught myself remembering the jaundiced remark made by an Australian friend; 'large chunks of Europe need a good clean up and a thick coat of paint'.

It was even difficult to admire Kalamata's pride and joy. In a grassed section of the *plateia* stands a memorial to the 1821 War of Independence. The three revolutionary heroes, Mavromichalis, Kolokotronis and the pistol-packin' priest, Papaflessas, gaze streetwards, while above them a fierce female, statue of liberty, brandishes her sword.

'That's the most unsubtle thing I've ever seen,' I announced, rashly.

'What was subtle about the War of Independence? What is subtle about war in general?' George demanded to know. I subsided, suitably crushed.

I also had difficulty in coping with the cock-eyed tricks time gets up to in Greece. No wonder the Greeks invented the word *anachronism*. In Kalamata, Mercedes and Alfa Romeos glide down the main street, while sun-blinkered drivers squeeze brakes whenever horse-drawn carts, donkeys or even hand-carts demand right of way. And such things happen more often than you would think. Bewildering stuff this was, all of it, to one accustomed to living in neat little compartments linked by a corridor of time which was two hundred years at its longest.

But I began to explore Kalamata, and to adjust to another, older world. I discovered that I could walk away from the main streets, up the broad steps beside Aghios Nikolaos's church, and find myself in narrow, winding streets where tall, crumbling houses loomed against the sun, where greenery spilled over rusting balconies, where black-scarved women stood, stared and gossiped. Here and there ridged, biscuit-coloured urns acted as flowerpots for cascades of fuchsia, doorknockers shaped like aristocratic hands with long, slender fingers, invited, and the sight of several wrought-iron Lions of St Mark hinted at a Venice long vanished.

Soon *tacky* and *seedy* became lost souls of adjectives, wandering, searching for other situations to describe. I could not apply them to the convent where a dozen nuns wove silk and linen while the scent of orange blossom drifted through the air. I could not apply them to the thirteenth-century castle overlooking the town.

Such descriptions became completely irrelevant when I gazed down on the ribbon of road threading its way through tucks of mountain to Sparta, or when I looked in the opposite direction towards the pleats and folds of Kalamata's own mountain, the Basket, which broods over the bright blue curve of Messenian Bay.

In Navarino Street the house with arches and colonnades, grey walls and balconies ablaze with bougainvillea compensated a thousand-fold for the concrete cubes of high-rise flats. And I dragged many an Australian visitor to view the tenth-century church of the Holy Apostles, a dignified little structure standing in the centre of the old market.

I even began to notice the jacarandas, gum trees and wattles I had not observed before. I was managing to see, at last, that surface impressions are not everything, that shiny, spotless veneers like the ones I had been used to, may not live up to their promise, may conceal a hollowness, may be lifeless.

I also began to discover other people who were still living in two worlds. *Kyrios* George, the tailor, was one. His shears paused mid-broadcloth when I mentioned Australia. 'Those were the days. How I loved my life in Australia. See that photograph on the wall? That's me in Collingwood.' Another George runs the Australia Restaurant, where decorative *objets* are empty Carlton Draught cans, where an idiosyncratic map of Australia, which places Tasmania level with Sydney, overlooks people dining on pizza and *smoaked* pork. *Kyrios* John owned a *zacharoplasteion*; over coffee and cakes he would reminisce about Punt Road, Commercial Road and Chapel Street. *Kyrios* Thanassis used to deliver mail to the school my sons attended in South Yarra.

I was not alone. All these people had liked Australia, as George had, and had never regretted going there. Why had they left it? 'Kalamata was *home*,' said one. 'She called me back.' I understood why. Roots are always difficult to sever; that word *home* is one of the most magnetic in any language.

Chapter 8

On 13 September 1986, the earthquake struck. Even here in the village the shock was strong. It is useless to attempt graphic descriptions of the moments of impact: noise resembling a bombardment, violent movement, clouds of dust, breaking ornaments, flying books, general mess and bewilderment.

'Why is the house jumping, Mum?' asked Alexander. As he and I crawled out from under the table, I said, 'That must have lasted three minutes.' 'Fifteen seconds,' estimated George. Later we heard that the seismologists had measured 3.9 seconds' duration and 6.2 on the Richter scale.

That knotty concept of time: how a mere four seconds' swipe from its devouring hand can change history, wreak havoc, destroy lives. That day the race was not to the swift, nor the battle to the strong; time and chance affected everybody. In that four seconds the *Kalamatianoi* became refugees in their own city.

The church of the Holy Aspostles succumbed immediately. Proud *Ipapandis*, the Cathedral, its clock stopped at 8.23 p.m., the moment of the earthquake, faltered at the second tremor, as did the town hall. As high-rise buildings fell, twenty people died, the electricity system failed completely, a whole village virtually disappeared, the road to Sparta filled with rubble, landslides became an ever-present danger, and water and food supplies were threatened. People began leaving immediately. A little later voices of protest were everywhere. 'She was only a young girl, I tell you,' a woman wailed to her neighbour. Her cry floated after me as I passed by. A coffin lid stood outside the church door.

In those four seconds the *Kalamatianoi* learned how fragile their own houses and existences were. Even I, who did not suffer at all, finally realized how irrational it is to assume that house/home will always be there, that the very words will always be magic, a talisman against evil and fear, that life is always predictable. But even the simplest dwellings are womb-like symbols of security and we feel grossly wronged when they are no longer there. My friend Cecilia, another foreign wife, was standing in the kitchen of her home when the front and back walls separated from the roof. Two young men tried to flee by car, and their own house fell on them: the ultimate betrayal. *Kyrios* Thanassis lost the apartment block which represented his life's savings, *Kyrios* John, his *zacharoplasteion*.

Some time later, I walked with George around the area where he had spent his school years. His old house was still intact, but the neighbourhood was greatly altered. Many buildings were wrecked; streets were either deserted or fringed by a few people simply sitting, stunned.

'I feel numb,' said George, seeing the landscape of his past blotted out. 'So much change in such a short time. The place will never be the same again.'

September 14 is an important day in the Orthodox calendar: the Feast of the Exaltation of the Honourable and Life-giving Cross. But many churches were no longer. One I passed was literally flattened; the dome sat on the ground and was still the highest part of the structure. Nevertheless, the remaining churches were packed that morning, and their bells rang out as usual, in defiance of death and damage.

'The sweetest sound I have ever heard,' said an English friend.

That morning, the same woman visited a hastily erected tent. Her friend's house was in ruins; as far as they knew, they had lost everything. But somehow they had salvaged a folding table, a chair, a spoon and a cup, and had managed to acquire a spirit burner.

'Please to come in and have a cup of coffee,' the Greek couple invited, dispensing hospitality in a makeshift house. Some things manage to transcend 'the gloom and eclipse of earthquake'. *Filoxenia, Filotimo.*

So in November 1986, it was obviously time to set things down in blue and white – definitely in blue – to submit oneself to the discipline of lists. A heading wrote itself: *Reasons For Feeling Ghastly.*

Number One: You have a minor ailment, which you were almost bound to get, but which has been exacerbated by the dizzying speed with which 1980s high-tech transport dumps people from one hemisphere into another. Right.

Number Two: You have not allowed yourself time to digest all the differences you think you know about, but which still have the shock of the new after only a short time away from them. Correct. George Eliot once stated that a difference of taste in jokes places a great strain on the affections. Differences in a great many spheres cause great strain, in my opinion. The customs officers at Tullamarine are pleasant, smilingly polite, humorous even, for heaven's sake. But I remind myself that it is easy for them: Australians of a certain age and background have the innocent good nature of people who have never been beleaguered or defeated. There is not the same consciousness of power play (despite what the feminists say) which is such an important part of Greek life. Ex-Europeans in Australia seem to me to have relinquished power play gracefully and gratefully.

'Thank God I don't live in Calabria anymore,' said a cheerful Italian taxi-driver. 'I live in Mulgrave and read biographies of Verdi instead.'

'There's no such thing as trust in Russia,' stated a solemn Ukrainian. (The mere thought of that sufferer does much to banish self-pity.)

Number Three: Everything is so easy in Australia. You have been seduced by the ease of communication, the small conveniences of everyday life, by the modicum of elegance so lacking in rural Greece, by comfort. True. (The water is off again today.) Here I made myself a note: visit Kalamata. The writing of the list was suspended while I did so.

I had been shocked and grieved by the earthquake of 13 September, and had felt guilty at having escaped very lightly. Soon afterwards, I traipsed the wrecked streets, trying not to believe what I saw: collapsed ceilings, glimpses of beds still made up underneath the rubble, chandeliers still hanging, flaunting their crystals uselessly in the morning light. Women were either silent and set-faced, doing their washing in plastic buckets, or weeping quietly into their handkerchiefs. Due in Melbourne at the end of September, I filed away a few statistics: 7000 tents means at least 20,000 people under canvas, possibly as many as 30,000. Seismologists say that the danger continues for fifteen days. Aftershocks measuring 4 plus are occurring frequently.

Imprinted on my brain were also some visions of the spirit of humanity reacting to suffering: the potplants lovingly lined up outside a tent, the caged canaries being tended and trilling deafeningly in thanks, the old priest pottering inside his tent, which he shared with a rose bush, the nine-month-old baby cooing and crawling on a heap of sacks.

But I knew that a week away would dim what I had seen. And so it proved. But then I saw it all again, because six or seven weeks had not made much difference to the physical appearance of the town. There are still tents everywhere, only now they have the depressing appearance of permanence, for brick and wooden floors have been constructed as a gesture against the Peloponnesian winter. Dismal little rows of washing flap from guy-ropes or improvised clothes-lines. Children squabble and play in the walkways between rows of canvas. The thought occurs, not for the first time, that perhaps the first part of a disaster is the easiest to cope with: shock protects, adrenalin flows, some action occurs in reaction to emergency. The real test comes later, with the dragging of time and the necessity to endure after the destruction of hope.

And so I returned to the list, feeling chastened.

Reason for Feeling Ghastly Number Four: Fear. Fear that you won't get back again to see the faces of the daisies in springtime, to see the puffy clouds making patches and patterns on green, fear that a cantankerous Fate may trap you here forever or, worse, alter the pattern irrevocably back there, change people, even remove them, fear that you have lost your way somehow.

But the only comforting thing about fear, I suppose, is that everybody experiences it. And some people have knowledge, which is worse. Once more I thought of the suffering Ukrainian, thankful to be in Australia, but certain he will never see his family and homeland again.

On to *Number Five*: You enjoyed yourself hugely, even while your puritanical soul shrieked, 'Hedonism. Vain puffery. Conceit.' You are not coping well with this bump down to alien earth. You are sighing for the lotus-eater land in which it always seems afternoon, a land where all things seem the same.

Perhaps the only country worth inhabiting is a state of mind? If my Melbourne is, as I suspect, the City of my imagination, then surely I can cart it around with me, dwell in it anywhere? I can close my eyes and will that sense of security (womb-like?) to return, will that feeling of relaxation to vanquish the recurring agony of dislocation. I can, when the old men growl and shoot glistening gobbets of saliva into the gutter, go back to Olinda and spring dampness and blue rinses and hear instead, 'It was such a *luvly* afternoon tea, Betty,' and perhaps decide that afternoon teas are not what I want, after all. Behind the old men, a notice tacked to the wall exerts its own contrasting charm: *I buy snails. 150 drachmae a kilo.*

Enough of the list. I begin to feel better. The Little Summer of Saint Dimitrios lasts and lasts, each golden day slipping by like painted beads on a string. Manny-from-over-the-road comes with cabbage and a bag of home-grown peanuts, 'because I haven't said welcome yet. How're your parents? You've got a cold, a bad one. Poor thing.'

Spiro calls from his shop as I go by. 'How's your *grippe*?'

'Still with me,' I croak, knowing that homesickness and the cold are exacerbating each other.

'*Tha perasi*,' he smiles, encouragingly. 'It will pass.' I know he is right, about both things.

The boys come home and fill the house with their chatter. Slowly I'm getting used to the sound of Greek again. When they go off to the soccer ground I take Ozzie-dog on his favourite walk. At five o'clock the rose light bathes the mountains, and already fine plumes of smoke are rising from the valley. Another beautiful, sun-filled day tomorrow. Beguiling, bewitching weather.

I close my eyes and open them again. I feel . . . well, okay. Yet somehow, I know I'll never be quite safe again. That other dog, the black one, will always be waiting in the shadows, ready to go for my throat. But then Ozzie licks my hand, we turn together and he takes me home.

Chapter 9

1989

IN the third year after the earthquake, reconstruction still goes on, and the streets of Kalamata resound to the stutters of *xenna*, as Polish labourers call and shout to one another. The restoration of the church of the Apostles is complete; the house on Navarino Street still stands, as does the unsubtle statue. The castle, with the arrogance of seven centuries, remains unchanged.

Immediately after the earthquake, the Ministry of Culture and Science began collecting the remnants of neo-classical statues and façades. Outside its tent a proud sign hung: *I Kalamata zei*. Kalamata lives. The adjectives *tacky* and *seedy* were, in a sense, more appropriate than ever in this ruined city, but they rarely sprang to mind.

Survival, let alone comfort and luxury, has never been guaranteed here, but life has continued somehow, changing shape slightly or drastically as circumstances (earthquakes, wars, occupations, famine: a long list) have demanded. Like their rocks and landscape, the *Kalamatianoi* endure. George knows that those who have stayed to face an uncertain future do so because they love the place and cannot imagine living anywhere else. Inconvenience, even privation, can be shrugged off. *I Kalamata zei*.

Chapter 10

1987

TRAVELLERS of a certain age carry more than suitcases. Their hearts are like back-packers' kits, hung about with odd collections: parcels, bits and pieces worn and often torn with memories, associations, vestiges of past education and experience.

When I set out for Ithaca, my extra luggage could have been imagined, a bright bundle knotted to a stick long enough to reach back to 1960, the year I made a slight acquaintance with Tennyson's 'Ulysses'. In 1987, aboard a ferry which moved slowly across an apparently endless bolt of blue wrinkled silk, I wrestled with recalcitrant memory.

> It little profits that an idle king
> By this still hearth, among these barren crags,
> Matched with an agèd wife . . .

The words stopped then, and others, lists of adjectives, strings of phrases, surfaced to fill the gap and drift about the imagination. Penelope: not an aged wife but a determined, wily woman, sitting at her loom, weaving, unravelling, maintaining her dignity in spite of an inward longing to lay about her importunate suitors with a shuttle. Ulysses: not old and disappointed, but cunning, adventurous, vigorous, tenacious. Other notions, concepts, reflections swirled around: Life (ah, that capital letter), old age, qualified loss, 'some work of noble note'. 'Ulysses', it seemed, had become a poem for middle life.

Then there was the sense of place united with the power of the word. Ithaca was an enchanted name, a kind of rocky, two-faced magnet, attracting yet repelling Ulysses, inexorably drawing all those with knowledge, however sketchy, of *The Odyssey*. Yet Ithaca itself is deceptive; the ferry follows the coast after Kephallonia for so long that you think there is nothing there. Tucks, folds, dense mantles of olive-green entice, lure, but do not deliver. Then, suddenly, a headland rounded, the port of Vathi springs into sight. And, thus stimulated, memory improves, even if certain words have to be checked on later:

> There lies the port; the vessel puffs her sail:
> There gloom the dark broad seas.

It is all just so.

A late addition to my extra bundle was Kavafis's poem, 'Ithaca'. Ever compliant, I felt that I had obeyed its instructions to the letter:

> When you set out for Ithaca,
> Ask that the journey be long,
> Full of adventures, full of things to learn . . .
> Have Ithaca always in your mind.

Have your own Odyssey, in fact . . . and I had had, in a sense. Mine had been longer than usual, starting as it did from the wrong hemisphere. Twenty-seven years were made easier by the fact that, in spite of a few buffets by life's billows, I had not had to deal with Polyphemos and assorted villains. But during the voyage a mental as well as a physical shift had occurred. Ulysses had become Odysseus (Othysefs); Latin had given way to Greek.

And there it was, the real thing still, in spite of 1987. Smiling, upturned faces greeted the ferry passengers, houses, modern ones as a result of the catastrophic earthquake of 1953, hugged the harbour, little boats rocked on the water, and millions of dollars' worth of luxury yacht lined the wharf.

We sauntered along beside the water, looking for the house belonging to *Kyria* Dellaporta. I longed for it to be the shoe-box sized and shaped one with the bright green walls and sea-blue shutters, its front row of roofing tiles edged in azure. But the Dellaporta house was a more restful biscuit colour, trimmed with bright yellow.

We settled in, dusk fell and pinpoints of light appeared on the mountain opposite. Tennyson spoke again:

> The lights begin to twinkle from the rocks
> The long day wanes: the slow moon climbs.

It did climb, too, becoming a perfect yellow disc beside the church tower.

The children drew our attention to the present, to strings of coloured lights, the thronged square, the tavernas, the locals enjoying the evening *volta* and parading in the high fashion which contrasted strangely with the tourists' casual garb. We ate at little round tables by the water, golden rings of *kalamari*, white chunks of *feta*, green twists of pepper, red slices of tomato; we drank yellow retsina. And while we ate, the deep moaned round with many voices. We heard Europe and the whole world; the tourists opened our ears to French, German, Japanese, Swedish, Dutch, the sounds of middle America and Manchester, and Italian, always Italian. We soon learned that many Italian words had crept into the island's Greek: grandparents are not *yiayia* and *pappou*, but *nonna* and *nonno*, the word for fear is *spavento*, mansion is *cazarma*. *Dellaporta* is much more Italian than Greek.

Later we listened to the voices of the past. At the water's edge an anchor reclines on a plinth, a memorial to all of Ithaca's lost seamen, 'those whom the waves embrace forever'. How many must there be, after six thousand years? And the shade of Ithaca's most famous seaman broods over the land still.

'You must go to the village of Stavros to see Odysseus's statue,' a neighbour told us. Foolishly, we thought she was referring to a much later Odysseus, one of the heroes of 1821.

'No, no,' she chided, 'I mean the statue of our King.'

On the beach, a *yiayia* was having trouble with her six-year-old grandson. 'Dimitraki,' she called, sternly, 'if you don't come out of the water this instant, I won't read *The Odyssey* to you tonight.'

Even in the world of anecdote, the past, recent this time, pressed in, and we were reminded that Australia and the Ionian islands had been partners in Empire and fellow-sufferers of a savage penal code until 1864, when independence came to the islands. Our neighbour related how her grandfather, as an eight-year-old, had witnessed the public hanging of a thief. The British, he said, always took theft more seriously than the Greeks did, but then Greeks did not have much property to protect.

Granted a last request, the thief asked to see his mother. When the woman, half-dead herself from worry, sorrow and poverty, appeared, the condemned man upbraided her. He said:

When I brought you an egg, you took it. When I brought you A chicken, you took it. When I brought you a goat, you took it.

The sombre poetry of accusation had lasted 120 years.

Every morning we awoke to a view of the mountain through slatted shutters. Once we swam off a beach shaded by gum trees and oleanders; there the sun shone a pool of light through a pattern of eucalyptus leaves; there, a little further out, the *Odysseus V*, a yacht crewed by four women, lazed across the water.

Taking a boat ourselves, we reached another beach. Perfection was the word we all agreed upon. Through ripples of green every striped stone was visible, bedded in sand the exact colour, we realized suddenly, of the Dellaporta house. The cliffs were marked by slanting striations in cream and brown, and topped by green tufts of bush. Walls of rock stood on three sides; a humped islet loomed in the middle distance; wisps of haze lay on the horizon.

We ate a huge ridged melon presented to us by the owner of the boat. 'From me to you,' he intoned gravely, handing us, as well, a knife the size of a machete.

Along the beach road our Greek-born son picked up long pieces of eucalypt bark and gazed at the contrasting colours and curling edges. The gums had been planted, we decided, by homesick Greek-Australians, for it was from Ithaca that the first Greek migrants to Australia came. In the *plateia*, at night, we met *returnees* from Australia, people who knew people we knew.

'I went to the Stavros *panegyri* on Thursday,' one woman remarked, 'and all of Melbourne was there!'

Many worlds fuse into one.

I said it, Ithaca, was the real thing, didn't I? But it wasn't, quite. If anything, reality split into several dimensions, and there was even an element of the surreal about the place. Images came floating up from the subconscious almost immediately, triggered perhaps by bright colours, the colours of childhood. The Dellaporta back gate was higher than the house; in a way, it was my unknown, remembered gate. In the blinding light, it stood and watched as I struggled with blue-and-white painted buckets; on the other side of the world, and almost a century later I was repeating my grandmother's experience of hauling water from a well. Other ancestors elsewhere had lived in low stone cottages by a sea less benign. Is it such tortuous ways that we repeat our childhood, return to our roots, make our myths reality?

Then there was the house itself, a *grandmotherly* house if ever there was one, filled with souvenirs, memories and little shrines: photos of ex-King Konstantine and side-whiskered priests, ikons of Saints Nikolaos, Fanourios, and Yerasimos, the Greek flag and a flagpole resting in a corner.

Different worlds came crowding in. On the table lay a photograph of a 1920s belle, inscribed *To Pete, with best wishes, Hellyn*. Hellyn, aspiring to who knows what heights with the altered spelling of her name, had a sweet smile carefully set in a cupid's bow, crimped hair and huge, melting eyes. A stamped notice on the back of the photo asked the recipient to 'kindly give credit to De Camp Photo Studios, 245 W 42nd St, New York City'. Rummaging in an unfamiliar drawer for a pair of scissors, I came across an old metal shoe-horn, again the bearer of information: 'Time Will Tell. Wear Sundial Shoes. H. Klein, 815 Sutter Ave. Brooklyn, NY.' And in the same drawer, an old pen surfaced, labelled 'WA Sheaffer Pen Co. Fort Madison, Iowa, USA.' Even objects make odysseys, it seems, and so do words.

We left one morning at seven. Although we had pushed off, there were no sounding furrows to smite. Instead the ferry moved almost imperceptibly on pearly-grey, slightly dappled water. But even though the setting this time was not quite right, the poem *Ulysses* still lingered, teaching the lessons which every schoolboy thinks he knows:

> Though much is taken, much abides;
> . . . That which we are, we are.

Mottoes for mid-life, not youth, we know now.

Ithaca, for us, was life, lessons, an experience. Let Kavafis have almost the last word:

> Have Ithaca always in your mind.
> Ithaca gave you that splendid journey.
> . . . You will have already realized what these Ithacas mean.

Yes – Ithaca, Dellaporta, the unknown, remembered gate.

Chapter 11

THE road to Igoumenitsa takes us to a part of Greece we have never visited before. Lakes shimmer to right and left; at other times we drive through bare canyons, like an imagined Colorado in miniature. But past Agrinio we also see the Cafeteria New York, boasting a huge neon sign in the shape of the Statue of Liberty, torch and all. What is the Greek for 'huddled masses', I wonder, briefly. I wish I could meet the owner of the cafeteria: is the statue a good business gimmick, or something more?

On the ferry we draw slowly towards Corfu's castle-topped crags, towards the tiers of buildings surrounding the port. As usual, we each bring our individual bundles of preconceptions with us. Mine have been largely formed by the brothers Durrell, while George's derive from his schooling, odd bits of reading since, and the reminders of the Venetian sway over Kalamata: swirls of wrought-iron, blurred shapes of the Lion of St Mark. It is hard to know what the boys expect. Doubtless some shreds of history and geography have stuck, for the older ones, at least, seem to have grasped the idea that the Ionian islands are 'different'. But they also have the idea that the islands are modern, cosmopolitan, the home of the jet-set.

I pay a visit to the Public Library, housed in the back portions of the stately British-built palace of St Michael and St George. I ask the librarian about traces of English in the island Greek. He is interested but discouraging. 'The British weren't here long enough. 1816 to 1864 is no time at all, really,' he declares. 'The Italians now, that's another matter. But let's see what we can find.'

He leads the way to the catalogue. The library is a place which confirms me in my preference for the past. High-ceilinged and airy, it does not seem to have changed in years. A woodstove with soaring yards of flue stands in the middle of each room, waiting for winter. Solid shelves and cabinets line the walls; bundles of news-papers, tied with string, pile high on vast tables. There are no computers or micro-fiche machines here. Later, when some children call to borrow books, the librarian opens an enormous ledger and notes titles, and names of borrowers, with a ballpoint pen, apparently his sole concession to modernity. The library consists of volumes in Greek, Latin, Italian and English, and in one corner I discover a collection of books donated by the British Council. John Buchan, Arnold Bennett, D. K. Broster and J. B. Priestley figure prominently.

The librarian, like most of his kind, polite and bespec-tacled, pulls at catalogue drawers in haphazard fashion, almost willing the packed cards, with Dewey classifica-tion numbers pencilled lightly in one corner, to give up their secrets. One drawer, yanked open abruptly, reveals empty yoghurt containers crammed with a variety of impedimenta; it is banged shut immediately.

Eventually I settle at an acre of table and delve into various books. One, about Commissioner Sir Frederick Adam, was written in English and Italian, but had been annotated in Greek. Who was that long-ago student who filled the margins with black-inked notes on accents and pronunciation, all written in a neat, precise hand?

It is not hard to deduce that four generations of school-children must have learned English during the British years. Of course it is practically impossible to estimate the extent of this influence, but Lawrence Durrell, as late as the 1930s, thought that echoes of English accents could be heard in the cries of Corfu's street urchins. Adam and that great philhellene, the Earl of Guilford, established schools on each island in the Ionian group. Today the numbers of schools and pupils seem pitifully small, yet, for the date of 1825, the figures represent a gallant achievement: quite some hundreds of children received at least basic instruction. The schools were apparently mod-elled on the Lancastrian system, and pupils studied Greek, Latin, literature, arithmetic, 'the elements of geometry' and English. As was to be expected, Adam 'also encour-aged the study of the language of the Protecting Power by a powerful stimulus, namely, that of promotion in public situations'.

Adam, his wife and Guildford also took an interest in 'female education' and engaged 'able instructresses from England'. But it is highly unlikely that the Corfiote women who became famous in the world of letters during the nineteenth century had attended any of these schools. Their 'able instructresses' and instructors would have been those hired privately by European aristocracy.

I briefly follow the trail left by Margarita Alvana-Miniati, who was born in 1821 during the British period, and died in 1887, by which time the Ionian islands had been Greek for over twenty years: a sense of great historical movements within the space of just one life is imparted immediately these dates are known.

Alvana-Miniati published in English, French and Ital-ian, and in English at least, was mistress of the florid Victorian style. Her historical sketch of 'the life and times of Dante' has a memorable beginning: 'In the darkness and clouds, amidst the storm of passions, the spiritual and temporal interests of mankind were struggling for supremacy.'

The house in which Lord Guildford was baptized into Orthodoxy stands a short walk away from the library. Now somewhat disguised as the bar *Tequila*, the house nevertheless bears a plaque inscribed in *katharevousa*. The name looks strange: *ΓΥΛΦΟΡΔ*. He is lauded as the 'great philhellene and founder of the Ionian Academy'. Although this institution, bravely begun at a time when the islands had no army, navy, literature, 'no national brotherhood of science and the arts' was allowed to languish after Guildford's death in 1827, it clung to life and is still alive today.

It is not long before I decide that our children are enjoying Corfu for all the wrong reasons. 'Look at all these shops!' they call, diving in and out of doorways, fingering souvenir stands and eyeing Yves St-Laurent T-shirts longingly. 'Look at the streets and buildings instead,' I instruct, for Corfu is like a waterless Venice: narrow streets twist and snake interminably, tall buildings crumble and peel slowly under the sun, and washing is strung, building to building, flapping high above the pedestrians. And suddenly, a corner turned, we stumble on little boys playing cricket, a first glimpse of what proves to be a consuming passion.

Elsewhere we discover the Golden Restaurant, staffed by two young and energetic waiters, one fair, one dark, whose Greek carries a different accent. We learn that they were born in Melbourne and lived in Pascoe Vale for [near Brunswick] sixteen years. Father, the cook, comes out especially to say hullo. 'How're things Down Under?' he wants to know. 'We're not sure,' we chorus and tell our story, for we have been 'returnees' longer than he has. He nods his head a trifle ruefully. 'The missus and I would go back to Melbourne tomorrow,' he announces. 'This place isn't what it was. All tourism. You'll never believe the rent I'm paying,' and he names a sum that sends our eyebrows sky-rocketing. 'But *ta paithia*, they like it here. They don't want to go back to Pascoe Vale. *Ti na kanoume? Ta paithia . . .*' His voice trails away, and he shrugs his shoulders, leaving me once more to ponder one of the facets of Greek life I find most incomprehensible and exasperating. All this work, struggle and sacrifice for the *paithia*. What about the parents and their lives?

But our boys, with the adolescents' certain instinct for glamour, discover the Club Med. beach, and are agog at the undreamed-of sports facilities: courts for every possible ball-game, a soccer ground where the commentary on the daily match is in French (this is salutary, for *not* understanding language is a new experience for them), the water-polo set-up, water-skiing, hang-gliding. They meet a boy from Jersey. 'Did he tell you about Gerald Durrell's zoo?' I inquire idly. This is too much to expect, of course, and they look blank. 'What he did tell us,' they say, 'is that he's been here a fortnight, and he hasn't been into town yet.'

'What?' I cry, aghast. 'You mean he hasn't been to the castles, to the museum, to Mouse Island, or even to the churches and shops?'

'Nup,' they reply, grinning happily. 'Great, heh? But he said he *might* come to the cricket match on Saturday!' It occurs to me then that this youth will have enjoyed a vastly expensive holiday without really knowing where he is, for it seems fairly certain that he will leave without having heard a word of Greek.

George wants a glimpse of Albania. It is painful for our offspring to leave the beach, but they soon become interested in counting and noting pub signs, firm indicators of the expatriate presence. We have already seen Churchill's English Bar and the Black Cat; now, as we drive north the lists force themselves upon us, for here we see the Pig and Whistle, the Irish Shamrock and the Tartan Tammies, and even the Kangaroo Bar and the Bora Bora. Among the inevitable advertisements for hamburgers are ones for Chicken 'n' Chips and English meat pies.

We find another beach which serves yet another luxury hotel. Across a narrow strip of water, Albania looms in bare humps through the haze. There another language is spoken, another mentality prevails and, from all reports, the clock has stopped. Albania is still not part of the modern world. I am ashamed of how little I know about it: memories of childish giggles over the outlandish names of its royalty, King Zog and King Leka, more sobering thoughts of anti-communist emigrés returning, parachuting perhaps on to this very strip of coast, there to be rounded up and shot in very short order. On this side of the water, activity is incessant: motorboats, water-skiers, yachts, topless swimmers are all indicators of the wealthy West at play. George stares through the binoculars.

'There's absolutely nothing stirring over there, nothing,' he states, flatly.

Culture time. Haunted by the vision of the fifteen-year-old philistine from Jersey, I drag three, no four, males in my wake. There are varying degrees of willingness to view the treasures of the Archaeological Museum and the Sino-Japanese collection, the kitsch gentleness of the Sound and Light show, which requires some adjustment on our part, as we have never seen one before, and the magnificence of the Achilleion. Occasionally, not often enough, I ponder my wisdom in doing this sort of thing, and try to compare my life with my children's.

Aged eight, my biggest treat was to be taken to Melbourne's museum. Siblings and I gazed at Phar Lap, model ships, displays of porcelain and reproductions of eighteenth-century English rooms. Or we went to the Public Library, where soft sounds are a feature: the creak of the wooden swivel chairs, the slap of shoes on lino, as people walk normally on entering and then try to tip-toe. There might be a squeak or two from the ladders, and there is always the clunk of the lift, but rarely a snore. In my time I have actually seen a dust-coated employee rouse a student from slumber with a mild rebuke. The smell of the library is pleasing too – a combination of old leather, hide preserver, dust, lino, ink and, on wet days, damp overcoats.

Because of my extreme youth and the fact that I was first taken to the library by my mother, I might be forgiven if I fancy my many visits thereafter as returns to the womb. It *is* rather like a giant womb, the library: you are alone in your pool of light and are only dimly conscious of other life not far away; movements are slower, more stylized, sounds penetrate from a distance. Old men, many of whom I have always thought of as being homeless, perhaps have a similar feeling when they come in out of the rain; to them the library must seem a refuge and strength, a very present help in trouble.

Emerging into Swanston Street after a longish spell in the library is the equivalent of a pre-Leboyer birth, with noise, harsh lights and commotion, a jolting and jarring into life after the peace of the protected and blurred atmosphere inside. Later, following Swanston Street down into St Kilda Road, I was overawed by the Shrine of Remembrance, that imitation temple, hybrid Antipodean Parthenon, bound to exert a powerful influence on the minds of the children of the fifties.

What else? Nothing much. Fleeting recollections of the Streetons and McCubbins in the National Gallery. The Geelong Art Gallery? Perhaps, but I remember nothing about it. School excursions took in places like the woollen mills, the salt works, and once, a quite terrifying visit to a sheltered workshop. Then there were no folk museums, no Soverign Hills to visit. The past is definitely a foreign country: Granny and I occasionally walked Pakington Street at dusk, in itself an unusual thing to do. 'Let's see,' she said, once. 'We might be lucky; we might find a television set on in a shop window.' And we did. And now I cannot recall who was more impressed by the flickering grey of technology.

At eight our children were taken to Mycaenae and Epidaurus on school excursions. Vague remarks about piles of rocks and the number of ice-creams eaten were the only responses we could prise from them. And yet. And yet, perhaps the remote past is not such a trackless wilderness to them. In Corfu's Archaeological Museum Dimitri and I stand together while he guides me through the mysteries of an inscription dated to the sixth century BC.

'Why do I have to bend my head to read it?' I inquire.

'It's called *boustrophedon*,' he explains patiently. 'They followed the pattern of an ox turning during ploughing.'

'Oh,' I remark weakly, thankful for this grasp of information, but ashamed, again, for if I have ever known anything about *boustrophedon*, it has long since disappeared.

But I do at least know a little about Gorgons, and stare at the gigantic one on display. She is more than three metres in height, and her grinning mouth and heavily lidded, bulbous eyes project an extraordinary power which the passage of time has done nothing to diminish. Snakes twine around her waist, and poke symmetrically out from behind her ears. On either side, her children, Pegasus and Chrysaor, and two lion-panthers, look understandably submissive.

A visit to the Museum of Asian Art does not require as large a mental leap as might be imagined. Here Japanese Edo theatre masks grimace from walls; here the boys read the words *T'ang*, *Ming* and *Ching* for the first time. All these treasures are housed in the British-built palace which later belonged to the Greek royal family; first we view the sumptuous throne room, then investigate items collected from more than a world away. West and East merge and mingle; tourists from anywhere and everywhere gape and goggle; phrases from a multitude of languages, and inadequate in any, sigh and whisper.

And we drive to the Achilleion, built by the Empress Elizabeth of Austria in the 1890s and later bought by Kaiser Wilhelm II. Elizabeth, a strange, doomed, wandering creature, empress to over fifty million people, spent at least some happy hours here in her dream palace, taking lessons in Greek and walking in gardens and hillsides. In the little chapel with its statues, paintings of Madonna and Child, and Christ before Pontius Pilate, its crosses, candles and prayer-stool, it is impossible to avoid thinking of that tortured life, with its Mayerling burden, which ended so violently in Geneva in 1898. Impossible, too, to avoid thinking of the Emperor Franz Joseph, who adored the wife who could not, or would not, live with him. Notified of her death, he exclaimed, 'Nothing has been spared me in this world'.

Now the palace, with its hosts of statues, the nine muses, Achilles, is a tourist attraction and a casino. So in a sense it is still a pleasure palace, although Corfiotes whose tastes run to green baize tables have to play elsewhere, so fearful are the authorities that the casino may ruin local lives. But ruined lives, after all, are part of the atmosphere; here and there it is possible to see pre-1914 photos of the Kaiser in summer holiday groups, posing carefully in order to hide his withered hand.

Part of culture time, and a very positive part, I told myself, was our visit to the Saturday afternoon cricket match. Here, every week, strands of history and language meet, on a pocket-handkerchief ground in front of the Palace of St Michael and St George. Everything is in miniature: the scoreboard, faithfully labelled in English, is tiny. This reduced scale has its effect on the game: a six is scored when a ball soars into the gardens of the adjacent mediaeval castle, or into the seats lined up for customers of the nearby *zacharoplasteia*.

The hitting of a six inevitably means a search during which time the Greeks miss no opportunity of relaxing and chatting. I fear for the horses drawing phaetons along the street, but so far they have been lucky. Parked cars do not fare as well.

'We've tried to tell *o kosmos*,' says a chatty Greek spectator, 'but they don't seem to understand about cricket balls.'

They probably do not understand the prices of such essential items, either, for we learn that each ball costs eight pounds to import from England. Out of the corner of my eye I see Nikolaos giving up hope of ever owning a cricket bat.

We settle down in the shade of enormous trees, and proceed to be noisily Australian. 'This beats the MCG any day,' I announce, for does the Melbourne Cricket Ground have waiters and a violinist prowling the outer? We drop the names of Australian Cricket greats from Bradman to Lillee for the benefit of Brits sitting close by. They smile tolerantly and order tea. Lawrence Durrell recounts that rock cakes used to be made for the more important matches; today there are no rock cakes, but it is still possible to order 'tzinger beer'.

I am forced to lower my voice as my sons inconsiderately ask me the meaning of arcane terms such as *silly mid-on*, *fine leg*, *two slips and a gully*. Of course my Greek fails over these, but fortunately our Greek friend engages in lively conversation about more basic terms. The field is sensibly called *to fill*, while *o batsman* and *o bowler* are exactly the same terms given a Greek accent.

Runs are *ronia*, pads are *getes*, the bat is a *palla*, and the wicket takes, again very sensibly, the Greek word for wood, *ta xilla*. Our friend is also informative about the state of cricket in the rest of Europe. There are teams in Malta, and in Holland, of all places. Corfu has four teams, but something has to be done, for this cricket ground we are looking at is the only one on the island.

Batsmen walk out and the fieldsmen take up their positions. I am somewhat bemused to observe two individuals who are wearing nothing but brightly-coloured satin shorts, hats and Dr Scholl sandals. It appears that these people are the umpires. Play starts, and we might be in Victoria or Northumberland. But the opening batsman is suddenly clean-bowled by a beautiful ball which curves inexorably towards the middle stump. Then there is an excited, staccato rattle and we are speedily brought back to Corfu.

The afternoon wears away. We do not stay until the end of the match, but we do see the star in action. We are inclined to snigger when we see him stalk out to the pitch, for we do not know, then, that he is a star. He is rotund, bespectacled, padded and gloved. He is very dignified, but strained pink flesh peeps through his shirt buttons. 'Oh, these unfit sixty-year-olds,' I mutter to myself, expecting him to suffer a heart attack at his first ball. He, meanwhile, adjusts his straw hat and settles himself at the crease.

At the first stroke we gasp. By the fifth we are entranced, for here is a master. With consummate ease he sends the ball crashing into the castle gardens time and time again, leaning gently on his bat while the search party retrieves the ball. To my inexpert eye, nothing seems beyond him: he sweeps, hooks, cuts and drives mightily. At tea-time we congratulate him, and he smiles, inclining his head. '*Efharisto poli.*' We leave then, and on our way ask a teenage player how old the star is. 'Seventy-five,' he replies, grinning at our disbelief. '*Sovara.*' Seriously.

Quite accidentally, we notice a sign pointing to the British Cemetery. It is only a few hundred yards away from the noise, fumes and bustle of the tourist-ridden town, but is a place of touching tranquillity, planted with pines and cypresses. Sad, shady, cypress. Here are all the reminders of colonialism: this could easily, at first glance, be a cemetery in India or Australia. Tombs are solid, huge, and inscribed with combinations of Victoriana and extracts from the King James Bible. Most graves are soldiers' and sailors', but as well, there are rows of graves belonging to wives, children and babies, for cholera was endemic in the Corfu of the past. Transplanted people often died dreadful deaths. Here and there more modern graves have stories to tell: one belongs to a young Australian tourist.

And then there are the graves and tablets belonging to more recent British expatriates. Simple inscriptions are evidence of deep attachments: *Resting in Corfu, a place so loved.*

One tablet touches me more than any other:

> *Jilly and Christian*

and underneath the Greek capitals:

> *APNAKI MOY*

My little lamb. Is this a foreigner's grammatical error? For only an extra A is needed to form the plural. But the Greek endearment says it all: love, longing, the connotations of the Good Shepherd, Greek rural life, all captured in an English person's grief. Jilly and Christian (who were they?) died on consecutive days.

155

It is a Friday morning in June. The British Airways flight to Heathrow is packed with returning holiday makers. On my left sits a much-travelled Englishwoman in her sixties. She has a house in Athens, a flat in London. We fall into conversation, and I learn that the woman on *her* left is from South Africa, and is about to pay Britain a visit after a gap of twenty years.

'I'm going for the first time,' I blurt out, sounding like a fifteen-year-old, 'and I'm *so* excited.'

My companion's face creases in puzzlement. 'You mean the first time in several years?' she hazards, as if correcting an error. I burble on.

'No, I'm Australian, and I've never been to Britain before.'

'Good heavens! Why, I thought you were British.'

Child of the fifties, a real cultural cringer whose self-consciousness about my Australian accent has increased rather than decreased in Europe, I am absurdly pleased by this. I am not a modern Australian woman at all, it seems, if a mere label means so much. Accents continue to be divisive, and I continue to be bemused by British attitudes towards them; somewhere I have read that survey results show that the four least valued accents in the British Isles are Cockney, Liverpool Scouse, Birmingham and Glaswegian. Dublin Irish and Edinburgh Scottish, on the other hand, rate high. Three weeks later, my host, whose accent I would describe as London academic, shudders: 'Goin' to Cornwall, eh? God, that West Country burr. Frightful. *How* I hate it.' I immediately determine to like it, and do – without effort.

But at Heathrow there is a positive plethora of accents, and I am amazed at their uniform politeness. *Pleases* and *thank yous* bounce effortlessly through the air. No wonder so many Greek sentences seem unfinished to my ear. On the way to the Newcastle-upon-Tyne flight I practise saying *Newcarsle*, as later I will practise saying *Uvinjam*, *Bellinjam* and *Annick* for Ovingham, Bellingham and Alnick. But the steward says *Newcassle* and *Fassen* all safety belts, please.

I have chosen Northumberland first, seeking out phil-hellene friends, for travelling solo twenty years too late is a daunting prospect. Feeling the need for bridges, I use friendship's ready-made ones, hoping that I will learn to dive off them eventually. For the moment the foreign-ness of England far outweighs the familiarity produced by a lifestyle faithful though transplanted.

And yet. And yet, as we drive to the village, I feel as if I am twelve thousand miles away. For surely this green is remembered from Western District Victoria, surely these stone walls are the ones first seen in childhood? Antipodean lives often seem lived in reverse order, and mine is no exception. At the end of the first afternoon, K. laughs and says, 'It's like having a mature child in tow, your seeing and commenting on everything for the first time in this way.'

Now I want it back, that first afternoon, with its strange mixture of custom and newness, when I see a dog in a shop being fed *sweeties* over the counter, when I am called *hinny* and *pet* immediately. *Pet* is a word from my grandmother-past; only one Australian friend calls me *pet* occasionally. Later I chart the endearments: *luv* and *ducks* in London, *loov* in Lancashire, *my love* in Cornwall, *flower* instead of *blossom*. No 'Aw, c'mon, Bloss,' here. And I briefly wonder about the origins of the grandmotherly *lovey-dovey cats' eyes*.

Here is a chance to relive a section of life the way I want to, to do things forbidden or impossible in childhood. I go to Mass twice, for K. is Catholic; it is interesting that a Saturday night dream features assorted ancestors looking stern, a hill made of marble to be scaled before the dread door of the church reveals itself, and a priest who quizzes the congregation in general and me in particular on the finer points of his sermon. But the service, once experienced, seems rather more casual than remembered Presbyterian and Methodist ones. All that is missing is a rousing chorus of 'Onward, Christian Soldiers'. In contrast, Orthodoxy seems frozen in the grip of time.

And one evening becomes the Wimmera of the fifties, for we go to a fair, far, far, bigger than the local agricultural show of happy memory, but much the same. Even the ground has been foot-churned to the right texture and shade of dust. I search in vain, however, for the rows of gaping clowns I had so longed to play thirty-five years before. As compensation there are stalls I have only heard about: roll-a-penny and coconut shies.

The right amount of glitter, tawdriness and unconscious humour remains. *Patronized by the Nobility* announces the sign above the boxing booth. At each end of the sign are painted pictures of Muhammad Ali and the owner of the booth, a slight, seedy little man dressed in a dinner jacket. Muhammad Ali is unaccountably absent, but the proprietor is there, still formally dressed, and now spruiking into a microphone. He imitates an aristocratic accent rather desperately, and a crisp cry of *Shaddup* punctuates his patter frequently. After half an hour's viewing of flesh being pounded, bruised and broken, I decide that childhood's yearnings for the boxing booth had largely been a waste of time.

The gipsy fortune-tellers are present in vast numbers, and all, it seems, claim descent from Gipsy Rose Lee. Their huge modern caravans are drawn up in rows, shining with mirrors, fringed with curtains, ornamented with plastic flowers, flanked by boards listing promises and skills. Know Yourself. Learn Something to Your Advantage. Advice to the Rich, Powerful and Famous, and To You. Palmistry, Tarot, Crystal-Ball Gazing.

As usual, I veer towards the past, towards the one-and-only traditional gipsy caravan in sight. Its shafts are down and horse or horses are missing. Instead, propped against the convenient railings are letters of gratitude, including one or two from the noblest in the land. 'The Prince and Princess of Wales have asked me to thank you most sincerely for your kind gift on the occasion of their engagement/wedding . . .'

The van itself is exquisite in red, cream, yellow and green. Each wheel-spoke has a fine stripe painted precisely down the centre, little shutters are fully functional, and carved bunches of purple grapes nestle in the shade of wooden leaves. The roof has a scalloped edge and a shiny chimney. Inside all is a-glitter and a-sparkle with mirrors, the mandatory crystal balls, and wind-chimes. Other impressions are of wreaths of chiffon, folds and tucks of tulle, dips and swags of curtain, and right away at the end of the caravan, what K. called the 'safest little bed in the world'.

Madame is a softly spoken, kind-eyed, friendly pudding of a person. I am uneasy. She takes my hands in hers, and spreads them out, smoothing them gently with her thumbs. Then she starts.

'You've shed tears, lady.'

'Haven't we all?' I remark, jocularly, and immediately wish I hadn't, for this is a jarring note which threatens the mesmeric formulae. Phrases float in space.

'You're from across the water. You've lost somebody.' Myself, perhaps, I want to say but do not. 'The man in your life can be led, but never driven.' Disbelief completely suspended, I could sit there indefinitely, enjoying the egocentric exercise, feeling soothed and lulled by words.

'I see success, darlin' – and happiness, luck and travel.' Five minutes pass, the session ends. Madame looks at me sharply.

'And don't *worry*, lady.' Nothing more. We say our goodbyes. I leave with the feeling that the final word has pierced the protective, ritual layers and has reached the heart of me. Worrying is what I am best at.

I begin a friendship with Newcastle Railway Station, a noble building which shows me the architectural inspiration for Australian stations. Schools, too, seem to have been transplanted without a change. But apart from the station and the stately Tyne, what lingers in the memory is the first sight of the soaring monument to Charles, Earl Grey, '. . . by whose advice and under whose guidance the great measure of parliamentary reform was, after an arduous and protracted struggle, safely and triumphantly achieved in the year 1832'.

Howick Hall, still the home of the Grey family, is the first mansion I am taken to see. Three storeys of dignified Georgian solidity, it gazes across sleek lawns, woodland and formal garden, yet is, I am told, thought so ordinary by English standards that it is not listed in any of the famous guide-books. The power of the word, and of habit: that such a place, such grounds, could or should ever be thought ordinary. And the paradoxical power of transplanted life mindful of Britain for generations – nothing is ordinary, yet many things seem familiar.

Back in Newcastle, the station and monument, with its sonorous words, are in sight of each other. From the station I set out for Scotland, gathering, in preparation, a few shreds of knowledge round me like a garment. In Edinburgh, I remember, *Gardyloo* had been a common cry, made when emptying chamberpots from tenements. *Garde l'eau*. St Giles' Cathedral, where Montrose is buried in the Chapman aisle, and where John Knox, the Cathedral's first Protestant minister, preached until his death in 1572. And the ill-fated Queen.

The train draws into Berwick-on-Tweed with its three

bridges. Somewhere a tartan sign says 'Welcome to Scotland'. Soon a woman bound for Aberdeen begins to chat. 'Ah, poor Mary. I'm from Fotheringhay, where she was executed, you know. Never mind, they gave her a magnificent funeral afterwards. Magnificent.' She repeats the adjective with an almost reminiscent sigh.

Later, gloomy, lowering Edinburgh becomes one of my favourite places. St Giles' is hard to leave. There I find myself suddenly staring at John Knox. The fact that he is now a statue matters little, for power emanates from stone, even, and years of Presbyterian church-going ensure that I know I am in the presence of one 'who neither feared nor flattered any flesh'.

Soon afterwards I discover the tomb of Archibald Campbell, Marquess of Argyll, 'Beheaded near this Cathedral AD. 1661. Leader in Council and in Field for the Reformed Religion'. Imminent execution concentrates the mind wonderfully; Dr Johnson was right. Chidiock Tichborne, for example, on the eve of his execution, somehow managed to write eighteen lines of controlled, poignant poetry, 'My prime of youth is but a frost of cares,' he began, and went on to secure his immortality.

While not blessed with a muse of quite this calibre, Argyll, sacrificed quite shamefully by Charles II, nevertheless uttered fine and undefeated words of admonition:

> I set the Crown on the King's Head.
> He hastens me to a better
> Crown than his own.

I continue to tread the trail left by persecuted aristocrats, but find, surprisingly, a family name which leaps from a list of deserters hung on a wall in Edinburgh Castle. The army life had, apparently, been too much for John Milne of the 66th Foot, of the Parish of Wolverhampton in the County of Stafford. In civilian life Milne had been a grocer, was listed as being 23 and three-quarter years of age and 5 feet six and a half inches in height. He had light brown eyes and dark hair and when last seen on 4 March 1835 in Plymouth, was wearing coat and trousers of fustian.

The bare bones of description, terse words filled in under appropriate headings, prompt questions, build bridges, create drama, breathe life. *Milne* is the name of the grandfather I never knew. Now I wonder what happened to the grocer from Wolverhampton; Plymouth was a convenient place in which to desert. It seems likely that if he escaped detection, and his nondescript appearance must have been an aid, he somehow managed to migrate to North America.

Thus engaging in a mild form of ancestor-hunting, that Antipodean obsession, I set off for Inverness, en route for Bonar Bridge, where the mother of my Milne grandfather was born in 1847. Only recently have I learned that Bonar Bridge, and not Inverness, was her birthplace. How often words, recollections, family legends fail.

It is a perfect day and I sit opposite an American student, appropriately named Heather, who has dreamed of visiting Scotland since she was seven.

'It sure is different from Missouri,' she sighs with deep satisfaction. 'Look at that. It's like watching the best movie you ever saw in your whole life.'

We both clutch at the familiar, using tags and labels to sum up visual experience. It is impossible to say anything new. I mutter about the 'land of the shining river', as sparkling threads flash past.

'Those sheep!' she exclaims. '"Sheep may safely graze" is all I can think of.' Later, as I absorb a little information about the Highland Clearances, the sheep lose their innocence, do not seem symbols of peace and content, but creatures much more ambiguous, threatening, destructive.

On the track of one great-grandmother, I find myself in a bed-and-breakfast place run by a vivacious redhead who bears the name of another.

'Weel, of course, Mackay's m'husband's name,' she announces with more than a tinge of scorn. 'I'm a Grant mesel'. Those Mackays were a low lot. Thieves, y'ken. And,' she lowers her voice, 'they even disguised themselves as *women* on occasion in order to escape the law or angry sheep-owners! Theer y' are!'

This news of transvestite ancestors, delivered at 8 a.m. over a plate of eggs, sausages and grilled tomato causes me to gaze meditatively into my teacup, while the Americans at the next table chatter energetically.

On the train the next morning I am struck by musical names like Muir of Ord, and Ardgay, which is Gaelic for *high wind*. The names are pleasant; some sights, such as that of the monstrous oil rigs in Cromarty Firth, are not.

Bonar Bridge seems a sleepy little place. Until the famous Thomas Telford built Bonar's first bridge in 1812, all trade and communication was by sea. The name itself comes from the Gaelic *Bhannath*, meaning *low ford*. It is ancient land, this, containing some of the oldest rocks in Britain, Neolithic tombs and hut circles. To the Norsemen of the tenth century, the area was *Sudrland*, the South Land.

When Paul Theroux passed this way, he heard a difference in accent, the last echo of Norn, the language of Shetland and Orkney, which was also spoken in Caithness and Sutherland. My ear is not acute or experienced enough to notice this, but I do manage to find out that the old riddle about the cow, four-stiff-standers, four dilly-danders, originated with Norn: *Fjórir hanga, fjórir ganga, fjórir standa upp à sky*, and feel a sense of achievement. The Hildina Ballad, its thirty-five verses noted down in 1774, is much more romantic, however, with the Earl of Orkney debating whether he should rescue a maiden from the glass castle in which she is imprisoned.

Today I am the only tourist in Bonar Bridge. But the woman at the Tourist Information Centre tells me that five hundred a week come in high season.

'Americans, mostly,' she says, 'searching for their ancestors.' A roll of the eyes. I tell her about my own small quest.

'Indirect result of the Highland Clearances,' she announces briskly. And indeed John Prebble documents an incident, attempted resistance to clearance, which took place nearby in 1854.

'Your great-grandmother was almost certainly a Gaelic speaker. Probably took ship from Glasgow.'

Glasgow alone must have seemed like the end of the earth, yet by the time she was twenty-one Ann Duff had sailed to Australia and had married David Milne, of either Dundee or Forfar, at Castlemaine in Victoria. She saw out her days in the northern part of that state, in heat, dryness and dust, far from soft green hills, the blue-grey of the Kyle of Sutherland and little stone cottages each topped by four chimney stacks. A pang of pity strikes; the finality of migration then was absolute. Did she migrate alone? No one knows. But now it seems significant to me, evidence of some small pattern in life, that she left one Bridge and ultimately settled at a place named after her husband's family: Milne's Bridge.

The local draper and an octogenarian named Belle are interested. The draper writes the date 1847 on his cigarette packet and generally takes the attitude that this particular year is as close as last year, or even last week. But all the Duffs are gone, ah yes. One branch to Canada, and one to Argyll, which sounds as if it might be almost as far, at least to the draper and to Belle. They suggest that I have to chat to the *munister*. Repeated rings at the door of the *Munse*, however, produce no response.

It rains in Norfolk. Does it ever *stop* raining in Norfolk? It is useless for people to talk about the endless horizon; all I can see is a wet, grey blur, all I can feel is a biting easterly. Yes, this is a climate for thinking, not sweating. If climate and landscape have their effect on character, and Henry James went so far as to aver that landscape *is* character, I now know a great deal more about great-grandmother Harriett, grim as the weather, with a nature, individual, hard, fashioned by the flint I have never seen before. Yet these influences made her a successful pioneer, and there are veritable lists of brave, gifted people who have called Norfolk home: Dame Julian, Nelson, Sir Thomas Browne, Elizabeth Fry, Edith Cavell, Alfred Munnings. Harriett rejected flatness for mountains, rejected other people's influences so that she could be her own person. The landscape, predictability, smallness, familiarity, were probably all reasons why she could not stay. Perhaps she also felt, but could not express, the effect of big skies and wide horizons, that there was nothing, as a Scots farmer explained to Ronald Blythe, in East Anglia, 'for a man to measure himself by'. But Harriett had moved to mountains and valleys, and mountains 'make a man think' because 'they are there for all time'.

I wander Norwich streets seeing the red letter boxes labelled VR and set in flint surrounds as some sort of symbol, or at least some sort of link between hemispheres and eras. Did the relatives left behind post their letters in these boxes? Perhaps. Perhaps, also, they doubted that their missives, penned with effort and posted at great expense, would ever reach their destination. But I know that some, at least, did.

Later, as the train rattles along to Acle, Harriett's married name flashes from a building near Brundall station. Once in Acle it is not difficult to find the church of St Edmund, King and Martyr. This is the church that Nana never saw, but knew to be not only absolutely real but an integral part of her. When she was ninety-one, she started in surprise on learning the name given to yet another great-grandchild.

'Tamsin. But that's my great-grandmother's name, her Christian name. She's buried in the churchyard at St Edmund, King and Martyr.'

And I, on a grey day, find the grave of Tamasine Hunn, mother of Harriett. Harriett's father, Jacob, did not die until he was eighty-seven, and the inscription from the book of Job which is just visible on his tombstone would also have been apt for Nana's.

> Thou shalt come to thy grave in a full age,
> Like as a shock of corn cometh in his season.

I am not alone in the graveyard. With me is a friend who has lived in Australia for twenty-five years. But her grandmother was born in Acle, and when J. emigrated she went first to Kerang. The name Milne's Bridge has meaning for her. Threads, patterns, words, bridges, lives linking or touching briefly across space and time: how unexpected and yet expected all this is.

We leave the lichened stones and enter the thirteenth-century church. Flint lasts. The font, made in 1400 but defaced during the Commonwealth, still has the power to move the onlooker who takes the time to gaze at the blurred Pietà, the man with angel wings, at the Lion, Ox and Eagle. On the wall nearby I find the list with its magic name: Ralph de Norwich, Rector of Acle in 1221. We squint at brass plates on the floor. The Rector, busily preparing for the children's Teddy Bears' picnic,

village and church both owe their names to the much older name of *Gwendern*.

The tourist attraction tin-mine is only a short distance away. At the entrance all visitors are equipped with hats, not tin, but hard plastic, and maps. A chill of apprehension deepens the further I penetrate the mine. I search for adjectives. *Claustrophobic, dark, damp, threatening*, all seem worn out, exhausted. Water drips continually on stone. The thought of all that weight is terrifying, although the real terror was the water, I learn. If the pump stops, we will be paddling at the end of half an hour; but it is some comfort to know that the mine takes five days to fill.

If the vivid adjectives escape me, at least I learn new nouns: *adit* means horizontal entrance or passage, *bal-maidens* were women, usually wives and daughters of miners, who worked on the dressing floor at the entrance to the mine. Once ore had been brought to the surface it was their job to break it into fist-sized lumps and to feed it into the stamps. I even learn about new ways of coping with injury and unemployment, for miners who could no longer work made models of mines to show in the streets. And I also learn about a new but still grisly way of death: on Tuesday, 24 August 1858, seven miners lost their lives by drowning in slime when a shaft collapsed and the levels filled with thousands of cubic fathoms of the stuff. Today's tourists can, for forty-five pence, buy facsimiles of the relevant newspaper reports; once again I read a family name.

Later, on yet another train, a Cornishwoman asks my name. 'Ah, the gentry,' she announces.

'Surely not my branch,' I demur.

'Well, definitely the *St Orstell* branch were of the quality,' she persists. 'Related to the Rashleighs, they were, had a lot of land, and they'd won most of it at the gaming tables.' I am forcibly reminded of the gambling streak, strongly disapproved of, but always there, in great-grandfather and great-uncles.

'At least they weren't mine-owners,' I say, gratefully, and tell her how all those old history lessons about Lord Shaftesbury had suddenly come to life when I saw a notice in the mine museum. With the passing of the Education Act of 1876, no child under the age of nine was permitted to go down a mine; if a child under the age of eleven was employed, he had to have passed the second standard of education. The pang of pity I had felt for Annie Duff had become as nothing.

The Cornishwoman sighed. 'Only yesterday, really, isn't it? Awful. Do you know, my love, that one mine was so rich and so extensive that little children had to stay down it for three days at a time?' We both fall silent, contemplating the horror of it.

At Taunton she leaves. 'Off on a holiday. Mind you don't put me in a book. By the way, did you know the Cornish always come home to die?'

Where is home, though? That word, that question again. Was there ever a person with so many choices of place in which to die?

And the rest. Brief stays in London, Merseyside and Lancashire. Fleeting impressions. Words linger in the memory just as persistently as sights. In Westminster Abbey I give up the struggle to photograph the effigy of Elizabeth I, and instead snap, and snap up, the inscription nearby:

> Near the tomb of
> Mary and Elizabeth
> Remember before God
>   All Those who
> Divided at the Reformation
> By different convictions
> Laid down their lives for
> Christ and Conscience' Sake.

In Poet's Corner I view the memorial to Caedmon, 'who first among the English made verses', and the one to George Eliot, bordered with the words: 'The first condition of human goodness is something to love; the second something to reverence'. For Greeks and cross-cultural children, I ignore Dylan Thomas and photograph Byron's words instead:

> But there is that within me which shall tire
> Torture and Time, and breathe when I expire.

Later, in Birdcage Walk, we tourists peer through the barred fence to watch the Foot Guards conducting a uniform inspection. The officer in charge greets us sarcastically. 'Good *morning*, ladies and gentlemen.' (He wishes us anything but, that is clear.) 'Autographs at the end of the session.'

To his men he does not speak, he barks. His is not a voice, but a collection of over-strained, polypped vocal cords, an opera-singer's nightmare, which soars, grates and squeaks in the wrong places. Or perhaps the right places? For here, on this parade ground, words, language, body language are all used to intimidate.

There must be more than this. And there is, for very soon I discover Colin, an employee of a firm which organizes walking tours of London. Colin is a gnome-like youth whose voice also grates and breaks because he has worn it out. On two consecutive mornings I tramp in his wake through mile upon mile of London streets. These tours are not well patronized: it seems that a combination of prolonged exercise and London weather does not appeal to tourists. But those who do choose to walk are enthusiastic, almost as enthusiastic as Colin himself.

He is passionately in love with London, and is master of fourteen different walks. Fascinated by the life of literature and art, he sprays his excitement, spitting words out in a flurry and tumble. Anecdotes about Wren, Dr Johnson, and Richardson are yelled above the traffic noise. 'Betcha haven't read all of *Clarissa*,' he grins at me. 'Betcha right,' I reply, and discover later that George Eliot once sternly remarked, 'We have fallen on an evil generation who would not read *Clarissa*.' At various points we stop while Colin pulls pieces of plastic-shrouded cardboard out of his pocket. 'I'll just read you what Goldsmith said about . . .'

Now the names take on shape: Postman's Park, once a paupers' graveyard, St Botolph's and other churches including St Bride's, with its wedding-cake spire, Dr Johnson's house, 'where we *know* he worked on the Dictionary,' pronounces Colin, and the Cheshire Cheese, 'where we do *not* know that he ever drank. Not proved,' says Colin, smiling as he shatters this illusion yet again. And the next day sees a list of words unfold: Queen Anne's Gate, Pall Mall, Jermyn Street, Savile Row, Regent Street, Hanover Square, Cavendish Square, Portland Place, all the way up to Regent's Park, with Colin expatiating on the subject of Regency London. I am tempted to mention Georgette Heyer, but think better of it. He dabs labels on every example of architecture worth mentioning: 'A fine example, very lovely' or 'extremely squalid' are his favourites.

In London all experiences fuse: the layers separate, then melt together again as I go to the *Angry Penguins* exhibition at the Hayward Gallery, as I hear a Greek in the Victoria Underground yell to his wife: '*Eh! Pou pas?*' Where are you going? I smile at the familiar sound, at those staccato words, and a flicker of recognition marks his face. Wife returned to his side, he marches off, leaving me a little homesick, for this is the only Greek I hear in four whole weeks. But this experience teaches me that I have at last formed an attachment to this language, whereas once I feared it would swamp me, baffle me forever.

At the Hayward Gallery, the names of Australia's greats sit beneath their respective paintings. Boyd, Perceval, Hester, Tucker, Vassilieff. But it is the Nolans I have come to see. The whole of Britain awaits me, yet I am drawn to this collection of Australiana for I may never have another chance to see these treasures at the one time, in the one place.

The glowing colours of 'Ned Kelly', the wit, those penetrating, moving eyes, are startling, yet it is to other paintings that I turn with an instant flash of recognition. Childhood memory leaps to life with 'Wimmera Landscape' and 'Kiata'. Kiata's angry sky and yellow and bitumen colours I remember, but 'Wimmera (Landscape with Train)' means more to me, for had we not lived near that very railway track? Everything is there: the straight lines which bend ever-so-slightly with the eye, the telegraph poles going on forever, the smudge of train-smoke, the geometrical buildings and their shadows, nine gum trees, no more, and the colours of desert dryness and drought, yellow, grey, dusty-green. London, England, Scotland, Greece, all disappear. I am back there again, twelve thousand miles and thirty-five years away.

An End and
a Beginning

Chapter 12

MY mother-in-law is a speaking woman. This gerund, present participle gone wandering and transformed into an adjective, may not be the word I am looking for. I do not mean that she is talkative, although she can be, very often. Rather, the whole of her speaks, expresses a point of view, indicates her station in life. Her black clothes call, 'I am a widow,' her headscarf, knotted different ways according to the weather or her current occupation, informs the trained observer immediately. A weather-beaten, gnarled right hand, quietly providing the general idea, if not the details, of years spent in manual labour, moves forward almost imperceptibly in certain company. It proclaims and commands, 'I am the *papathia*, the priest's wife. You will kiss my hand.' That same hand flies to her breast and strikes emphatically in moments of tension, or moves up and down in concert with raised eyebrows to express the Greek *oxi*, most often perceived by me, at least, in unambiguous capitals. NO. The head jerks back, the chin upward in that most disconcerting of Greek gestures. There may be an accompaniment of a sharp Tch!!, the tongue moving sharply and clicking against the hard palate, there may not be.

But Greeks love to talk, and older ones, at least, are still convinced of the power of the word. When gorgons rise from the sea during storms and demand of the captains of tempest-toss'd ships, '*Pou einai Megas Alexandros?*' – where is Alexander the Great? – the only safe answer to give is '*Zei kai vasilevei*' – he lives and reigns. Any other answer guarantees the destruction of the ship with all hands. '*Na meen avaskathi*,' breathes Yiayia, warding off the Evil Eye – may it not be envied.

For the Evil Eye is jealous of anything good and beautiful, from sprouting beans, buds on flowers to newborn babies. It was a long time before I learned not to admire tiny babies, such admiration being an integral part of me, and the expression of it culturally determined. How could I *not* admire creatures so absolutely beautiful, untouched but knowing, creatures deliberately designed to stir the heart and earn praise? I demanded to know. Slowly it became clear that such mellifluous adjectives as I used were potent, participating in the nature of these babies, and thus tempting the Eye to do its worst. And so I learned to dry-spit if I simply had to admire. *Ti omorpho moro!* What a beautiful baby. Phtou. Phtou. I spat, against the power of the Eye and whatever other evil was threatening. I spat in his eye, I always thought, my mind making a leap to the Australian expression of irritation.

But when Yiayia talks, she talks. Now eighty-two years old, she is preoccupied with the past. For her, words re-create it. *Ti thimamai. Ti thimamai.* What I remember. She sits and spins, out of a word-thread, a tapestry of old times. I see her mother, another *papathia*, the Panayota of the old photograph, swathed in ankle-length layers of dark clothing, scarves concealing her hair and face, and learn a new verb. You won't find that in your dictionary, says George, grinning, but I track it down, eventually, in a very large Greek one. Μπαμπου-λώνω, to conceal the face. Ach-oo, *kakomira*, ill-fated one. And she was indeed ill-fated, in anybody's language;

she bore fourteen children. Only five survived to adult-hood. Then one young man died, and another sailed to America and never returned. *Pethane noris*. She died young, my mother. But *o papas* . . . through all these trials Papayeorgi endured, certain in faith, sure of the power of that Word he invoked every Sunday and feast-day. *Kyrie Eleison. Christos anesti ek nekron*. He sat with his books and his papers, rolled his own cigarettes, wisps of tobacco in thin paper, organized the women into the work of subsistence farming: the olive harvest, the rais-ing of the animals, the spreading of the manure, the vegetable garden, the fig harvest, the wheat harvest high up in the mountain village. He could read. *Ixere gram-mata, o pateras mou*. He knew his letters.

And knew, certainly, how Greek society was built on three words: *timi, pallikaria, filotimo*. Honour, bravery, generosity. But *filotimo* is not so easy to pin down. Pride, ambition, self-respect, sensitivity – the synonyms multi-ply and still it proves elusive. The meaning of some words soaks through pores rather than through brain-cells or ears, and *filotimo* is one of them.

But although these powerful words bound the elements of life, economic, social and emotional, together, and although *o papas* wrote these words, and others, on sheets of paper which sailed away to America, they were not enough to bring the first migrant son home.

Now the second migrant son, who returned from Chicago in 1936, regrets that the letters are all gone, that he did not save even one of them, that the entreaties in inimitable handwriting are gone for ever. For surely handwriting is as definite a mark of individuality as a voice? Although it can, of course, assume a persona: every fourth Thursday Yiayia has to sign her name on the back of her pension cheque. She seizes the pen stiffly, subduing it, sets her teeth, presses firmly with her hand and moves the unfamiliar stylus forward at a snail-like pace. *A. Μπούρα* flows, no, trickles slowly out, suggesting a ponderousness quite foreign to her nature. Once she wrote *Αφροδίτη*, and I felt her transformed into youth, beauty, a different person with a real, powerful, overwhelmingly evocative name.

Few women of Yiayia's age can read or write, yet they are so steeped in folklore and religious imagery that words often spring out of them almost as formal and polished as poetry. One morning I was stopped by a woman I did not know, but who knew me. Without preamble, she gazed at me solemnly, and intoned: 'You deserve a crown of gold and ivory'. Of course, I asked her to repeat herself; I was sure I had either misheard or misunderstood. She did so, and I was still at a loss. 'Er, why?' I asked. This was the signal for an outpouring on the subject of my great virtue and self-sacrifice in leaving my own family and *patritha* and coming to my husband's. In short, I was to be compared with Ruth. I had said, 'Whither thou goest, I will go,' and here I was.

Touched and amused and more than a little thankful that she did not know the real me, I walked home on an uplifting cloud of vanity. I still upbraid my family on occasions when I feel hardly done by: 'Don't forget! I deserve a crown of gold and ivory.' Often the thought occurs: what would an Australian have said? Probably nothing, or at most: 'Yer doin' orright, mate'.

Here modern fads like the words and concepts of psychology, sociology, self-development, adolescence, adjustment, neurosis and peer-group pressure might as well not exist. Another grandmother, a neighbour, has little patience with her grand-daughter's desire to be a modern, liberated young woman, and still less patience with her interest in fashions, makeup, pop music, boyfriends and their motorbikes. 'She used to be such a dear little girl,' this *yiayia* laments, 'but now Satan has taken her away'. Good, evil, white, black, light, darkness: there seems to be no grey area in between. The no-man's-land of doubts, fears, maybe's and perhaps's is missing. Nor are good and evil abstract notions. Satan wears a black leather jacket and rides a Honda as surely as he once had cloven hoofs and carried a pitchfork.

Still another woman, old and barely coping with a dying husband, tried to soften his rebelliousness by pointing to the ultimate example of goodness. 'Our Little Christ suffered for us, my golden one, now it is your turn to suffer for Him.'

Everything is clear cut, obvious, concrete, and what seems verbal extravagance in English is entirely natural in Greek. Greeks, old rural ones at least, have their ideals still intact, and such idealism is reflected in their speech. Greeks will describe their mothers, for example, as madonnas, goddesses, golden blankets covering them, while in my middle son's exercise book one year, I found a poem carefully transcribed for Mother's Day: *Mother*.

> You are my greatest love
> You are my guardian angel
> You are my protector and my help
> You are the sun of our house.

Memory calls again: I hear my French teacher reciting irregular verbs from twenty-five years away. He seemed ancient to us, and rightly so, for when we mentioned his name at home, Mum exclaimed, 'But he taught maths. He taught me!' We looked at each other, sure that our teacher must be at least ninety.

He knew his job; he knew his subject. French grammar was a playground to him, through which he tip-toed, trampled, gambolled and frolicked as the mood took him. It was easy. For many members of the class, however, it was not. When he had tried, and repeatedly failed, to make us see the beauty of the subjunctive, its forms and the constructions in which it occurs, he gave way to a fit of exasperation. 'I might as well be hoeing carrots in Lara!' he exclaimed hotly. But he did not give up.

He was self-conscious about speaking: all French teachers were then. At a time when France was at least a month away by ship, few State school teachers had ever been outside Australia. Nevertheless, we had a taste of French literature. It did not matter then, that it was a mere sip and nibble at an enormous repast. For if the irregular verbs had faded, other ghosts return to haunt. The most substantial of these is the schoolmaster in Daudet's story, *La Dernière Classe*. France has been defeated by Prussia; the next day schoolchildren of Alsace–Lorraine are to begin instruction in German. Trembling with emotion, the teacher, M. Hamel, exhorts his pupils always to remember their French, never to let it go: '. . . *Parce que, quand un peuple tombe esclave, tant qu'il tient bien sa langue, c'est comme s'il tenait la clef de sa prison.*'

Most of us, to whom speaking any language other than English would seem the direst punishment, understood, even if dimly, the rightness and sense of this moving command. But none of us could suspect the misery and sense of isolation produced by hearing only a jangle of sound in the ears, the horror of grasping no meaning and being able to communicate none. We had not the vaguest idea of what the Papadopouloses, the van Cleefs and the Sanguinettis had suffered.

Nor had we any idea that striving with our own language would help us towards a freedom of another sort. We could not believe that any foreign invader would force us to stop speaking English, but we did realize that our very thoughts were limited by the confines of our spoken and written word. None of us understood that the more flexible, versatile, precise, exact, and familiar we became in English, the more our thoughts could expand, the more freedom could be ours. In that utilitarian age post-World War II, we knew little of Latin and Greek, did not grasp that Greek had been spoken for nearly 4000 years, had no notion that the Ancient Greeks all that long time before had succeeded in developing a language with an astonishing capacity to express precisely feelings, emotions, mental states and requirements.

We knew still less about language acquisition, the way in which we inherit sentence patterns from the immediate, distant and long-distant past. We never noticed the way in which toddlers attempt to reproduce phrases and sentences, although Dad had pointed out the original way in which our three-and-a-half-year-old brother requested two Ryvita biscuits and jam: 'I'd like a shut-up together raspberry cardboard, please.'

Our ignorance, too, of orality, was profound, so profound that it has taken me years to see that literacy itself is a kind of exile; literate people are so often cut off from the richness of superstition and folklore, from much beauty and adventure. We are also separated from the mentality of orality: my reaction when Yiayia says, 'But he *can't* be on television today; he died last week,' is to laugh and shake my head. But for people who are part of an oral society, memory, recollection, methods of recording and communicating are all different. We are forever separated, Yiayia and I, and not only because we were born in different countries and have different mother-tongues. She is an inhabitant of an island I can never reach, but can only glimpse from afar as the river of modern life, literacy, bears me slowly away. She, in her turn, often seems exiled from her own grandchildren by her use of old-fashioned, countrified language. I know

Greek words she does not know; she knows ones I can only hear from her; like her, such words are slowly dying.

When I met Howard, I began to understand about inherited sentence patterns, about both the static and dynamic nature of language, its completeness and incompleteness. Howard was only fifteen years younger than Grandfather, and spoke like him. It was not merely a matter of accent and expressions used, but a rhythm, a type of placement which I, no linguist, find difficult to explain. There was a familiarity in the balance of Howard's phrases which I welcomed with relief. I saw him and spoke to him very seldom, but felt at home as soon as I did so. Swift's definition of style applied here: to me, Howard was adept at the use of the proper words in the proper places.

Now other teachers call down the corridor of recollection. One showed us how a sentence worked, how it changed when a phrase went wandering, how necessary it was to know your tools before you could build anything. The blackboard filled, emptied, filled again with lists of the parts of speech, phrases, clauses, complements, adverbial adjuncts. Never start a sentence with *and* – and now I commit that sin frequently. Never start a sentence with *because* – this sin I find much harder to commit. This teacher was the superintendent of the local Presbyterian Sunday School, and this fact gave his teaching added power, the weight of Holy Writ, the vastness of ultimate authority. He would not let us play, take liberties, experiment with language, use slang. Rules were rules and there to be obeyed.

Another, however, knew the rules, taught them well and then showed us how they could be bent. He loved colour and concrete imagery. 'Goog, you melon-headed chump!' he would roar, quite without malice, as Tom, a sweet-natured but dull boy with an egg-shaped head, made simple spelling errors and muddled adverbs and adjectives yet again. Both teachers, as far removed from Socrates in time and space as they could be, made us practise the art constantly: sentences, paragraphs, sets of instructions, invitations, acceptances, thank-you notes, full-scale letters, descriptions, adventure stories; we wrote and wrote.

We also practised the old-fashioned art of handwriting. Today's ball-pointed, fibre-tipped generation is sorely deprived, never having known the feeling of power that comes with the mastery of the steel nib. Magic flowed and sputtered down on to the page as we recited inwardly the rules for copperplate, light up, heavy down, and studiously resisted the temptation to be waywardly modern and cross our t's. Instead our t's were looped as we wrote five times, carefully, and for as long as it took:

Australia, the island continent.

Now I find it very difficult to do, but am glad I knew how once upon a time. I do not know whether I will ever feel about a word-processor the way I felt about the steel nib and my Parker fountain pen. Even the boy who mixed the ink and poured it into forty-five ink-wells every morning had a kind of glamour.

Yet we took it all for granted, never thinking too much about language, writing, speech, communication, except to feel vaguely resentful if we heard a private school, Toorak, or English accent, for it was an axiom, then, that Australian accents, even of the middling sort, were ugly, flat and harsh, and somehow, strangely, indicative of mental and cultural inferiority. We would have been mightily amazed to learn that other cultures would fight, and had fought to the death, over issues of language. In his book *Hellas*, Nicholas Gage recounts, for example, how rioting occurred in Athens in 1901, as a protest against the translation of the Gospel into demotic Greek, and how spectators died in a fight which broke out when the *Oresteia* was presented in the demotic in 1903.

Later, I was, indeed, bemused by the idea that language could be changed by Act of Parliament, but had the distinct feeling that George Bernard Shaw, for one, would have approved of the Greek attitude: of necessity the emergent Greek nation of the 1820s created *katharevousa*, its official language. Now demotic is the official language, despite the fevered protests of many who still favour the 'pure' *katharevousa*. Language, in the past, has been a hotly political issue, with the left favouring the democratic demotic, the right clinging to the exclusivist high Greek. More recently, the Socialist government abolished the old system of breathings and emphases in written Greek, insisting instead on a *monotonic* system, in which stress marks, and stress marks only, are used on words of more than one syllable. I heaved a sigh of relief over this piece of legislation, as all those *oxeias* and *perispomenis* had proved too much for my natural indolence. But now my eldest son wrestles with Ancient Greek, his task made all the harder by this legal simplification of Modern Greek.

Should the Greek government be also fighting a rearguard action against the pernicious influence of English, as the French government is? Appalled by the incursion of expressions such as *le weekend, le fair play* and even *le jerk*, the *Institut* is doing its best to safeguard the purity of the language. There is to be none of this lazy *le computer, le software* nonsense: honourable French words attack the dangerously monoglot world of new technology. *Un Walkman*, for example, is not French: *un baladeur* is the preferred noun. Greeks are showing little resistance: they refer to *ta computer*, but call, very confusingly, pocket calculators *ta computerakia*. And in France there is tension and divided feelings over proposed alterations in spelling and removal of the circumflex.

In the meantime, arguments still rage, even among ordinary people, over the respective merits of the two styles of Greek. I sat and listened while one such battle was fought on our balcony one summer evening. Kosta, a bright young polymath with a love of engineering, science, folksong and literature, was fervent in his praise of demotic, declaring *katharevousa* to be an artificial language imposed on the people. George's brow darkened as he listened and then argued back. My own view, which I had no chance to express, was that you cannot hope to keep language in a mummy-case, no matter how hard you try. I attempted to follow the meanderings and convolutions of their reasonings but my mind kept wandering off on tracks of its own.

While it is difficult to imagine Australians becoming fevered on the subject of language, it is fair to say, I think, that they enjoy playing with their own brand of English and revel in the effect such play can have on English speakers from elsewhere. Even as I write, the drama critic of the *Sunday Times*, in an effort to account for the continuing appeal of Dame Edna Everage, is concentrating on the matter of accent, maintaining that the English 'love being conned, twitted, insulted and injured by people with outlandish pronunciations'.

Recently, resentful of expatriate English people's comments on the Australian accent, I was telling an Australian visitor how such remarks tend to make me retreat into a kind of reactive argot; the temptation to utter remarks like 'Stone the crows and starve the lizards' at five-minute intervals almost overwhelms me. I informed him how I recount, with a straight face, the tale of the pilot of a smallish plane discouraging a late, importuning passenger by laconically uttering the immortal phrase: 'Sorry, Ocker, the Fokker's chocka'. My visitor gave a great crack of laughter. 'Great stuff. Keep feeding it to them. They fall for it every time – they love to think we really speak like that.'

And surely Mr Hawke's appeal is firmly based on that Strine accent? I like to think that he has taken elocution lessons, not in order, like Edward Heath, to learn Received Pronunciations, but to ensure that his diphthongs will remain forever ambiguous, his nasal tones always a signal to Everyman that here is a sympathetic soul who understands Everyman's every complaint, whim, fad and fancy.

As well, there seems to be more than one kind of diplomat: those who take care to preserve the careful accents of Melbourne Grammar and Trinity College, and those who know well that a broad Australian accent, lavishly peppered with rural phrases, will instantly wrap the solitary expatriate in well-remembered warmth. It matters little that such an expatriate may have been a city dweller all his life, for in his heart every Australian, be he bank-clerk or barber, sees himself as a doughty contender against fire, flood and drought, the strong, silent, bronzed type made famous by John Masefield and Anzac.

'Gotta find a gum tree,' muttered one servant of Government at a crowded Greek dance. On his return raffle tickets were being sold in aid of a local charity. 'Oh, the old chook raffle, eh?' he asked, of no one in particular. No formal farewells for him. 'Thank yer mother for the rabbit in the morning, luv,' he sang out at departure time. Next morning I felt lonely.

The family knew well language's power to persuade, puzzle and entertain, and experimented endlessly, with varying results. One great-grandmother, Kate, could not abide being out of the limelight. At family gatherings she would, as a matter of immutable routine when not getting enough attention, rush across the room, arms flung high, shrieking, 'My God, my God, I'm dying!' She knew that silent drooping in a corner would have no effect whatever on her noisy descendants. But her melodramatic proclamation did not, after the first few times, have much effect either. Nevertheless, it has gone down in family history. This fact would doubtless have pleased her.

Great-grandfather Robert was a dedicated ventriloquist and had to be almost forcibly persuaded, in his old age, to refrain from hiring the local hall for the brilliant concert he was sure he could give. He practised for hours on end, often in the middle of the night, and was master of various monologues in which he played all characters. One such item was entitled 'The English Railway Porter', in which he would be both porter and a female passenger, who would list the items of her luggage in the following order: 'I've got three trunks, four bundles, an umbrella, a flat-iron, a gridiron, a piece of string and two children.'

Now phrases come and go, reminding me of other times, other places. Grandfather would sigh reminiscently about his youth: 'Ah, those were the days when men were men and women were glad of it.' Our father concentrated on places and people.

'Who told you that, Dad?'

'The man outside Hoyts.' Or 'Joe Blow'. Or 'Jim Flick'.

'Where's Hoyts?'

'The other side of the black stump.' As a child, I had a permanent vision of vast desert with a solitary, lightning-charred stump sitting, marking some mysterious boundary. In the same way I had a picture of *Annie's room* – *up in Annie's room* being the invariable answer to the question 'Where is it?' Annie's room was a vast cavern full of treasure, missing items, even people, who were lost, stolen or strayed.

Then, 'Where're you going?'

'All the way there and back to see how far it is.'

Mum, on the other hand, preferred parody, and this preference guaranteed education of a sort for us, because, to ensure her own satisfaction, she had to ensure that we knew the original.

'Hail to thee, blithe pussycat!' she would greet us. 'That's a horse of another feather,' she would announce when a subject was changed. And, darkly, 'Strong cheese is binding.'

Her imagination was peopled by figures from the past, in particular by two widows, Mrs Coffey and Mrs Nolan, who come down to us as loveable characters, ineffably wise and dressed like pictures in a book in floor-length black, hair-nets and bonnets. Mrs Coffey had two claims to fame: one was that, as a girl, she had danced with Ned Kelly. How strong, firm and short the chain of Australian history is. The other consisted in her firm pronouncement that 'You're a long time married and a long time dead, Marjie.'

'She never indicated which state was preferable,' Mum would add with a wry laugh.

Traditional Greek women also had firm views about marriage, views which have been recorded by sociologists and immortalized in poetry: Παντρεύτηκες, σκλαβώθηκες, γιατι ο Θεός το θέλει.

You married, you became a slave because God wills it. Να χορέψει να χαρεί τώρα που είναι νιο παιδί, γιατι σαν θα παντρευτεί μες στα βάσανα θα μπει.

Let her dance, let her be happy while she is a young child, because when she marries she will enter into torture.

Yet every Greek woman wanted to be married, and to become a mother. Motherhood was the crowning achievement of a traditional woman's life. It was only after she had produced a child, preferably a male one, that the traditional woman could enjoy independent status. Until then, she was at the beck and call of her mother-in-law. As in most countries, mothers-in-law do not enjoy a good press in Greece. My neighbour, Stavroula, an eighty-two-year-old widow of great heart and girth, often seizes me by the arm and declares, 'Ah, my golden one, how fortunate you are in your *pethera*. My mother-in-law, now! Ach, if a knife had been plunged into her heart, no blood would have spilled forth, not a drop!'

Blood would certainly spout from Yiayia's heart, for it has not turned to stone in spite of her hard life with its many trials: poverty, drudgery, deaths of children, almost constant war, and fear, fear, fear. But she and other women knew little of lives outside the village; it is only now that they are beginning to comprehend the privileges others have enjoyed, to realize that the world is a much larger place than they had thought. Ξυπνήσαμε, says Yiayia, opening her eyes wide, acting out the word, as she so often does. We woke up. One word describes the whole process of awakening consciousness, the movement from darkness into light, drastic, almost jolting change.

Small wonder, then, that these women, building existence on the firm foundations of *timi, pallikaria* and *filotimo*, and modelling their domestic lives on the example set by the Holy Family, should seek some consolation in the power of the Word. Every Sunday you may see them, sitting and standing by turns, right hands with the first two fingers joined to thumb, making the sign of the Cross, lips moving in an echo of the liturgy, the language of which they barely understand.

But 'genuine poetry', T.S. Eliot stated, 'can communicate before it is understood'. And Orthodoxy *is* poetry, with the appeals to the senses made through the flickering candles, the wisps and perfumes of incense, the steady gaze of the icons, the sheen of gold and silver, the richness of white, gold, purple, crimson and blue robes, the representation of the twinkling firmament above, the taste of the elements, all united in the ancient chanted hymns. Everything combined, Paul the Silentiary wrote, in order to drive 'away the dark-veiled mist of the soul'.

Take any of the famous English definitions of poetry, and the Orthodox liturgy conforms. Whether poetry is the best words in the best order, the spontaneous overflow of powerful feelings, originating from emotion recollected in tranquillity, the surprising by a fine excess, and it is all of these, combining and overlapping, matters not. For the Orthodox worshipper returns to his liturgy, which strikes him as a wording of his own highest thoughts, the most beautiful, impressive and widely effective mode of saying things. Words and thoughts unite and fly up to the Pantocrator, whose face gazes from the dome of almost every church.

It is significant that scholars consider religious poetry to be the only original Byzantine achievement, exhibiting complete control of metre and thought, and that, once the liturgies were complete, with all the feast days having their own special hymns, the point of writing disappeared, and the quality of the poetry inevitably began to decline. But religious poetry became a weapon against the barbarians and a light of hope during the Ottoman occupation, as well as the foundation of other literatures: Russian, Southern Slavic, Rumanian, Syrian, Coptic and Armenian. Words formed a many-linked chain which the modern Orthodox still grasp firmly today.

The concept of the Word is all-powerful. Romanos's great hymn 'Mary at the Cross' is a dialogue between the suffering Christ and His suffering mother. The imagery reinforces the notion of the death being an outrage against Nature: Mary is a ewe who sees her own lamb taken to the slaughter. Later, she cries in protest, 'Alas, how is my light snuffed out . . .' She pleads with her

Son, 'Speak to me, O Word; do not pass me by in silence.' Christ eventually replies in subdued triumph, 'I now exist, I, the Word, who in you became flesh'.

In his Christmas hymn Romanos uses the concept of *word* in different ways. Constructed around the repeated phrase *Ο προ αιώνων θεός*, God of all time, the poem through natural images, images of life, paradox, suggests the miraculous power of Christ's birth, and the place of the birth in history. In the cave where Christ was born, 'has appeared a root never watered, blossoming forth forgiveness; in it has been found a well never dug, a well from which David once longed to drink. In it a virgin has given birth to a child and at once has brought an end to the thirst of Adam and of David'.

The wise men have followed the 'star that would solve the parables of sages, their utterances and riddles'. On hearing 'these strange words' Mary kneels and worships her Baby, who then bids His mother to admit the Magi to the cave: 'Bring in the men whom I have brought with my word; for it was my word that shone before these men who are searching for me; to the eyes it is a star, and to the eyes of the mind a power'.

In the mighty Akathistos Hymn, the Panagia is hailed as the 'abode of God and Word', as 'the mother who bore the Word'. Her transcendent power reveals worldly strivings as but pale shadows of perfection.

> Hail to you who show the philosophers to be fools
> Hail to you who prove men of letters to be men of no wisdom
> Hail to you for able disputers have been shown to be idiots
> Hail to you for the fashioners of fables have been made to wither.

Before the Virgin, 'mother of god, we see wordy orators as voiceless as fish'.

Silence appals. It is significant that the wordy orators

have their powers die within them, are rendered speechless, for clamour is a positive force.

An eighteenth-century folksong, its roots obviously deep in the Byzantine era, recounts the last mass in Santa Sophia. The splendour of sound was a vital part of the liturgy: 'God, Earth, Sky and the great church rang the bells. There were 400 sounding boards and 62 bells, a priest for each bell and a deacon for each priest. Both Emperor and Patriarch were chanting and the pillars of the huge building were shaking. But as the worshippers were about to begin the hymn of the Cherubim, a voice came from the sky, and the Archangel commanded: "Stop the Cherubic Hymn . . ."' That one word Πάψετε signals the end of an era. Darkness and silence envelop like a shroud pierced only by the sound of the Panagia's weeping and the Archangel's instructions. 'It is the will of God that the City fall to the Turks. But send a message to the West asking for three ships to come.' The ships were to rescue the Cross, the Holy Bible and the Altar. In the silence of defeat, a frail thread of communication is to save the faith, together with a stronger promise made by the Archangel to the suffering Virgin: 'Hush, lady, do not weep so profusely; after years and after centuries, they will be ours again.' Πάλι με Χρόνους, με καίρούς, πάλι δικά μας θα είναι.

The influence of that promise, that phrase, lingered for five hundred years and lingers still in the minds of some. The thread can be traced through to modern literature, and every Greek child has been asked the question: Πως θα πάρουμε την Πόλι; How are we going to take the City? Implicit in the question is the notion that the City must be retaken. One attempt was made in 1922 and ended in catastrophe: the Great Idea crumbled to dust while Greeks and Armenians died horribly, while another Greek city was obliterated, and while more than a million Orthodox survivors fled westward. Many of them could not even speak Greek.

Scot Thomas Carlyle wrote that 'Speech is of Time, Silence is of Eternity'. This knowledge Greeks carry around with them like a burden. It often appears to an outsider that here silence is not peaceful, therapeutic, restorative, innocent, but dark, brooding and threatening, a memory of nothingness, of that time before the Creation, a looming space with the capacity to remind one of the grave. Such a space must be filled, and is.

The power of the women and the Word reasserts itself with every death. The death-knell sounds first in the village. Then the thin wails of the *miroloyoi*, the words of fate, begin, more chains stretching back to a remote past and forward to the unknown future, for it is almost as if words fly ahead to prepare a resting-place for the deceased. And, for the time, words fill the awful emptiness of death, the yawning of the grave. The corpse lies in his coffin, while the women wail of his virtues, his deeds, his faith, his beauty and their dreadful sorrow at his leaving. In Athens, when a public figure or theatrical celebrity dies, people throng the streets and applaud, filling the air with loud clapping, an act of defiance, almost, against the last and complete silence.

For, in spite of Christianity, the Orthodox religion, at times of death, harks back to an earlier era. Charon it is who dominates, taking the soul to the savage heart of Hades. Charon is such a potent symbol that an Olympic Airways pilot named Charos changed his name so that his passengers would not hear the grim message, 'This is your pilot, Captain Charos, speaking'. I laughed hysterically when I first heard this tale, immediately labelling it as a Greek example of suburban legend. But George knew the pilot, and earnestly assures me that the tale is a true one.

The sense of darkness, decay, an end, is uppermost. There is also a sense of burial rather than of eternal life:

Aς είναι ελαφρύ το χώμα που θα σε σκέπασει. May the earth which covers you be light.

And now Yiayia thinks and talks increasingly of death. She and her brother, who is two years older, have long discussions about death, and which one of them is likely to die first. There is almost a rivalry developing, it seems. Each has received instructions from the other. 'When I die make sure you come and wail for me.'

If brother Dimitrios dies first, Yiayia will sing the *miroloyoi*, and already my traitor imagination is forming and reforming words and phrases. Yiayia would be horrified if she knew this, for surely I am meddling with powers about which I know nothing?

> He travelled far across oceans and seas
> He did great deeds
> He brought honour to our house
> Fine warrior that he was,
> And then he returned to us from
> The *xenitia*
> And made us glad.
> With brave sons, sturdy as trees, he
> Made our name live again,
> That which was dead and lost.
> He was a poet and a singer
> And now his voice is still
> Now he is going on his final journey
> Never more will he return to us.

She will not stop there, of course. The speaker will speak on almost as long as her strength lasts, calling to the playmate of her childhood, urging him back, knowing he cannot come, dwelling on the beauty of his youth, now lost forever, recalling their parents and the siblings who have gone before. She will fill the space of silence for as long as she can, but knows that her words, inevitably, will sink in it and lose themselves, disappear, as we ourselves will disappear one day.

Chapter 13

WHEN I lived in Australia, one word passed me by. I had heard it, even used it about my own household, but did not feel its meaning until I came, *we* came, to live in Greece. The word is *cross-cultural*, itself a hybrid.

My brother made me a present of a tape recently. I hummed along with the Bushwackers' Band, failing memory struggling to supply a word or two here and there. Then came a song I had heard only once before. 'And the Band Played Waltzing Matilda' is the stirring ballad of an original Anzac who returns, legless, to Australia. I stopped humming as the singer detailed the feelings of futility and rejection, the sense of the passing of time making sacrifice meaningless:

> . . . Tired old men from the tired old war
> And the young people ask
> 'What are they marching for?'
> And I ask myself the same question.
>
> But the band played 'Waltzing Matilda' . . .
> And the old men they answer the call
> But year by year those old men disappear
> Then no one will march anymore . . .

Sobered, touched and moved, I listened. But the brass band rendition of 'Waltzing Matilda' at the very end of the song was totally unexpected. I burst into tears, sobbed for minutes, in fact. Not again, I thought disgustedly, fearing yet another crippling attack of homesickness, something which had once been merely a word, but now has real shape, presence and effects. Not again. 'Waltzing Matilda' has never even been a favourite song. Why this reaction?

For the rest of the morning I sought answers to the question. Various words and phrases floated in and out of my consciousness: nostalgia? Mondayitis? low blood sugar? middle-aged sentimentality? Words, melodies, as triggers for me, whereas sights act for other people? For I once sat in the stand at Melbourne's Olympic Park when the Piraeus soccer team, Olympiakos, streamed on to the ground holding aloft an enormous Greek flag. The Greek sitting next to me, all six feet and sixteen stone of him, wept unashamedly into his handkerchief. And he continued to sob his way through the Greek 'Ethnikos Ymnos'.

Later, when the big boys, Dimitri and Nikolaos, came home from school, I determined that they had to listen to this song.

'Come on, Dimitri, you ought to listen to this song.'

'Oh, yeah?' he queried, helping himself to thirty drachmae for the essential sports paper he buys every day.

'Terrible, aren't I?' he grinned, racing off.

'Horrible,' I agreed.

I often think that Nikolaos is the most Australian of my children. He listened to half the tape and to the whole song. He bit his lip and looked rueful. 'That's really sad,' he said, 'but I like the "Theme from Ben Hall" better.'

Parents have delusions about their children. My chief one is that my children are Australian, like me. But they are not, and, regularly, clear evidence forces me to face this fact. For Niko 'And the Band Played Waltzing Matilda is merely a sad song, among thousands. For me it is much more, because it concerns the psyche of Australia, the myth of the past and the powerful spell it continues to weave, the self-searching and sense of loss, and, specifically, a personal feeling of regret for what I see as my own ancestor's four wasted years of youth.

So they are Greek, my children, but I cannot allow them to forget their Australian roots, for their own sake as well as mine. I am quite shameless about emphasizing Australianness. Even though I cannot quite imagine myself living permanently there again, I love my country. In Bicentenary year, Professor Manning Clark was asked what he most appreciated about Australia. He said he was tempted to say: I like the whole bloody lot. How well I understand the temptation.

At any one time our living-room is littered with pages from the *Age*, the *Sun*, the *Times on Sunday*, the *Australian*, while copies of *Overland* and *Island* magazines are being hoarded carefully. *For the Term of His Natural Life* was compulsory television viewing, but *The Colour of the Creek* was not, for it had been dubbed in Greek and sounded completely artificial, while even the title had become *Golden River*. The big boys complain that Alexander and I have seen *Crocodile Dundee*, while they have not. They have all sampled the works of Banjo Paterson, Henry Lawson and Mrs Aeneas Gunn.

Besides, Australia sits in a jar on the bookshelf. Sometimes I empty the contents into a bowl for the sheer nostalgic pleasure of burying my nose in mouldering sprigs of wattle, heath and acacia. The pot-pourri is old now, but I cannot bear to throw it away. I finger the gum-nuts and trace patterns in powdery pollen, while the bush scent drifts. The smell of dust and rain is missing, but I make do. One day a New Zealander comes to call, and sniffs appreciatively. 'This house even smells like Australia,' she says, sighing.

And one Australian visitor could not believe her ears when, having heard the boys talking in Greek for half an hour, an anguished bellow in the best of Strine rent the air: 'Mum! Mu-um! Where's the Vegemite?' How strange it is that that black and yellow jar is in itself a national symbol, which will probably always remain ours, given the reluctance of other cultures even to sample the contents. A high-ranking member of the Foreign Service, currently stationed in Athens, makes afternoon tea of toast and Vegemite every day, bringing an important element of Antipodean culture to the Near East. But I doubt that his Greek colleagues ever share this daily ritual.

In 1980, the first miseries of homesickness upon me, I was walking along congested Vassilissis Sofias, Athens, beset by gloom and smog in about equal proportions, when I saw a white T-shirt approaching. Emblazoned on its front was a huge picture of a Vegemite jar. I literally squealed with excitement at the wearer: 'O-oh, Vegemite!'

'Yeah,' he remarked, cocked one eyebrow and walked on, leaving me staring after him. As a tourist, he had no interest in meeting a fellow Australian. So I watched home and childhood walk away.

As we are a Greek–Australian family it is fortunate, I suppose, that we live in such a convenient geographical position. For Dimitrios and Nikolaos, at least, Gallipoli (*Kali Poli*, the Good City) and the Dardanelles feature prominently in the geography and history syllabuses of Greek schools. The fact that Australian fought Turk in 1915 supports my children's Greekness and their sense of Australian and Greek being on the 'right' side. Such feelings are reinforced by the sentimental attachment older Greeks have to Australians, remembering the Australian military presence during World War II. Occasionally I wonder how German mothers discuss the war with their offspring.

Alas, we have not yet visited Gallipoli. It seemed more important, in 1984, to visit Istanbul. Then I took only my luggage; George took his race-memories as well. He does not even call it Istanbul. It is Constantinople, or more often, The City. For him, and for millions of others, it is still a vital part of the Greek world, if not in fact, in the collective consciousness. Many Greeks realize the ambition of a lifetime by visiting Istanbul; a large number of them return saddened by the vision of the Greek world's remnants in Asia Minor. Istanbul is virtually the only place in Turkey where Greeks are now permitted to live, and of a population of over 100,000, only 4000 are left. The Patriarch, still regarded as the spiritual head of Greek Orthodoxy, is permitted to wear clerical dress in the street, but other clergy are not.

We had planned to arrive on a Monday. The City fell to the Ottoman Turks on 29 May 1453, a Tuesday, and Tuesday remains an inauspicious day throughout the Greek world. It took Sultan Mehmet II two years of determined planning and action to conquer Constantinople. He had wealth on his side; a Hungarian engineer named Urban first offered his skills to the Byzantines, who could not afford to pay for them. The Turks could, and for them Urban designed cannon, the largest of which had a barrel of seven metres and fired balls weighing 600 kilograms. Yet The City's mighty walls withstood a sustained bombardment for six weeks. The frustrated Sultan ordered the building of a roadway from the Bosphorus to the Golden Horn, and had his ships dragged along it, so that they could attack the lightly defended Horn, until then kept safe by a floating boom. Even so, the Turks nearly gave up as the defence continued and the Emperor, Constantine XI Palaedogos, rejected Mehmet's peace proposals. But one of the many gates in the walls was left open; people like to say it was an accident but words like *bribery* and *corruption* spring immediately to mind.

On that Tuesday, as Turkish troops entered The City, the Emperor Constantine tore off his imperial vestments and flung himself into the fray beside his men. He was never seen again. When the victorious Turks poured into Aghia Sophia, Justinian's miracle and centre of Byzantium, the priests, according to legend, seized the holy vessels and melted into the walls of the sanctuary, there to wait until Constantinople was Christian once more.

Since then, to quote Carlo Levi, 'Many years have gone by, years of war and of what men call History,' and in spite of the Archangel's promise, Aghia Sophia is still not Christian. Huge circular boards, lists of Caliphs, dominate the interior, and garish stained-glass, starkly modern, has been installed in the windows of the 'museum'. The Panagia was right to weep during the last Mass; perhaps she is weeping still.

The boys had not been too sure about visiting Turkey, and George even wondered whether they should restrict themselves to speaking English in the streets of Istanbul. And of course, the trains being what they are, we arrived on a Tuesday. At first the boys were shocked by the sights of Graham Greene-land: the squalor, the seediness, the grey landscape of buildings where alley cats prowl up cobbled lanes, washing flaps from one tenement to the next, faces stare from behind barred windows, and where rubbish eddies in the drains. But it was only shortly afterwards that we all noticed the contrasts: the magnificence of the skyline, marked by Aghia Sophia, the Suliemaniye and the Blue Mosque, the razzle-dazzle of the Grand Bazaar, the strange beauty of the muezzin's cry, the throb of the ferries zig-zagging their way across the water, and the Bosphorus Bridge slung like a mighty hammock between Europe and Asia.

The people fit somewhere between the seediness and the magnificence, for above all The City is people and pulsating life. White-robed Arabs shepherd their children along the streets; little knots of devout Moslem women strain through taut black veiling to gaze at shop windows; jeans-clad Turkish girls and youths rub shoulders with older women, modestly clad in long skirts and headscarves. And of course, we were most interested in the Turks, who seemed to be quiet and friendly people countenancing the cultural mix about them with the apparent tolerance born of familiarity.

'Do you think they look different from us?' asked George, after we had spent two hours wandering the streets. 'No,' I replied, 'you all look much alike.' It is true that many inhabitants of Istanbul are obviously of Greek origin, having become Moslem and Turkish over the centuries. To an outsider, this apparent similarity adds another dimension of futility to past and present tensions.

Soon all reservations about speaking Greek had gone as we discovered how many Turks speak it still, and as we observed the local accent. Dimitri and Niko began a treasure hunt for 'Greek' words in Turkish, and were fascinated to hear George exclaim over words and phrases he had not heard since the death of his grandparents. And everywhere we went, taxi-drivers offered us cigarettes, bakers and shop-keepers presented the children with cakes. Often our progress along streets and lanes took longer than expected because of the number of people who wanted to pat Alexander's head or pinch his cheek. All three boys, then, saw the human face of 'the enemy'.

I viewed Aghia Sophia as a masterpiece of early engineering, as an aesthetic wonder, as a ruined shell of past glory. I remembered Justinian's triumphant cry of 'Ho, Solomon! I have outdone thee!' George walked in, stood, and stated simply, 'I am here,' and then shivered at the thought of being in the centre of the Byzantine world. His father, priest Papadimitri, never had the opportunity to see it, and the 'I am here' was a statement of accomplishment as well as an expression of wonder. Aghia Sophia inspires awe and respect, but not, I think, sadness, at least not in one who is not of the Orthodox faith. Sadness strikes in other, more personal, situations.

The day we went to meet the Patriarch it was raining, falling down so hard that carts were ankle-deep in water and gutters were swamped. At the gate of the Patriarchate an outsized red flag hung and dripped. Inside, where we expected chatter and a bustle of activity, there was only silence. Two secretary-priests and one maroon-clad bishop occupied an office; a rusty-bearded, black-clad aristocrat, another visitor, snapped irritably at the boys. Upstairs we were ushered into the presence of His Holiness Dimitrios I, who was dressed as a parish priest and working in a room so modest as to be almost austere. The audience lasted five minutes; outside in the soaked garden the thought of his isolated world-within-a-world was almost unbearably depressing. He is an exile who has never left home.

It was still raining on Sunday when we went to find a Greek church. We found the church of Aghia Triatha, the Holy Trinity, but arrived too late to hear Mass. The service had just finished, but there were only four people standing in the churchyard. A grey-haired woman with a gentle, smooth face paused under her umbrella and said, 'You're from Down There,' her words proclaiming simply an age-old unity, a refusal to acknowledge wars, politics, separation. The church was large and the white and gold iconostasis was evidence of former wealth. Pew after pew bore family names, long-faded. The one man inside lit a candle, spoke to us and wept over his memories. The sadness of 'I remember . . .' echoed in the empty space.

Until 1980, when I migrated, I had little understanding of what it was like to be a member of a minority group. I thought I understood, but I was wrong. I had always been in the majority: I was a WASP, for want of a better label. In Greece, as a minority of one in a traditional village society, I learned. And in Istanbul, as I emerged from the gloom of the church into the silent, humid rain, I realized I had seen a minority bearing the heavy burden of the past. There is no future: at the church of Aghia Triatha, even the undertaker is running out of work.

There are several categories of cross-cultural children, and our children fall into two. Dimitrios and Nikolaos were born in Melbourne, Alexander in Athens. Dimitrios and Nikolaos watched the see-saw of a marriage, as I dipped from the heights of knowledge about one society to the depths of ignorance about another. Alexander has never had this experience: his father has always been the authority on his environment. He knows that I am different, but such knowledge does not seem to be a burden, for that is the way things have always been for him. He has no hesitation about speaking English to me in public, whereas Dimitri took years to do this.

Alexander is the image of his father. *Omios Yeorgis!* the old men exclaim, delightedly. Just like George! Yet George, probably because of his migrant experience and the associated feelings of embattled isolation, finds it extremely difficult to criticize any feature of Greek life. Alexander has no such inhibitions, accepting and rejecting, naturally at this stage, according to his feelings.

A month into his first school year, he came home clutching two little squares of paper. Further investigation revealed that they were cheap little prints. 'Holy pictures,' he told me, solemnly. One was a fairly standard portrait of the Panagia and Child, while the other showed God in the process of creating Heaven and Earth. He is suspended in the firmament, robes, beard and hair flowing, hand outstretched towards a fiery sun. Earth is already present; Africa, the Atlantic and the Americas are shown on the blue globe, while Australia is conspicuous by its absence, in darkness presumably, on the other side.

'Interesting,' I remarked in my usual guarded fashion. 'Is there any particular reason why Kyria Maria gave you these?'

'Oh, yes,' he beamed, happily. 'I have to put them under my pillow every night and they will help me with my schoolwork.'

'Oh,' I remarked, feebly, playing for time, while George exclaimed, brightly, 'What a good teacher you have!'

The bile of scepticism rose in my gorge, but I swallowed hard and said merely, 'Just remember that you can't leave everything to the Holy pictures, won't you? *You* have to try as well.'

'I know *that*,' rebuked my six-year-old, pityingly.

He and Kyria Maria form a mutual admiration society, but he still feels free to criticize. By now, she had taught all three Bouras boys, and probably thanks Providence daily that there are no more. She has been affectionate towards each one, but has realized, too, that she cannot expect unquestioning belief from any of them. This year Alexander is critical of her clothes. Kyria Maria is a statuesque matron and currently dresses in full mourning which is relieved only by the gold cross which bounces on her ample bosom. There has been a death in the immediate family, but Alexander remains unimpressed by her discipline.

'*When* is she going to wear some colours?' he asks periodically, describing in minute detail the fashionable garb of his much-loved kindergarten teacher, Jenny. One day he had an item of news.

'Kyria Maria wore brown boots today,' he announced hopefully. But the black raiment continues to be worn.

At times Kyria Maria, admirable character though she is, tries my patience sorely. She demands that her pupils attend church every week but, whereas Dimitri and Nikolaos used to trot off obediently every Sunday, Alexander is not keen. Early in the year, however, he drew me aside and said, 'Do you know what *she* says? *She* says that Christ will not like us if we don't go to church.'

Overhearing, Niko rolled his eyes and exclaimed, '*She* hasn't changed!'

I often feel myself on uncertain ground, but this time the ground was not merely shaky, but riven as by flood and earthquake.

'Teachers *can* be wrong, you know,' I began, carefully, 'and I think Kyria Maria is wrong about that. The Bible tells us that Christ loves us always. He's not going to worry about church attendance.'

'H'm,' he mused, struggling a little inside. His spirit finally rebelled. 'Well, I don't care. I'm not going to go if I don't want to.'

The other boys have similar conflicts, but whereas Dimitri is quietly sceptical and draws no attention to himself, Nikolaos nearly always feels that he has to make a stand. The class of fifteen-year-olds is apparently uniformly cynical about religion, but when the teacher recently invited all the boys and girls to make confession to the priest who had come to the school for just this purpose, Niko found, somewhat to his consternation, that he was the only one to decline the opportunity. In front of the class the teacher demanded to know the reason for this. Niko quietly stated that he has been prey to doubt for quite some time. A girl student immediately proclaimed, 'Your mother's done that to you.'

Quietness ended. My son, highly indignant, roared the Greek equivalent of 'Pipe down, you, and leave my mother out of this'. When he told me of this episode I fought to repress my oft-recurring thoughts about the nearest Qantas ticket office, and forced a calm question.

'What did the teacher say?'

'Nothing,' he replied, shortly.

Cross-cultural children are often, but not always, bilingual as well. Sometimes, as I crank myself up to speak Greek and hear the protesting grind of cogs, wheels and sprockets as I change over from English, I imagine that such children have a handy button in the brain, which enables such effortless switching from one language to another. Yet for Dimitri, Niko and Alexander, Greek, of course, has a very definite edge over English and George comments that their English is of a specific type, anyway.

'These boys speak *Gillian Bouras* English,' he remarks, wryly; and I am forced to admit that I use far more Australian expressions now than I ever did. This practice is another defensive weapon in the armoury of the expatriate. Yet I can feel these phrases ossifying; they are no longer common parlance in Australia, surely. But apart from the often unconscious usage of expressions from the past, I consciously try to convey the idea that language is, at least in part, a fascinating playground, where one may have fun and games, and take care to introduce my sons to expressions like 'Give us a geek' or 'Let's have a squizz'. For when one language dominates another, the second is very often in sound working order, but lacking in colour.

So, 'Don't be a nincompoop!' I cry, or 'Don't be a dill/

drongo/donkey'. To the question, Why? I give my grandfather and father's reply: 'Because y's a crooked letter and can't be made straight'. And so on. Like generations before them, Dimitri and Niko have puzzled over that elusive object, 'the wigwam for a goose's bridle'.

Acquisition of vocabulary is another difficulty when one language dominates another; vocabulary loss is a graver problem. All the boys have the disconcerting tendency to stop short in the middle of an English sentence. In the case of the older ones, looks of horror dawn as they realize that a vital English word is missing. Alexander, of course, but Dimitri and Niko too, tend to take refuge in the use of the word 'thing'. I chide them for taking the lazy way out, but must admit that I am guilty of the same practice when speaking Greek. *Pragma* is such a convenient word!

Bedtime stories are not exactly a restful ritual, either, when we have to stop for frequent explanations. Of course, I have always made things (that word again) hard for myself. Years ago, I recall, I was determined to read John Masefield's *Jim Davis* to the junior males. It is a yarn which swashes a good buckle, after all. But oh, the agony of it! I have still not forgotten the frequent stops for words like 'isolated' and 'repeat' and the pauses every two minutes to answer questions like: 'What's a bee-skep/nightrider/Rector/combe/moor?' I made a stern effort and we finished the book; I hope I'll get my reward in heaven.

Problems in usage abound. English prepositions are notoriously difficult for Greek speakers. 'I'm going *at* school,' announces Alexander happily most mornings.

'No, you're going *to* school,' I correct automatically, wondering how many reinforcements are needed. Niko has overcome his particular difficulty by now, but for a long time he was unable to form a simple past in English,

and devised a neat stratagem to cope with this inconvenience: he often spoke like a character from the King James
version of the Bible: whereas Eve said, 'The serpent
beguiled me and I did eat,' Nikolaos used to say, 'Dimitri
did pinch my chewing-gum and I did hit him.'

It is hard to avoid translation from one language to
another, it seems. For example, in Greek, the same word
is often used to express the English *make* or *fix*. I became
so desperate over hearing 'I'm going outside to make the
puncture in the bike,' and like pronouncements, that I
decided on drastic action. I remember screeching, 'The
next person I hear making that mistake, or saying "open
the television", or "close the light" will be fined twenty
drachmae, and I mean it!' (I also remember muttering to
myself, 'Gotta hit them where it hurts, in the pocket,'
and almost immediately pondering whether either
Dimitri or Niko would have understood that particular
sentence.)

It is also inevitable for expressions to acquire new,
humorous twists. I was once watching television when a
singularly plain personage appeared on the screen. 'Dear
me, she's no oil painting,' I remarked, idly. Some time
later, Dimitri pointed at another individual not particularly blessed with beauty and announced, 'He sure isn't a
painting by Leonardo!' And the expression, 'You're the
little white hen who never laid away' has become, in our
household, a shortened version. Protestations of virtue
are always met with a cry of 'Ah, but you're the white
chook!'

If being a cross-cultural child is difficult, then being a
cross-cultural parent is often more so. For Greeks of
George's generation, social change has occurred at lightning speed: they cannot keep up, and see no reason to try
to do so. George, for example, sees no need for sex
education of any kind, because he himself never had any.
'I was a farm boy,' he says, and shrugs. Set in my

middle-class Western ways I am naturally horrified at the thought of a country environment being sufficient and have always endeavoured to answer the children's questions honestly, albeit with a sinking heart. After all, I have led a sheltered life! But like the multitudes of parents everywhere I struggle to provide guidance on matters such as AIDS, pornography, drugs, relationships and teenage sex.

I try to remain relaxed, and if we can treat such subjects fairly lightly, so much the better. I particularly enjoyed the episode involving the old priest, recounted by the boys in the first week of school. At that time Papastathi usually takes it upon himself to deliver a few words of advice. On this occasion he exhorted the male students: 'Be good, conscientious students, obey your parents . . . and don't go looking at those naughty girlie magazines on sale at Spiro's shop!' Our children, at least, were not slow to sense that priests may know a great deal about basic good and evil, but are somewhat ignorant when it comes to concepts such as contrasuggestibility.

'He certainly knows where the magazines are!' hooted Niko. Dimitri, however, had a specific question to ask; significantly, he asked me and not his father.

'Does Baba read girlie magazines?'

'Er, no,' I replied, 'at least, not as far as I know.'

'Why not?'

There was nothing for it but to answer in straightforward fashion. 'Well, I asked him that once.'

'What did he say?'

'He grinned and said he'd never been able to see the point in just looking.' Dimitri gave a great shout of laughter and went back to his homework.

It is also a tricky business observing traditional customs which seem to be dying hard. Seventeen is a popular age for brides in the village, and when Dimitri was in the equivalent of Year 10 in the Australian system, two fifteen-year-old girls in his class became engaged to be married. The father of one of them is a cousin of George's and, one day, I overheard him boasting about marrying off his daughter.

'Poor baby,' I sighed.

'What do you mean, baby?' he roared. 'She's nearly sixteen. It's *time* she was married.'

'Of course,' I grumbled later to Dimitri, 'there'd be a right old stir if you become engaged at sixteen.'

'What?' he cried, pale with consternation. 'Another of your crazy ideas. *Boys* don't marry early.' (And indeed, Greeks of my acquaintance had been horrified and had told me so, when my brother married at twenty.)

'Why shouldn't they, though?' I challenged.

This was too much. 'Males are *different*,' he announced loftily – as if that mere word solved everything, summed the situation up.

When I see my children with Australian adolescents I realize the extent of their Greekness. I realized this, too, when I took them to Australia in 1985. It was Alexander's first visit, and Dimitri and Niko had been away five years. But they felt completely at home, to the point where they knew many TV commercial jingles off by heart. I first noticed my sons' Greekness, I suppose, when they started singing one of these commercials and dancing to it – in the shopping centre of Waverley Gardens. Their grandfather couldn't believe his eyes; certainly there were no Australian teenagers bending and swaying along the concourse.

On a more recent occasion we took the boys to Athens to meet four Australians, two boys and two girls, all aged between fourteen and fifteen. After initial awkwardness felt by all, the afternoon and evening settled down into a pleasant social occasion: everybody played volleyball, ate Chinese food and genuine Four 'n' Twenty pies, and talked about school, sport and pop music. At one stage the hostess murmured to me: 'Your eldest son, so mature.'

'Mature?' I queried.

'Oh, yes. He's in there with the others, completely at ease and keeping up an endless flow of conversation.'

'Oh, I see. Well, yes,' I commented, somewhat ruefully, mindful of my daily struggle to get a word in edge-wise in conversation at home.

'How was it?' I asked after we had returned to our hotel. 'What did you think of the Australian kids?'

'Oh, we had a good time,' was the reply, but Dimitri, as usual, had the last word.

'Those Australians,' he said, shaking his head, 'they're so *quiet*!'

'Yes, I thought they were *lovely*,' I remarked with a degree of fervour.

'You would,' he retorted, grinning.

Interesting enough, I was talking to our hostess's daughter a month later. She was telling her mother and me how she had been to visit a Greek friend. The friend's little brother had been playing table-tennis with another small boy.

'It was incredible,' said Victoria. 'Every time he scored a point, he'd jump on the spot, yell, and then run around the room waving his arms wildly.'

'But of course,' I said.

She looked at me. 'All that energy down the drain – and think of how long it takes to finish the game!'

'I know,' I answered, 'but they love the drama of life, and they get the most out of every moment.'

'H'm,' was the doubtful comment.

She will probably observe, as her stay in Greece lengthens, the way in which Greeks will create drama to fill a boring gap, to enliven dull routine. Of course many Australians do this, particularly those with Celtic ancestry, I venture to suggest, but for Greeks it seems to be a deliberate, conscious choice. Niko (is he the most Australian of my sons, after all?) provokes his brothers in order to get his own and other people's adrenaline flowing. I long for a quiet life and ask him why he does it. He grins wickedly. « *Ας έχουμε κάτι ατμόσφαιρα* », he chortles. 'Let's have some *atmosphere*.' It seems to me that we have *atmosphere* all the time. George creates it, too. «*Είστε όλοί χικσάκια* », he announces, Hellenizing my maiden name and blaming the boys' Australian heritage for every idiosyncrasy and show of bad temper. In his view, Greeks are models of perfection and placidity.

Years of living in Greece have had their effect on me, of course. A colleague in Australia once told me that I had a major problem.

'You're too quiet and nice,' she told me briskly. Ugh. This in the age of Germaine Greer and the assertive woman. I could not decide which charge was worse. But now, in Australian company, I often feel over-dramatic, garrulous and noisy. I over-react, naturally, to the sheer comfort of meeting Australians, and babble with excitement. They put up with me with unfailing politeness, and while I love the Greeks, with their colour and drama, nothing, at least for me, can take the place of the laconic sense of humour which is so distinctively Australian.

We were once at a Carnival dance attended by a certain number of people in fancy dress. Suddenly a grotesque figure entered, a skeleton, whose grinning skull and luminous bones were truly frightening to behold. While the Greeks around us screamed, yelled, reared back and gesticulated wildly in repulsion, the Australian on my left remarked casually, 'Jeez, that reminds me. Better drop the mother-in-law a card tomorrow.'

214

Chapter 14

VINDOLANDA, Northumberland, and Pylos, Messin-
ias, were both homes to large settlements and armies.
The bright moor and Homer's sandy Pylos were also
home to inventories, the lists of essentials which create
their worlds for us. But Vindolanda, the later settlement,
is more personal. The anonymity of Linear B does not
prevail here; the long distance of the past shrinks a little.
On a lady's slipper a cobbler has stamped his name:
Lucius Aebutius Thales.

On thin sheets of wood professional scribes wrote
letters and soldiers' lists which catalogue such mundane
items as socks, sandals and underwear. The birthday
party invitation sent by Flavia Severa to Lepidina was
also written by a scribe, but contains lines added by the
hostess herself, and is the first female handwriting from
the Roman world. Another note records the gift of fifty
oysters made from one man to another. The kind soil of
Vindolanda kept these records safe until 1974, when it
yielded them up. Treasures continue to be found.

To the tourist of the 1980s, the settlement looks solid,
invincible. Thoughts crowd: birthday parties, oysters,
the social round, the trappings of comfort. It is hard to
remember that this was a frontier. On the other side of
the Wall, however, strange tribes spoke jarring tongues.

In an intelligence report, mention is made of the *wretched Britons*, the *Brittunculi*. This is the first known use of such a word: fear and contempt creep through it. So the Romans watched with purpose and waited for the barbarians.

The thought of the letters fascinates. Picture a scribe pushing his freezing fingers, taking dictation, dreaming of the Rome he may never see again. Picture the officer, saying what he must, reporting, but also writing to family and friends. He delivers the letters to a courier seated on a stamping horse, wondering as he does so whether any reply will ever come along that frail thread of communication. Rome, warmth, sun, seem very far away.

The power of the word. How people love and fear it. How they work out, plump for, insist on their own authorized versions. Much later, further north of that same wall, a language would be persecuted almost to extinction. In 1746 Dr Johnson began his Dictionary; the same year the battle of Culloden was fought, a battle compared with the Black Death for its effects and far-reaching consequences. Now the onslaught of twentieth-century tourism cannot disguise the fact that bleak Drummossie moor, six miles from Inverness, is one of the saddest places on earth. By modern standards of carnage, Culloden was not a big battle, but the figures speak for themselves. The Duke of Cumberland lost fifty men, the clans lost two thousand. More Highlanders were to die, horribly, in the battle's aftermath. But that day in April also saw a way of life and a language begin a slow death.

Later Dr Johnson reported that the Highlanders had only their language and their poverty left, but that even their language was being attacked on every side, mainly by means of the weapon of education: new schools had been built and taught only English. And what Culloden began, the Clearances and forced emigration very nearly finished.

With the passage of time it has also become clear that roads, one of the simplest, most obvious marks of progress and so-called civilization, have been one of the most potent factors in ensuring the death of ethnic languages. Roads are an ambiguous presence, guaranteeing continuity in that they enable isolated communities to live on in the same places instead of abandoning their villages. But with every gain there is almost certainly a loss.

Persecuted Gaelic has, in the end, fared better than tolerated Cornish. The 1981 Census Report indicates that the number of Scots who can speak Gaelic is increasing; of the speakers of Gaelic, 42 per cent judged themselves able to read and write the language as well, an increase of eleven per cent over a ten-year period. Roderick Mackinnon's *Gaelic*, in the Hodder and Stoughton *Teach Yourself* series, has run through seventeen impressions since 1971.

Cornwall, in the meantime, has often been described as an area of language death. Yet visitors to the area can buy bilingual postcards, and even newsagents' shelves boast volumes entitled *Simplified Cornish*. The *Guinness Book of Records* for 1988 notes that there are now three hundred students of Cornish; it seems likely that this number will increase. And in 1989, £6000 was spent on the first revision of the Cornish dictionary for 55 years. Perhaps Dorothy Pentreath, said to have been the last speaker of Cornish, who died in 1777, and was buried at Mousehole, rests a little easier now.

Dr Johnson, ambivalent towards the Scotchmen, as he called them, was much surer of his feelings towards Greece. 'The grand object of travelling,' he stated unequivocally, 'is to see the shores of the Mediterranean . . . Almost all that sets us above savages has come to us from [there]'. He was equally convinced of the value of the Greek language. 'Greek, Sir,' he informed Lord

Chesterfield, 'is like lace; every man gets as much of it as he can.' Such a view has, broadly speaking, remained in fashion: nearly two hundred years later, the English novelist Elizabeth Taylor would make one of her characters state that learning Greek at school was like storing honey against the winter.

Things were comparatively simple for Johnson. Dying in 1784 as he did, he was spared the spectacle of the emergent Greek nation of the 1820s seriously debating the problem of the new state's language. What would the doctor have said about those, a not insignificant number, who favoured French? He would certainly have had much more sympathy with the one or two American legislators who wanted Greek to become the language of the new United States.

The imposition of *katharevousa* on modern Greece meant that a split, not only in society, but often in individual consciousness, was almost guaranteed. Virtually two separate languages developed, dividing the powerful from the powerless, concentrating authority in those who read, wrote and spoke *katharevousa*, excluding those who knew only *demotiki*. Thoughtful people, both great and small, have debated the effect of this development for years and at least one authority on Modern Greek literature has condemned this bilinguality in no uncertain terms: « *Αν δε φταίει αυτή γιά όλες τις κακοδαιμονίες μας . . . δεν είναι όμως ανεύθυνη . . . »* If all our misfortunes cannot be blamed on this, it must bear some of the responsibility.

Language divides, isolates as well as unites, creating conditions of exile even within close-knit communities. As Catholics in Ireland say *Derry*, Protestants *Londonderry*, so the post-war Left in Greece favoured *demotiki*, the Right *katharevousa*. Now conservatives of a certain age are most critical of the introduction of *demotiki* as the official language of the Greek state, and even more critical of the monotonic system of writing. Greece, of all countries, illustrates the truth of Philip Howard's statement that 'the political battle is fought in the lexicon as much as in the ballot-box and the assembly'. Even in Australia, where society is often accused of being apathetic about politics, and praised as being 'classless', ways of speaking were, and perhaps still are, socially divisive. The elite of my youth *always* said *darnce* and *carsel* instead of *dance* and *castle*, but in Europe, language and politics seem inextricably mingled.

In Greece words are coloured weapons during and between election campaigns. KKE graffiti bristles in red along rough walls, New Democracy slogans shout in blue, while PASOK's messages stream in green above the party emblem of a sun. There are always initials in capitals, so that adjustment to Greek life becomes a matter of having a mental filing system for an entirely new set of initials. Somehow it seems so much more difficult to remember OTE than Telecom, DEH than SEC, EOK than EEC.

Language which is ours and not ours. Primitive forest people, I am told, use loving words to describe their home. The forest is *ours, our mother*. Outside the forest fringe live people who regard the forest with fear and loathing. Their words are full of warning: the forest is *dark, dangerous,* a place where a man may be *lost forever*.

So in traditional Greek villages, small children learned the power of the word early. Gossip swirled around them, and they were trained to report it from street, churchyard and *kafeneion*, not maliciously but as a source of vital information, so that they and their parents would know what the out-groups, the *not-ours*, were doing. At the same time the children were taught the necessity of silence, for they, small guardians, were never to tell the family's secrets.

Language and the individual's need for it. Picture the life of Irish Christy Nolan. Until he was eleven years old, his fine intelligence was trapped in a disabled body. His body, because of a difficult birth, had exiled his essential self from the world. Images, words, metaphors, similes, whole poems were locked in his mind, sealed by his prison, his feeble frame. Now modern pharmacology and modern communication technology have provided a channel for them all, but have provided a mystery as well. For there seems to be no explanation for the protean, multiple richness of Nolan's vocabulary which was apparently immediately obvious, for the power and precision with which he writes, for the archetypal images which he employs. One word of explanation must suffice: genius. The poems and writings which he set down first remind the reader of clotted cream: one of nature's delights and bounties, but to be tasted only a little at a time, lest it prove indigestible.

His remarkable mother says that words have always been his toys. He learned to read, and listened, listened, listened, so that now his compositions reflect conversations, English, Gaelic, as well as the world of radio and television. Words were his way out of a world made chaotic by his physical handicaps. He needed words, and still needs to shape them, to set them down, at first labouring mightily with his unicorn stick and typewriter, now working more easily with a computer.

Here in the village there are women who have taught themselves to read and write, or who have refused to let one or two years' schooling be lost. Kyria Ariadne is a bubbling, intelligent eighty-four-year-old who writes letters determinedly, reads anything she can get her hands on and still welcomes the chance to practise the English she learned when she lived in the suburbs of Melbourne for three or four years more than two decades ago. She was over sixty years old then, but she bought herself an appropriate book and learned the essentials. She also taught herself to write shopping lists and still chuckles to think of her forays into a different world. 'Buying milk in bottles seemed so strange,' she remembers.

And yet the thought intrudes. Would she have been better off illiterate? For, paradoxically, Seamus Heany himself suggest that language and facility with it, diminishes life. Through the poetry runs constant praise of silence, wordlessness, the genuineness of simple people who lack book-learning. Julian of Norwich was only one 'simple unlettered creature' to whom revelations were made. Our deepest contacts do not need words, and can be harmed by them. The passionate politics of Ireland are crystallized in a poem apparently concerned with grammar. In 'From the Canton of Expectation', Heaney writes of the optative moods of the past being shattered by the young and their 'grammar of imperatives'. He himself searches for one at least who has 'stood his ground in the indicative'. But I will always remember, and admire, Kyria Ariadne and the widow outside the newsagency in Kalamata.

For the deaf and blind, language is different. Are they always afraid, not having that ability to shape with language which we take for granted? But is there a sense of privilege at being set apart in a particular way, at having other means of communication sharpened? It is hard to know, human nature and envy of the majority being what they are.

It is a sobering thought that even one fault in a gene can make language different. With a colour-blind great-uncle, father and uncle, I am the carrier who determined my second son's perception of the world. Red–green colour-blind, he knows, and I know, that sometimes he speaks another foreign langauge, is in another land. Pink, purple, brown and maroon are concepts wreathed in mystery for us both. For I know that my perception of pink is 'normal'. He knows that what he calls pink is not what I see. He makes 'mistakes'. And sometimes he seems deprived, even slightly handicapped: he cannot, for example, see pink clouds in a sunset. But what does he see? And how can he explain?

So to the split, often deep, between language and reality. A research project at the University of Wales shows that friendly, encouraging phrases of speech used by a computer will seduce computer users into treating the mere machine as a human being. The experts consider that it is vitally important for computers to put their users at ease; it apparently matters little that the users have their perceptions altered in such a way.

Christa Wolf speaks of *logos*, the word as fetish, as being perhaps 'the deepest superstition of the West', but point out that the Christian mediaeval poet celebrated and promoted a unity between God and Man. Then there was no gap between langauge and reality. But now, when we know that a nuclear holocaust is a more-than-distinct possibility, we fumble along with the language of the past. There *is* no language to describe a concept which will be far worse than anything we can imagine.

Industrial man, Wolf says, is a divided soul, living in a kind of intimate exile. He functions as a different person in the spheres of work, assembly, home. And language splits along with soul and function. Scientific words are used at work, political ones in the assembly, private ones at home. These last are the only genuinely human words. Increasingly, too, the literature of developed nations is a different language from that of computer-speak, the market-place, the laboratory.

If language originally developed as part of man, as a necessary channel for the heavy burdens of dreams and the unconscious, a vital means of salvation and release, we are now faced with the prospect of great loss. Perhaps we are already enduring it, as the 'genuinely human' words seem to decline importance, to be becoming less and less significant to a greater and greater number of people. And for loss of words read loss of self, loss of spirit.

I often wonder about people trapped in a bilingual environment late in life. Are there any race-memories left in Sutherlandshire, for example, of the gradual death of the Norn dialect, the ascendancy of Gaelic, and the subsequent persecution of that language? Of the latter there must be: the tourist information staff at Bonar Bridge painted a word-picture, no less vivid because of its succinct phrases, of a bewildered people, struggling with a few words of English, to communicate with factors who viewed Gaelic, for the most part, as barbaric gibberish. Wolf's question takes on particular importance under such circumstances. 'How quickly does loss of speech turn into lack of identity?'

The Highland Clearances effectively removed a whole generation from the land and wrenched people to the new environments of Glasgow, America, Australia, where the next generation would grow up speaking the language of the enemy. I have not seen Harold Pinter's play *Mountain Language*, but feel sure it is a modern play which utters both a warning and an ancient cry of pain. According to the critics the play lasts only twenty minutes, but has no need to last longer. An officer of a dictatorship confronts waiting mountain women and informs them, 'Your language is dead. Any questions?'

What does this process do to people's consciousness? As I lurch from one language to another, I often have the feeling that what I say in Greek is not absolutely real. For my English words, learned, picked up, acquired, absorbed, have grown with me for more than forty years, and determine my perception of the world. But in Greek there is no conviction, no affirmation from unconscious or gut, if you like, because I came too late to it. Sometimes I view Greek words much as I still occasionally view Greek bank-notes. Toy money.

For those who are not Chomskys, who have never heard of linguistics, semiotics, symbols and signifiers, does *firinn* have the same resonance, connotation, meaning, warmth as *truth*, *maise* as *beauty*? For me at least, αλήθεια and ομορφιά will always be different. Eliot's 'every phrase and every sentence that is right' seems impossible to achieve. *Home* for the speaker of English an never be right as σπίτι or *dhachaidh*.

Even starting to learn a second language in nursery school or earlier still in infancy may be too late to achieve *rightness*. The *Sunday Times* reports that Parisian researchers have discovered that infants sucked much faster on experimental teats when tapes in French were played to them. The same message played in colloquial Russian 'meant' nothing to these babies. When the words were played through a filter designed to simulate aural conditions inside the womb, researchers noted the same effects.

Certain words, then, signal security. 'It's all right, Mummy's here,' countless generations of mothers have petted and soothed; how many mothers have ever added, 'and she is frightened too'? Very few, for words as talismans are mothers' business, translatable Rocks of Ages, able to be hidden in. Words are chosen, words are omitted, and gain and loss add up to explanations, whistles in the dark.

And great words, shaped and preserved, are security as well as myth and magic, proving that no one is ever quite alone, that all people have suffered spiritual isolation, been in 'disgrace with fortune and men's eyes'. They also show that people have dealt with fear through words: fear of the dark, invasion, threat by fire, sword, monster, his own undisciplined self, through what Virginia Woolf referred to as 'hard, white, imperishable words'.

Words sustain a long wait. The asking of questions

produces hope. When there are no questions, hope is dead. Rhigas Pherrhaios died in 1798. In his famous *War Hymn*, he asked the question: 'Young men, how long must we live in mountain passes, lonely like lions . . .?' He never knew the answer, but others provided it.

Solomos's *Hymn to Liberty*, destined to become a much-loved national anthem, links past and present, slavery and freedom, darkness and light, forging a chain of words between the European, Italianate seven islands of the Ionian and the rest of Greece. And always present is the consciousness of the heroes of the past: in the Eth-nikos Ymnos their 'sacred bones' are invoked as the very source of *Eleftheria*, Liberty. In the folksongs of the eighteenth and nineteenth centuries, many of which originated centuries earlier, the power and might of the heroes and their dignity in death is emphasized. Indeed the natural world was so in awe of Digenis, that Death envied him, ambushed him and 'wounded him in the heart, snatching away his soul'. Such folksongs, the Cretan poems such as *Erotocritos*, and the Orthodox liturgy, kept Greek alive, kept a vision of a separate Greece and a recognizable Greek character firmly before an enslaved people. Language is indeed a key to the prison door, a thread to cling to in exile. It is said, still, even in this philistine day and age, that a great many Cretans can recite sizeable chunks of *Erotocritos*, a long romantic poem which celebrates the transcendent power of love.

Seferis maintained that 'our words are children of many people . . . and are nourished on blood'. Words everywhere are nourished on blood, while blood, and the shedding of it, often points out the futility of words. Writing in his diary after the Suvla plain retreat at Gallipoli, General Sir Ian Hamilton said, 'My heart was grown tough amidst the struggles of the peninsula, but the misery of this scene well-nigh broke it . . . Words are·

no use.' Here is the ultimate despair of a man who used words as a weapon, as propaganda, as comfort, and who loved them.

In the 1970s Eleni Fourtouni translated the works of Greek poets, 'whose voices, because of political insubordination, had been silenced'. The Junta well knew the truth of the Greek proverb: *Η γλΦσσα κοκκαλα δεν έχει, καί κόκκαλα σακάει.* The tongue does not have bones, but breaks them.

The poet Jenny Mastoraki, who almost died from the injuries inflicted on her by the police on the night of the Polytechnic uprising in 1973, wrote of 'this silence . . . nurtured inside four walls' which 'was meant to become a song . . . my song'. Cruel silence, imposed through brutal intention or simple negligence: Prince Charles Edward Stuart never bothered to write to Flora Macdonald once he had escaped to safety. In English cotton mills how easy it must have been not to attempt to talk above the incessant chatter of the machines; how easy it was to become deaf and thus have speech and the ability to communicate changed forever.

In Durham Cathedral a married couple lie. Their deaths occurred within a few months of each other, and both are acknowledged by epitaphs which anticipate Victorian sentiments at their most inflated. The deceased of 1823 are lauded in approximately twenty lines of prose punctuated regularly by words such as 'rectitude', 'benevolence', 'exemplary', and phrases like 'unrepining resignation to the will of God', and 'an affecting interest to their sorrows'. In the face of carnage on the battlefield, Sir Ian Hamilton felt the impotency of words; in the face of death from childbirth and premature illness, the mourners left behind looked to words as a means of shaping and lessening grief, of doing something about that last journey, that final exile.

Words can comfort. Even the names heard in childhood, and our own names, act as a solace. Nana's comment, when her last brother died, was striking in both its resignation and desolation: 'Now there's no one left to call me Harriett'. And still I remember, smile and sigh over the scraps of Longfellow's poems which obviously impressed her, and which my mother has passed on. Memory becomes a patchwork of mingled phrases. 'A Psalm of Life' seems to have been a favourite.

> Tell me not, in mournful numbers
> Life is but an empty dream

. . . was one quotation which alternated regularly with another, which was always used with an ulterior motive:

> Let us, then, be up and doing.

And one verse was thought to be particularly inspiring:

> Lives of great men all remind us
> We can make our lives sublime,
> And, departing, leave behind us
> Footprints on the sands of time.

Comfort may have little to do with artistic merit. This thought occurs nearly every time I mumble my favourite lines from George Matheson's famous hymn:

> I trace the rainbow through the rain . . .
> I lay in dust life's glory dead,
> And from the ground there blossoms red
>   Life that shall endless be.

Doubt came and conquered, but the remembered power of the word still impresses.

Yet words and the power of the word are always attempting to leave us. Even Dickens moaned that if he missed writing for as little as one day, it took him a week to start writing again to his satisfaction. Ted Hughes maintains that language is something unnatural in the animal world, and that only 'constant, communal effort' prevented, and can prevent, its disappearance.

And so the poets struggle, to much greater effect than the rest of us, certainly but struggle they still do. Eliot, for one, knew well the despairing nature of striving and wrote of words that 'strain . . . crack and sometimes break'. He also expressed the single-mindedness of the task:

> Trying to learn to use words . . .
> For us, there is only the trying. The rest is not our business.

In Greek, Takis Varvitsiotes wrote that:

> . . . our words die
> Faster than even a day

while Dimitris Tsaloumas's *Hypochondriac* has

> . . . a shout so weak
> it can never reach God's ear

Only the trying. In the slums of the huge cities of the United States experimenting educators began, fairly recently, to teach Latin to underprivileged, deprived children. A somewhat unexpected result, for the notion of transfer of training has been taboo among educators for generations now, was that these children's performances began to improve in *every* subject. Now I read that Latin is being reintroduced in American city schools at such a rate that the supply of teachers can hardly keep up. While continuing criticism of Latin centres on the fact that it is a dead language, that very truth means that it carries no racial or class distinctions for children who suffer from both. Paradoxically, it has power, almost a healing power, because part of its original force has drained away in history.

On Holy Island, Northumberland, Eadfrith the scribe, having first been to visit his friend Bede at Jarrow, sat in the Priory's scriptorium and made his copy of the four gospels. His task took him at least two years, and, according to Illich and Sanders, 'brings into sight the watershed that separates the oral from the descriptive mind'. He made all his pens himself, mixed soot, glue and water for ink, and used forty-five different colours for his illuminations. This labour of love was undertaken as part of the preparation for the elevation of the remains of St Cuthbert in AD 698. Shortly after finishing his exquisite copy, Eadfrith became Bishop of Lindisfarne and never wrote or painted again.

But he had assured a continuity. Marauding Vikings forced the monks to flee their island in 875, but they took the gospels and the body of St Cuthbert with them, and eventually settled at Chester-le-Street. There priest Aldred added an English gloss to the Latin. And Aldred, in his colophon, guaranteed immortality for Eadfrith, scribe and artist, Ethelwald the bookbinder, Billfrith the anchorite and jeweller, and for himself.

Almost a thousand years later Kosmas the Aitolos, later canonized for his efforts, dedicated twenty years of his life to travel. He went from Greek village to Greek village, preaching, teaching, advising, trying to arouse the collective consciousness in the cause of freedom. He founded countless schools, and his actual words have survived, even if the schools have not.

Far better, my brother, to have Greek schools in your country than to have springs and rivers; because springs water the body, but schools water the soul. And insofar as you teach your child his letters, then he can call himself a *person*.

Grammata, letters, words often fall short, yet we make do, cling to them and use them, no matter how ineptly, in moments of crisis. In 1845, families evicted during the clearance of Glen Calvie sheltered in Croick churchyard;

there, literate persons scratched messages and names on the church windows. John Ross, shepherd of the Parish of Ardgay, presumably felt bound to clutch at immortality in this way, as did C. Chalmers and Ann McAlister.

As these words, mere lists, conceal pain, so other words, unexpectedly, are only surface, to those who do not know. Thus British and American audiences are intrigued by Crocodile Dundee's laconic lexis: G'day, Yeh, Nuh, while an amused Englishwoman told me that she had once met two other women from Australia.

'They came from that place – what do you do call it? The Outback? They had faces like roadmaps, and I couldn't understand a word they said!'

Twice a week, foreign women meet for language lessons in a chilly prefabricated building, relic of Kalamata's earthquake. Our Greek teacher is proud of her language. Ah, the richness of it, she boasts. We have so *many* words in Greek. We, her pupils, tend to bristle at this, being equally convinced of the richness of Swiss–German, French, Italian, Serbo-Croat and English. English has 500,000 words, I muttered rebelliously one day, even if the average person used only 10,000. She remained unimpressed, even when I informed her, in chauvinistic mood, that *our* Shakespeare used 30,000, and that this exceptionally wide usage was one of the measures of his genius.

All sorts and conditions of people are chauvinistic about language. A landowning relative of mine gave a last-minute warning to his daughter as she was about to leave for England. 'If you come back here saying *field* instead of *paddock*, then you're no daughter of mine!' Even the humblest Greek rushes to tell you that modern Greek has umpteen words, not quite synonyms, for *stone*. (Ah, the importance of geography, geology, topography, all Greek words.) In desperation I searched *Roget's Thesaurus* one day and discovered that English has approximately sixty nouns, again not quite synonyms, for *boat*. Can it be true that the Arabs have fifty adjectives for *desert* and *sand*? It seems highly likely. And I have just read that the shepherds of the Andes have more than sixty words for the colour brown in sheep's fleece.

But how many of these words will remain in their language forever? Languages fuse and thus change each other. It is now possible, for example, to make lists of what people call 'Ocker Greek'. I used to count the words: marketa, choppia, steaki, carro, Commercial Ro; every suburb in Melbourne had been given a gender: *to* Koburgo, *ee* South Yarra. In Greece the language now has the nouns *to stress*, *to process*, *to provlima* (instead of the older *thiskolia* or *difficulty*), *to spray*, *to wax*, *to blender*, and a host of others indirectly introduced by the likes of modern psychologists, Siemens and IBM.

The Greeks are a nation of talkers, and have always prided themselves on their boldness of speech. For at least three thousand years they have been fascinated by ἔπεα πτερόεντα, winged words. In Ancient Greece, poets, rather than priests, were teachers of moral and religious truth, and today's Greeks still look to Homer and poetry rather than to science; the *Iliad* and *The Odyssey*, Herodotus and Loukianos are all studied in a modern Greek translation as early as the first year of secondary school.

As Aeschylus said that his own tragedies were 'fragments from the great banquets of Homer', so today's educated people know at least a few Homeric tags, if not whole sections of the epics by heart. Horace Walpole said that the ancient Greeks 'have been dead so long they have exhausted their power of deceiving'. Lessons in morals and grammar could be learned from even such a wily character as Odysseus. Generations of English public schoolboys learned his expression of bravery and fortitude: 'Endure, my heart; far worse hast thou endured.'

Greeks remain proud of the fact that poetry written in Greek represents the longest uninterrupted tradition in the Western world. It will be some time, surely, before they will want to write poetry by computer, or will be satisfied with the computer-speak definition of a sonnet as an algorithmic system of prompts. Surely they will always prefer to think of poetry as something divine, to think of the man from rocky Chios being given the gift of song by the gods as compensation for his blindness?

While the 'man in the street' may neither read nor write poetry, he remains fascinated by language; even people with little formal learning know which common words are of Turkish origin, and can tell which part of Greece a stranger hails from as soon as he opens his mouth. A weekly television game is among the nation's most popular. In it, competitors, shoppers and pedestrians, are asked the meanings of various words, and are asked to match definitions with various obscure or esoteric words. Yet, George, in his early days in Australia, asked a fellow-worker the meaning of the word *reckon*.

'You Australians use it all the time,' he said, having been struck by the frequency of the question 'What d'ya reckon?' and sentences beginning 'I reckon . . .'.

'Yeah, well,' came the reply, 'I reckon it means . . . just *reckon*.'

I agreed with George that the very presence of words often tantalized. You had to wrestle with them, force them to give up their meaning or else be mesmerized, dazzled, made impotent. I was seventeen before I read:

Batter my heart, three person'd God; for, you
As yet but knocke, breathe, shine, and seeke to mend;
That I may rise, and stand, o'erthrow mee, and bend
Your force, to breake, blowe, burn and make me new . . .

It was just as well, I needed my strength.

At twenty, I howled down the phone to my mother, in complete despair at having to face a certain examination question.

'He's just too big,' I wept.

'Who is?' she asked, patiently.

'Milton,' I sobbed. 'He just overwhelms me, swallows me up.'

'Forget him,' she advised, succinctly.

I did, temporarily, but always remember the packed lecture theatre and the Professor, his gown green with age and tattered by time, reciting the first two hundred and forty lines of *Paradise Lost* faultlessly, pausing at the end to wipe a tear from each eye. 'Theatrical old toad,' grunted a mature student sitting on my right. Surely there could not have been two hundred and forty lines of recitation? Yet that is the number I have fixed in my mind.

But if words meant agony, they also meant amusement, particularly in retrospect when unwitting mistakes were recalled, understood and then relished. For years I thought the local Catholic school, St Liborius's, was in fact named after a St Laborious, and had visions of a work-worn saint wiping drips of sweat from a weary brow.

My mother had a collection of mistakes. During the singing of the children's hymn, 'Jesus Loves Me', countless children had carolled: 'They are weak, but *tea* is strong.'

Later, in my arrogance, I derived amusement from the struggle migrant friends had with English. Socrates once announced that money and business affairs had to be handled most efficiently or else dire consequences could result.

'You're right,' I agreed. 'Absolutely.'

'Yes,' he advised, in a meditative tone, 'unless you're careful, you can end up *bugger-up.*'

'Er, end up *what?*' I enquired, cautiously.

'You *know,*' he replied, impatiently. '*Bugger-up.* You have to go to court.'

Light dawned. 'Um, ah. *Bankrupt.*'

'Right. What did I say?'

Eventually, it was my turn to be laughed at as I confused the Greek words for *bamboo*, *drinking straw* and *squid*, with hilarious results, as I bought glue instead of greaseproof paper, and as I used farmyard words in Athenian drawing-rooms, for Greek is full of traps for the unwary. An Australian friend living in Greece, once – but only once – confused the word *reduction* (as in sale-price) with the word *abortion*. Holding up a bolt of material she asked politely, 'And how much is the abortion?' The sales girl stared, crimson-faced.

It is only now that I truly appreciate struggles with language. Struggling with my own I accepted as a fact of life. But I was married to my Greek husband for twelve years and had moved to Greece before I really understood that struggling with a foreign language was, and would remain one of the most painful parts of exile.

George himself discovered, long, long ago, the frustration of trying to learn a language in a formal way with those who used it informally at best, carelessly at worst. In his early days in Australia, he acquired a grammar book and set about earnest study. He had occasion to ask his work supervisor a question.

'Excuse me sir, what is a past participle?'

'Eh? A what?'

'A past participle.'

'You got me there, George. Too hard for me. Big words always were.'

George's interest in grammar was shared by Theo, who was doing an English course. 'My teacher says there are ten parts of speech,' he moaned, 'and I can only remember nine.'

'Let's ask somebody,' suggested George, in whose breast hope always springs eternal.

'Mr Smith,' began Theo, tentatively, 'can you remember the parts of speech? I can only think of nine parts of speech in English, but there are ten.'

'Crikey, are there?' remarked Mr Smith, scratching his head. 'Fancy that. Can't help you. Sorry, mate.'

Words have come to mean catharsis. Peace is achieved through outpouring. Did I realize this, dimly, whenever I heard my father shouting in his workshop at recalcitrant hammers and disobedient nails?

'You dirty, rotten, lousy, stinking pig of a thing!' he would bawl. Sometimes this string of epithets actually seemed to act as an incantation, and the tools behaved. But, always, he seemed to feel better.

Still, words may not be powerful enough. Communication may fail; language may baffle. The Phaistos Disk symbolizes Crete, Greece, and also the secrets of language: ancient, mysterious, unique, defying analysis. The Disk sits on its plinth in the Heraklion Museum, goggled at by thousands, while the pictograms, the ridged heads, hands, fish, axes, grouped and sectioned, guard their own secrets, hiding them in the snail-shell spiral. No chain, no bridge here – yet. The little stick figures are silent. They are lost to us, and yet not quite lost. Perhaps they will one day speak. Until then, like all words, decipherable or not, they remind us of the first poetry of our lives. They are like Kavafy's *Voices*: heard in dreams and imagination, their sounds faint 'like far-off music in the night, which dies away'.

Chapter 15

His name was Howard, but he never used it. Instead he had chosen a Greek name: Athanasios. What's in a name? you may ask. And I would reply: a great deal, in this case, because Athanasios means *immortal*. In Australia Howard had been given only a short time to live; in Greece Athanasios defied doctors. In Australia, time had a limit; in Greece, time kept stretching, years multiplied and Athanasios lived on, his name becoming sort of a guarantee.

George met him first. They were in the foreign language bookshop, both buying copies of *The Times*. Howard was a towering, impressive figure, reported George. He had smooth white hair and not much Greek.

'I knew he was Australian the minute I saw him, but he didn't want to talk about Australia. He *did* say he was from Port Melbourne originally, but he kept insisting that his name was now Athanasios, and that he had converted to Orthodoxy. Oh well, all expatriates are eccentric.'

'Indeed?' I remarked, in schoolteacherly fashion. I remember lifting an eyebrow and muttering about words and labels. But actually the achievement of mild eccentricity is one of my ambitions, so I rather regretted not having been in the bookshop at the right time to view this likely model.

I kept a sharp lookout in the streets from then on, but Athanasios seemed to have disappeared. George hoped he had gone back to Australia.

'He's seventy, I'm sure,' he said. 'Too old to be struggling with the language and all the rest of it.' 'All the rest of it' was a convenient, George-ish way of mentioning and summarizing all the trials and tribulations of migration. For George had been the archetypal migrant: torn in two, racked with longing for what he had left behind, his life in Australia very much formed by his Greekness and his desire to go back to Greece. Every cliché about migration had taken on startling immediacy for him. 'All the rest of it' was a light, casual phrase which skimmed the surface of the migrant experience. It distilled a single word: pain.

But Howard preferred the struggle and the pain, or so it seemed, for in spite of George's hope, with its in-built power and logic, he stayed on in Greece. Months passed, however, and I still had not seen him. Then he wrote me a letter. He had heard of me, it being a small world, and would like to meet a fellow-Australian, as he knew of no others in Kalamata. Could I call? Of course I could. I knew of no other Australians, either.

It was mid-winter. We drove through the pouring rain, up and down narrow streets, searching for the right address. Eventually we found it, and Howard answered the doorbell after walking down twenty-seven steps.

'How do you do?' we mumbled, all three of us ill-at-ease. I proffered a jar of home-made jam.

'Thank you,' Howard said, firmly. 'I'll enjoy that.'

A careful, tentative friendship began to develop, based on notes, letters and an exchange system. Howard would write to let me know that 'a stack of *Bulletins*' had arrived. He would leave them just inside the lobby door, near the electricity meter. I left whatever I had: cuttings from the *Age*, an English magazine or two, snippets of information about Australia which I thought he might have missed.

'It all helps to stop us from feeling too lonely,' he wrote once, and I had a strong impression that while he could set such words down on paper, he would never have been able to say them. Speech was too intimate, too threatening. In any case, he never mentioned loneliness again. Howard was a shy man. I suspected, too, that he always had been lonely, and regarded such a condition as being almost natural.

But even shy, solitary men cannot live by reading alone, and so I left other things behind the front door: more jam, home-made biscuits, rock cakes, boiled fruit cakes. He was older than George had thought, I discovered, much older than my father, and every old man likes home-cooking. So I reasoned, and Howard admitted as much.

'My mother, now,' he stated, staring down at me through dark-rimmed glasses, 'made superb Cornish pasties. She was a wonderful cook, Mum.' I quailed. Was this a hint? Surely he must have known that no other Cornish pasties would ever be like Mum's? But one day I would make pasties, I promised, one day.

We met very seldom. I knew little about him, except that I felt comforted whenever I heard his accent or received a few lines through the post. He knew little about me. Perhaps we did not need to know much. For Howard, at least, words, questions, answers, information, never seemed important, and so, for example, he never appeared to worry unduly about learning Greek.

'I try,' he said, one day, 'but I'll never learn it properly. I know that.' Slowly, however, a few facts built themselves into a structure, and answered the question George and I kept asking ourselves: Why was he here?

He had cancer. His Australian doctor gave him two years, three at the most. Well, Howard said to himself, no point in sitting around waiting to die. I'll do something I've always wanted to do. I'll go to Greece. And he did. And stayed and stayed. He referred to cancer as *the enemy*. 'It'll never get me,' he declared, 'I'll never let it.' He believed that Orthodoxy was his weapon, his new name Athanasios, the deathless, immortal one, a talisman. 'Call me Thanassi,' he urged, but I never did. In fact, I never even called him Howard, but always used *Mr* and his surname, very formally. Now I have a vague feeling of guilt about this, as if my failure to use his new name lessened the power of the word, weakened it in some way, deprived him of some protection.

Once Howard and I happened to be in Melbourne at the same time. I rang. That day I was not comforted by his voice. I had those accents all around me; I had returned home. He sounded like a stranger, anyway, sad and distrait, and his voice sounded distant, much further than a suburban line away.

'I don't like it at all anymore. Everything's changed. It's all different and it's not home. I've changed my ticket and I'm leaving early. I'm *going home*.' There was a definite emphasis on the last two words.

I hung up quietly, incredulous. He was so ill. He had had three operations in a Greek hospital and now here he was, turning his back on Medicare and comfort. He was braver than I could ever be, but I don't think he ever thought of bravery, just of the way things were for him. He strode boldly to meet his new world, and to face it, while I clung to my old one, looking back and sighing. And my inability to use his new name was surely symbolic of my clinging? How *could* he give up his old self?

We returned to Greece separately and resumed our

separate lives. He was in remission and walking miles to the beach and back, swimming regularly. I had a vision of his tall frame striding along the streets of Kalamata, his togs and towel tucked under his arm. Was he a little boy again, swimming at Port Melbourne, or at least remembering? I did not know.

He was ill again during the winter, but stayed on his feet. Once I climbed the twenty-seven steps and visited him in his tiny room. An ikon of Aghios Athanasios hung above his narrow bed. Underwear was boiling on the stove. Awkwardly I asked him if I could do anything. 'Nothing,' he replied, firmly. 'I'll be right. Did I tell you I visited my doctor in Melbourne?' He laughed with satisfaction. 'The bloke's jaw dropped. "You're supposed to be dead!" he said. "Well, I'm not, am I?" I said to him. Doctors! What do *they* know? They're not always right, that's for sure!' And the subject of washing, help, support was neatly turned aside. I left another fruit cake.

Spring came, bringing good weather, swallows and wild flowers, and I thought of Cornish pasties again. Howard was invited and said he would be glad to come. An indifferent cook, I prayed over the pastry and willed my creations to be as much like Howard's Mum's as possible. But George came home alone.

'A friend phoned,' he told me, 'and said that Howard was too ill to come. But he hopes to come another day.' I think I knew then that he would never manage it. The boys gobbled up the pasties; to me they seemed tasteless.

It was strange that I looked for him again on the morning before the earthquake. But all the shutters were closed fast. 'He's all right,' declared a little girl playing nearby. '*Kyrios Thanassis* is all right. *Perapataei akoma.* He's still walking . . .' He seems to be sleeping late, though, I thought. I went looking again some time after the earthquake. There was damage everywhere and the whole neighbourhood was deserted, but Howard's huge block of flats had come through unscathed.

Soon it was December again. The weather turned bitter, and George, on leave from work, was cursing and grumbling about the olive harvest. I wrote to Howard, but the answer came from a friend. He had tried to get in touch with George at work, he said, but had been unable to do so. He was sorry to have to tell us that Howard had died peacefully in his sleep in hospital and had been buried in the local cemetery.

I could not even cry. Instead I wondered about the funeral. Howard had had Greek friends, but I did not know them. I did not know the *papas* who had converted him. Howard's life had been a Greek one. An English friend had attended the funeral, I knew, but he had probably been the only foreigner there. Part of me felt that I should have been there too, one Australian saying goodbye to another. But Howard had said goodbye to Australia long before, and had already said goodbye to me.

A month or so before he died, I received a rolled parcel and a note. 'I'm sending you a souvenir,' he had written, 'and I know you'll look after it.' The souvenir was the last issue of the *Argus*, dated 19 January 1957. In January 1957, I was eleven years old, a country child who had just moved from a Wimmera township to Geelong, a city which, in contrast, seemed almost as strange, bustling and sophisticated as the New York and London of my imagination. I was about to start secondary school and a conventional, comfortable life. If anybody had told me then, that thirty years later I would be reading the *Argus* in the Peloponnese, I would have thought him mad.

I stared at the yellowing pages, at the banner headline YOUR LAST ARGUS, and, influenced by L. P. Hartley, reflected that the past is, in some ways, the most foreign country of all, with its own barely accessible language. The paper is crammed with references to Khrushchev, bodgies and widgies, Jack Davey, Victoria Shaw,

pounds, shillings and pence. The birth of Princess
Caroline of Monaco was imminent, and Melbourne's
public was debating Princess Grace's choice of names. All
this made up not another country, but another world, I
decided. But I *am* looking after the souvenir, and have
wrapped everything, in a way, in mothballs: the paper,
Howard's past and mine, that other world.

Since Howard's death the questions have become more
insistent. Why did he keep the *Argus*? What was his past
life really like? Had he really turned his back on it so
easily? And, perhaps the most important question of all:
why is it that Greece attracts the lonely? I can hazard a
guess at this last, at least. In Kalamata there is no silent
suburbia, no rattle of lawn-mowers making the only
sound on Sunday mornings, no anonymity. Noise and
people are always *there*, filling your ears and getting
under your feet. (Perhaps Port Melbourne was like this
sixty years ago?) Greece is a landscape, a word-scape, a
people-scape, which makes loneliness like Howard's bear-
able. In Greece, in Kalamata, he, I think, felt lapped in
vibrant life even when he was dying, even though he
lived alone in a little attic sheltered by an awning over a
tiny balcony. His own life was nourished by the life of
the town.

I was not part of the world he had made for himself
here. I merely appeared at the edge of it every so often, a
reminder of the past, a little like the edition of the *Argus*.
When he was ready he let that past go completely, and
posted the last vestige of it to me. It was appropriate,
therefore, that I had not known about his death in time.

'You're not to worry about me dying,' he announced
once. 'My friends have their instructions. They know
what to do.'

I still have the feeling that Howard is buried in alien
soil. But perhaps Howard died a long time ago, on the

other side of the world? Athanasios, the immortal one, beat off more than one enemy, died peacefully in his own time, answering to the name of his choice, having chosen the place of his death. It is a long, long way from Port Melbourne to Kalamata, and the distance was measured in more than miles. Howard began it. Athanasios finished it: a triumphant journey.

A FOREIGN WIFE
Gillian Bouras

'In 1969 we bravely organised two weddings. An Orthodox ceremony was then a legal requirement of the Greek State, but I wanted some English spoken over me as well. The first service passed in a sort of blur. Too late I realised that my squarish veil arrangement was not suited to the wearing of crowns . . . and I became rather confused about kissing hands and books . . . A short time later I walked down a familiar *fleur-de-lis* carpet towards a Presbyterian minister who welded familiar words and music into a brief service of blessing. It was George's turn to be confused.'

Gillian Bouras is an Australian married to a Greek. From the ambiguous position of a foreign wife, she writes of life in a Greek village. Her fellow villagers fondly regard her, the migrant in their midst, as something of a curiosity. They, in turn, are the source of both her admiration and her perplexity.

MILK
Beverley Farmer

Whether writing about being an Australian woman in love in Greece, or waiting at the airport for a small son, or being old and embedded in everything that has gone before, Beverley Farmer isolates moments of human experience with almost unbearable clarity.

She charts the distances between people, their place in light and landscape, their failures to love and be loved or even to sustain each other more than momentarily.

These are deceptively simple, extraordinarily attractive stories, set in Greece and Australia, by a gifted and original writer.